Divergent Lives

First printing, 2012

Published by: Lahongrais Books

Cover Design Copyright © 2012 Minnie Lahongrais

Cover Design by Reneé Groskreutz, Ralph's Design and Deli, LLC

Edited by Andi Reis, Ralph's Design and Deli, LLC

To order quantities of this book at a discount, contact:
Lahongrais Books: 347-338-8513
Minnie@MinnieLahongrais.com
www.minnielahongrais.com

ISBN: 0-9884-0160-6
ISBN-13: 9780988401600
Library of Congress Control Number: 2012952370

Divergent Lives

Minnie Lahongrais

Lahongrais Books

2012

Dedication

For Mari and Dayne

I have two eyes without which I cannot see.

It is through your eyes that I see the

possibilities.

This is for you.

143

Table of Contents

Acknowledgments

A story like this cannot be written alone. It took many hands to oil this machine. I would like to acknowledge some of those hands.

First, my daughter and grandson: Mari and Dayne, through thick and thin, you listened to my sometimes-outlandish musings and didn't make me feel like you were "yes-ing" me to death. Thank you! Love you guys so, so much!

To Bernice Winbush, Sharon Kalani, David Munkittrick, Todd Mobley, Dominick D'Avanzo, Benjamin M. Burt, Esq., Geovanny Murillo, Matthew Queler, Joon Yoon, Monica Hearne, OB/GYN, Pierre Bazin, Robbi Somers Bryant, Jorge Salgado Reyes and a host of others–we spent many hours talking over the phone, discussing plot lines over meals, emailing, Skyping and texting. For that I thank you, from the bottom of my heart, for taking the time out of your busy schedules to help me figure things out.

To my Twitter and Facebook friends who understood and supported me when I disappeared into my writing cave, a heartfelt thank you.

A special, deep-rooted thank you to Ralph's Design and Deli. You guys are awesome! Andi Reis and Renee Groskreutz designed a beautiful cover and an awesome book trailer for me. Andi was phenomenal during the editing process. When you find a team like this, you can't go wrong!

So many, many people were involved in bringing this story to you. If I inadvertently omitted your name, I apologize. Know that I am extremely grateful for any words of support you have offered me.

With Gohonzon, everything is possible!! NMRK!

There is no real cure for a sociopath.

"One must feel sorry for those who have strange tastes, but never insult them. Their wrong is Nature's too; they are no more responsible for having come into the world with tendencies unlike ours than are we for being born bandy-legged or well-proportioned."

Marquis de Sade (1740-1814), "Dialogue the Fifth" *Philosophy in the Bedroom* (1795)

Chapter 1
Adina: March 21, 2002

Adina Rosario Cruz's meeting went longer than expected. She picked up her phone again and again to check the time. She really disliked Friday afternoon meetings. Looking out the window and merely glancing at the suits around her, she wasn't hearing anything but white noise. Suddenly, everyone was standing.

She gathered her papers and stood, making polite good-byes to those next to her.

Then she was off, locking her office door, down the hall and taking long strides to the elevator. Doors open. Her heels clicked along the granite lobby, and with only a few more strides, a powerful rush of trench coat, purse, wind and hair, she emerged from the glass revolving doors onto the sidewalk. She lifted her face into the cool, spring air for a moment and glanced down to notice the sky's beautiful orange glow enveloping her arm.

She signaled a cab that was letting passengers out at the curb. It wasn't an unusual occurrence. Her office building was at a busy intersection and she rarely had to wait for a ride home. She hopped in as soon as the previous passengers exited the car.

"Hi. 1212 Delafield Avenue in Riverdale, please. You should take the Henry Hudson Parkway to exit twenty-one. I'll direct you from there," she instructed the cab driver and settled into the back seat.

"Yes, ma'am."

His gaze lingered a moment in the rearview mirror.

"Thank you."

She clenched her jaw at him in response. He looked away.

Rummaging through her pocketbook, she pulled out her smartphone and turned it off.

Adina was anxious to arrive home to Tommy. It was their anniversary and it would be a game-changing evening for the two of them. He rang her earlier that day and asked her to please be home at a decent hour. She promised to do so.

She leaned her head back and closed her eyes.

Adina Cruz and Tomas Ortiz met two years ago. She often saw him at the gym of their newly built condominium complex. Prior to their official meeting, he had discreetly watched her as she worked out. Never in her wildest dreams did she ever imagine that she would now want a long-term relationship with him.

Though very attractive, she didn't see herself in the same light others did. Of average height–five foot four inches tall–she was curvaceous and had big brown eyes. Very thick, wavy, shoulder length dark hair which was just starting to go salt and pepper topped it all off. Her voice had a sultry tinge to it with an almost untraceable "NuYorican" accent, which only became apparent when she was excited or upset.

Tommy, as he liked to be called, was six foot two, with a head full of medium length thick dark hair that was also beginning to grey at the temples. Like Adina, he had classic big, brown eyes with full lashes. Adina loved him very much, especially with his solid build, and she was brutally attracted to him. Here is where things started to deviate for them.

She wanted more from this relationship than either of them thought Tommy was capable of giving. Adina's desires were unconventional, dark even. She wanted more than just run-of-the-mill sex. Vanilla, some would call it. She was curious about different sexual activities. She especially enjoyed games that included inflicting pain, role-playing, and bondage. She liked to experiment with toys that she thought enhanced the sexual experience, like blindfolds and riding crops, and she wanted Tommy to join her in these activities.

Adina was sexually curious and open-minded where Tommy wasn't. He was very conservative in almost everything he did, but even more so when it came to the bedroom.

The one thing they did have in common was that they both came from loving homes, though tragedy struck early in Tommy's life. She often wondered if this affected his ability to allow himself to be uninhibited. His parents died when he was young, and his best friend's family took him in after the tragedy.

Now in his early forties, he desperately wanted to start a family of his own. He knew he would be a good, loving father but when the subject of children came up between them, the conversation usually became very heated. He couldn't understand why she wanted to do the things she did. They talked about her sexual interests often, and he still couldn't understand it. Ultimately, the last tête-à-tête came almost a year into their relationship, culminating in an agreement.

At that time, Tommy offered Adina the space she needed, to do whatever was necessary to satisfy her curiosities. He grudgingly agreed to wait for her to decide about the future of their relationship. Tonight, the night of their second anniversary would be the night the year-old agreement would come to an end.

However, unbeknownst to Tommy, Adina had already made up her mind. After a solid year of meeting and going out on dates with men she met at various work-related events, she realized that it was indeed Tommy who made her the happiest. So what if he wasn't into the experimentation? She knew he was solid as a rock. She knew he loved her. Why else would he allow her the room to explore this part of herself? She decided to really make an effort to focus more on their relationship. She would just have to learn to adjust. The last guy she met at one of those functions didn't measure up anyway, and she hadn't been with anyone else since then.

"Ma'am, I'm approaching your exit. Which way do I go?"

The cabbie abruptly brought her back to reality. Shaking off her thoughts, she gave the cab driver directions. She was home within five minutes.

❧⚬❧

Adina and Tommy lay in the afterglow of their passion. The light of the full moon brightly shone down upon them through her bare bedroom window; casting a somber light over the two of them.

"Please stay the night, Tommy. I want to wake up and see your face first thing in the morning."

Tommy chuckled and turned his face towards her, smirking mischievously, with one hand behind his head, the other on his chest.

Determined to get her way, Adina continued:

"We're going to get married, aren't we? Shouldn't I be allowed a taste of what it would be like every day for the rest of my life? I mean, seriously; think about it for a moment. When a girl buys a pair of shoes, she tries them on, doesn't she?"

Tommy could not be happier than he was right at that moment.

⇜⇝

Who would've believed that just a few hours earlier, as he cooked his special meal for the love of his life, he was mentally preparing himself for the end of their relationship? Though he loved her with all his heart, and always would, he had no choice when he gave her a free pass to explore. He knew there was a possibility he could lose her in the process, but he just couldn't do it anymore.

Who was he kidding? He couldn't do it a week into the agreement, but he *did* agree and he *was* a man of his word. As hard as the last year had been for him, the idea that she was out with those other men was slowly killing him. He couldn't stand the thought, so he poured himself into his work at the precinct because it would help keep his imagination from working overtime during that period of their relationship. He hated the images he had of her in bed with these men. He thought he would go insane.

Now, a year later and hoping for the best, he left work early, picked up groceries then headed straight to Adina's apartment. He didn't live with her, but he kept a set of keys that she had given him in case of an emergency. He let himself into her place. Contemplative, he began preparing for their evening together.

To his surprise, Adina arrived when she said she would. She appeared noticeably different to him. There was a new brightness in her eyes. No, this wasn't the Adina he had been expecting. The woman he just had dinner with seemed so happy it made him happy. It wasn't long before he knew why.

During dinner, Adina announced she was no longer interested in seeing other men. She promised Tommy she would make a renewed effort to solidify their relationship because she realized how much she loved and needed him. She admitted she no longer wanted to take any chances with their future or her health. She said she was fully aware this process of hers, this search for what most people would consider unconventional, also put her at risk of losing him forever.

Hearing her say those words, to have her finally commit to the relationship, made him delirious with love for her. He impulsively surprised her with an unexpected wedding proposal right on the spot. To his amazement Adina said yes, putting the cherry on top, so to speak.

⋙⋘

"You've never asked me to stay the night. Do you really want me to?"

"Yes, I do."

"I'll have to go home and get a change of clothes for work tomorrow."

"Then you should go now and come right back. I'll run a bath while you're gone and I'll eagerly await your return."

He leaned in and gave her a long, passionate kiss.

"I'll be back before you get done with your bath, I promise."

She nodded as they gazed in each other's eyes. He caressed her face with his fingertips, then got out of bed, dressed and left.

Adina leaned back into her pillow, stretched her arms over her head and stared at the ceiling, smiling. She was extremely excited knowing that she was now embarking on this new journey with Tommy at her side.

⋙⋘

In an empty apartment still under construction across the small courtyard, a man stood watching Adina with a full, unobstructed view through a large window, his form hidden in shadow. He held in the crook of one arm a large bouquet of purple and white orchids, arranged in a heavy crystal vase. Becoming angrier by the moment, he stood riveted as he watched Adina and Tommy writhe and tangle on the bed. Unblinking, nostrils flaring, and consumed by the heat of jealous rage, the stranger continued to watch as Tommy rose and left the room. Soon after, he heard Adina's front door slam shut. He turned his attention back to Adina as she lay in her bed. Both were woozy; Adina from the lovemaking; the stranger with barely controlled anger.

Walking away from the window, he headed toward the back door of the empty apartment and stepped through it. He furtively glanced around the courtyard, pulled the door closed behind him then turned toward Adina's apartment. He leaned in quietly as he approached and tried the knob. It wasn't locked. He stepped softly, deliberately into the foyer and closed the door behind him. He evened his breathing, reined in his anger. His intended was nearby.

He stood, just listening and watching for a full minute. Then a sudden rustle of sheets and mattress springs as Adina alit from her bed. He heard air whistling through pipes with the rush of water as it flowed into the tub.

She must be preparing a bath, he thought.

He continued to listen intently. Then, he heard the soft sound of her bare feet on the wood floors as she walked in his direction.

He stood frozen in place. He stopped breathing.

Not only was he hiding in the shadows of the foyer in Adina's apartment, but he was also hiding in the dark, evil place in his head as well, and he underwent an imperceptible change within.

જન્જ

Not bothering to get dressed, Adina got out of bed and went into the bathroom. She opened the hot water spigot, adjusting the temperature to her liking as it whistled. A thin film of steam quickly covered the bathroom mirror. Satisfied the water was hot enough, she turned and headed to the kitchen. She wanted a glass of wine to sip while she soaked and thought about Tommy.

Guided by the bathroom light, she headed toward the front of the apartment.

I didn't hear Tommy lock the door, she thought.

Suddenly, she stopped. There in the semi-dark hallway, she felt a presence near the foyer, just around the bend from the hall.

"Wow! That was quick," she whispered.

A big, beautiful smile spread across her face.

Thrilled Tommy was back already, she waited for him to announce his return. But he didn't. The foyer remained dark and silent. She took a step forward then stopped.

"Tommy?"

No response.

"Tommy? Is that you?"

Her eyes became large as saucers, trying to focus on the form in the darkness.

There was only silence.

Her throat constricted with fear and she squeaked: "C'mon, Tommy! Stop playing!"

Loud thumping in her chest. But none of that stopped her from taking one tentative step forward followed by another. The wood flooring suddenly felt cold under her bare feet, and chills rose up her spine.

Reaching the end of the hallway, she groped for the light and turned to face the front door. She stood motionless as her eyes tried to focus on the shape in the shadows. Standing in the foyer, a figure lurked in darkness. The way he stood, as though he were ready to pounce, kept her frozen there like a deer in headlights.

She was so stunned that she couldn't even try to be modest. Coming to her senses, she reflexively crossed her legs. One arm moved to cover her breasts, the other to her crotch.

"What the hell are you doing here? Get out of my house right now or I will call the police!"

She screamed, loud and indignant, her voice cracking.

Strangely calm, this figure growled.

"You will do nothing of the sort. You betrayed me."

Terrified and realizing her vulnerability, Adina turned and ran back to her room, locking herself in. She leaned on the door, her bare ass against it. Yet feeling numb, she shook uncontrollably. Now her tears slid over her grimace and down her chin.

"Where's my fucking phone? Fucking phone, goddamn it!"

She fumbled and reached for it on her dresser without moving from the door. She could hear her own voice chirping and gasping somewhere outside of her.

WHAM ...Vibrations rocked her body. Bursting into tears, her body jittered as the intruder's body hit the door from the other side.

Frantic and wheezing, she fumbled for the phone's power switch nearly dropping it, remembering she had turned it off for the night.

Desperately scared now, she glanced over at the bed with the rumpled sheets—the bed where she and Tommy had just made love. The air in the room was still thick with the scent of musk. The severity of the situation hit her as she continued to press her body against the door. She was struck by the reality that if she didn't get help, she would not live to see Tommy again.

Adina shook the phone and prayed for a signal before he could get in so she could call for help. But this madman continued slamming himself against the door. With each body slam against the only barrier between her and insanity, Adina bounced against it, unable to keep it shut.

"WHY?"

She screamed then moaned in despair. She shook the phone in her sweaty hand again as if that would make it magically find a signal and finally become operable. Then, like a car roaring to life on a cold winter morning, the phone was alive.

She wouldn't get her chance to call for help.

His grunt, a heave and she was knocked forward. He was in the room with her.

Adina screamed as she slid across the newly shellacked and slippery floor.

"Help! Somebody, please help me! Help!"

Her heart raced and beat so hard it felt as though it would burst from her chest. The sound of her blood coursing through her body pounded in her ears. Alternately crying and gasping, she desperately tried to catch her breath. Unable to control her bladder, it emptied onto the floor. "What do you want?? What do you WANT FROM ME!?"

Her voice cracked again in her attempt to sound more angry than scared.

It was then that she realized that she knew this man! She knew him! No time to ponder this. She looked around the room for something she could defend herself with.

"Shit! Fuck!"

Finding nothing, she cursed herself for living such a Spartan existence.

She glanced toward the window and considered thrusting herself through it in order to escape the madman about to overcome her. But all the windows in the complex were double- paneled storm windows.

I'll probably kill myself before I could even crack it, she rationalized.

But she tried anyway, not thinking to just open it and jump out.

The crazy intruder lunged across the bed at her, just missing her. At this point, her common sense mobilized by adrenaline kicked into high gear, and Adina finally tried to open the window, but it wouldn't budge! It was stuck!

"Fuck!" she cursed just as he threw himself at her once again, this time reaching her and grabbing a handful of hair.

He swung her around to face him and as he did, she tried to grab on to the dresser for leverage. All of her perfume bottles, her hairbrush, jewelry and other knick-knacks went flying when she was unable to find purchase. Everything that was on the dresser hit the hard floor with a scattered crash.

The intruder smacked her in the face with an open hand, making her head swing violently to the right. Her cheek grew hot.

It burned.

Her ears were ringing.

That first blow was immediately followed by a second; this time served with the back of his hand, causing her head to swing around to the left. Tears stung her eyes as the force of the two blows caused her to bite down on her tongue. Pain and blood exploded in her mouth.

This time she saw stars.

Her neck hurt.

She became dizzy.

She spit at him. Blood mixed with saliva slid down her chin. He began yelling something at her but she couldn't put his words together. She heard nothing but buzzing and her own frenzied breathing. She watched his lips move and made out the word "whore."

Before she could make sense of what was happening, he was at her again.

Grabbing her by the shoulders, he threw her up against the wall. The back of her head rebounded from it–hard.

Bright lights shot before her eyes as she struggled to maintain consciousness. Slowly sliding down the cool, hard surface, she finally crumbled in a heap and shook her head.

When she looked up at her attacker, he didn't seem that big to her.

I just have to out-maneuver him, she strategized.

She tried to get back up, but he was standing over her and reaching for her once again, snarling down at her. She felt drops of his saliva molest her cheek. In utter horror, she punched outward.

The maniac grabbed a hold of her neck with both hands and brought her to her feet as he squeezed and shook her violently, lifting her a few inches off the ground. Her legs dangled.

Gasping for air and quickly beginning to lose the will to fight, Adina had little energy left within her. But, she reached up with one hand to stick her thumb into his eye. She tried to balance herself on his arm with her other hand. He tried to peel her hand away from his face with his right hand, and as he did, he continued to press his left thumb to the base of her throat. Adina tightened her core and swung her leg back with a grunt, then quickly and forcefully kicked him in the groin as hard as she could with the ball of her foot.

Mercifully, the madman released her and brought his hands together to cup his crotch. She was amazed she landed on her feet when he let her go. Coughing and fighting for air, she was extremely shaken. In that split second, his head swung low as he gasped from the impact of Adina's blow, giving her a window of opportunity. Taking a chance, she head-butted him as hard as she could. She was amped up and fighting back now, propelled by the need to survive–it was clear his intent was to destroy her. The skin on her forehead broke upon impact and a knot quickly rose over her brow bone where she made contact with him. The pain cut a wide swath through her body.

He growled through gritted teeth as he stumbled backward toward the bed, coughing and still holding his crotch. He spat words about killing her. Adina gasped for air and the scratchiness in her throat became worse. She still struggled with the dizziness that threatened to overcome her.

Unable to focus and her legs like rubber, she held her hand to her forehead. It was bleeding and it hurt like hell too, but she knew she would not have another opportunity to get away from him if she didn't get out of the house fast. She absolutely had to find a way to escape his clutches. It was now or never because if she had to continue fighting him, she knew she would lose.

Finally, with every last ounce of strength she had, she ran out of the room and just as she reached the front door, he was upon her once again. She was trapped.

He body-slammed her against the door.

Her face smacked into it.

Blood flowed from her broken nose.

Lightheaded and weak, Adina desperately continued fighting to get away.

Frustrated at how close he came to losing her, he grabbed hold of the heavy crystal vase he had placed on the floor when he initially entered the apartment. He swung it over her. Water and flowers spilled everywhere before he slammed it hard into the back of her head. Her skull instantly cracked open like an egg over a hot frying pan. She slid against his body and he stepped backward, letting her fall face up at his feet with a soft thump.

∂∞∞

As he looked down at her body, Adina's killer slowly came back to his senses. He couldn't believe what just happened! Desperate, he grabbed at his hair, alternately running his fingers through it and pulling on it. Tears had begun to well up in his eyes as he whimpered. Deep in his chest, there was a rumbling and he began to pace. He looked everywhere but down. Finally, he threw his head back and growled.

He dropped to his knees, drew his face into his hands and began to cry. Then, abruptly, he stopped. He rose to his feet, seemingly transformed, and looked down at Adina's inert body.

His face softened.

"What have I done? What have I done?" he asked out loud to Adina's still body.

He actually loved Adina. She was the only woman he thought understood him. She never seemed to judge him. She made him happy and he felt like a human being worthy of love when he was near her.

In the past, he had tried to get her to see how much he cared for her. That was why he had the flowers. They were to be a gift for her. The only reason he was there at all that night was to declare his love for her in person before she did something stupid like marry her boyfriend. He really just wanted to talk.

But, recently he had begun to regret ever telling her that she should work things out with the boyfriend. He hated that he wasn't persistent enough when he told her he didn't think she should be going out with all those other men. He really just wanted her for himself. But he was shy and he was afraid of rejection. All he wanted was to tell her that he loved her and now she lay dead at his feet.

Crouching down beside her, he leaned down and gently kissed her on the tip of her shattered nose, the way one would a child. He pulled some of her hair over her burst skin and oozing wounds. A dark, raised bruise was now prominent on her forehead and he wanted to cover it. He didn't like to see her hurt like that.

"Half a second ..." he murmured.

His eyes were red rimmed and tears threatened to flow.

"If you had gotten the door open just half a second sooner, you might have survived; you might have gotten away.

"You know me. You're the only one who knows me," he whispered to her as he reached out and caressed her face.

He brought her eyelids down tenderly.

"But you failed and because you failed, you were dead before you hit the ground."

The intruder looked around. Telltale gray matter–Adina's brain–spilled out through the hole in the back of her head, which lay atop the beautiful orchids and pink baby's breath originally intended as a gift for her. Regret filled him.

"I'm sorry! I am so sorry, Adina! Please forgive me!" he cried.

He apologized over and over, but seeing her lying there, vulnerable like that also aroused him.

Having these feelings at a moment like this wasn't anything strange for him. He was always aroused when he fought to get what he wanted. He could feel his desire for her reach a feverish, uncontrollable level.

He reached down to touch himself in search of relief. He took a step back then slipped his hand down his loose fitting pants and began to massage his member. He rubbed himself for a short while before he felt the sticky liquid of pre-ejaculation fluid in his palm.

But he knew release would not come for him. It never does. Frustrated, he wiped his hand on his leg and stepped over Adina's naked body. He looked down at her, at the flowers that were strewn everywhere, then back at her again.

"Please forgive me," he whispered.

A single tear slid down his cheek.

Appearing outwardly calm, he put out the light in the foyer, turned the doorknob and walked out. Scarlet gel mixed with her brain matter contrasted sharply against the blond wood parquet flooring.

᷏᷒᷍

Twenty minutes after having left Adina, Tommy exited his apartment, which was two buildings over on the north side of the complex. As he walked to his fiancée's place, he blissfully relived his evening with her in his head. He wondered about the kind of diamond she might like on her engagement ring. What shape diamond would she like? What about size? Did size matter to her? He decided she would probably want quality over size. Then he wondered if she would even want an engagement ring. He realized he didn't know the answer to that question and resolved to ask her when he got in.

As he walked through the large courtyard, he finalized plans for their upcoming wedding in his head, even though they hadn't chosen a date yet.

Did she want a big wedding or would she prefer to just go to City Hall? he wondered.

Maybe we could just have a civil ceremony and spend the money we would have otherwise spent on a wedding reception on a honeymoon instead.

Where would she most enjoy going if she chose a more lavish honeymoon?

He was practically giddy.

Tommy was really struck by the fact that he didn't know these things about her. Well, he figured he would just have to fix that as soon as possible.

As Tommy approached Adina's front door, he suddenly remembered that he had not locked it when he left earlier and chided himself. He hoped that she did when she got up to prepare her bath. There were a lot of strangers in the area because of all the construction going on in and around the complex.

He and Adina were one of the first shareholders in this brand new community and many of the units had still not yet been sold due to the recession. Then there were the ones that had been sold and were currently being remodeled by construction contractors hired by the new owners.

When he reached the door, he turned the knob. It was unlocked.

Damn, he said to himself.

He entered and reached for the switch to turn on the light. His foot slipped on something in the entranceway, causing his body to tense. Distracted, he pulled his hand away from the light switch and put his hand out to the wall for balance.

"What the hell is that?" he exclaimed.

Probably just the new shellac, he thought, but his heart raced a bit. Then he brushed the thought away thinking that working with the police for so long had rubbed off on him.

Paranoid.

Adina was so neat he teased her all the time, even saying that she was anal about housecleaning. He once suggested in jest that she see someone about her problem because he thought she had a bad case of what he called "housekeeping OCD."

Shaking off the feeling, he chuckled softly. Still, with skittering, incomplete thoughts he hit the light switch and looked down at his feet. The surreal vision before him would only allow him to collapse to his knees.

His eyes focused on what he saw.

Naked and laying in a pool of blood amid broken purple and white orchids was his beloved Adina.

ॐ

Mason's phone began to vibrate against his hip, startling him. He saw it was his boyhood friend.

"Hey, Tommy! What's up?"

"Mase–! Something ... ta-terrible has happened!" His breath caught on every syllable.

Tommy was almost incoherent.

"Whoa! Whoa! What's wrong? Calm down!"

"It's Adina! Someone's broken into her place! She's hurt! She's hurt and it doesn't look good!"

"What? What's going on? What happened?"

"She's not moving! There's blood all over the place!"

"Ok. Listen to me. Hang up and call 9-1-1! Don't move and don't touch anything! Do you hear me! Don't move a muscle! I'm on my way!"

"Ok. Hurry! GOD!" Tommy nearly moaned with despair into the phone.

Tearing out of his seat, Mason gave Adina's address to the desk sergeant and asked him to send a car over there right away. He busted through the precinct doors to his car, jumped in and tore away. He was at his destination in ten minutes flat.

Upon arriving at Adina's home, Mason flashed tin at the patrolman standing in the doorway and asked where the witness was.

The patrolman nodded toward a police car where Tommy sat staring wide-eyed straight ahead, rocking back and forth in the back seat.

"Who's the responding Sergeant?"

"Sergeant D'Avanzo, sir."

Mason nodded and turned to look in Tommy's direction once more, then turned away and stepped over the threshold. He didn't have to go far to see that the place was swarming with police and forensic personnel. Just beyond the entrance, he saw the body–presumably Adina–lying on the ground in the foyer under a yellow tarp. This did not look good.

"Sergeant Jones! I understand you know the vic?" Sergeant D'Avanzo called out in greeting as he approached.

"Yes. What do we have?"

"One big mess. It was a while before we noticed the tub had overflowed.

"In any case, the witness, one Tomas Ortiz, states he and the victim, identified as Adina Cruz, were in an intimate relationship. They had dinner, had sex ... "

"Made love," interrupted Mason as he put on cloth booties.

"Er, made love. Sorry. I'm sorry. I understand you know them; my condolences, sir."

"Yes, I do. Go on."

Mason was annoyed by Sergeant D'Avanzo's flippant remark.

"Well, the witness, Tomas Ortiz, says that he too owns an apartment in the complex. Apparently, they had dinner, he proposed, she said yes and they ... were intimate. Afterward, she asked him to spend the night. He stated that he had never spent the night with her, but he agreed and left to pick up some clothes at his apartment.

"He stated he was only gone for twenty minutes. When he returned, he found her like this.

"I'm declaring it a homicide and I'm bringing him in for questioning."

"He didn't do this."

"We need to follow procedure, Sergeant. I know they're your friends, but the evidence, as it stands right now, points to the fiancé. We both know that when something like this happens, the perpetrator is usually someone the victim knows. We always start with the person closest to the victim.

"I promise you, Sergeant. I will make sure the investigation proceeds within guidelines."

"I have to talk with him."

"Sergeant, you'll have to do that at the precinct. I'm sorry. I've got to go now. I'll keep you in the loop. Hang in there."

"Thank you. I would appreciate anything you can do to expedite uncovering what happened here."

Mason looked over at Adina's body. He wondered what the hell happened. A technician who had been working on her was putting away his equipment nearby. Mason approached and asked him to lift the tarp. He had to see for himself what condition Adina was in.

His heart broke when the technician did as he was asked. It took all of his will not to look away. She looked like she put up a fierce fight. He knelt to take a closer look.

There were marks on her neck; bruises on her cheeks. Her lower lip was busted.

She must've hit her head on something in the struggle, he concluded.

And I hope it was the bastard who did this. His lip sneered as the thought caught him by surprise.

He scanned her body. She was naked and he blushed.

Adina was his best friend's fiancée. He should never see her like this.

His eyes travelled to her hands. They had been bagged.

"Good. There may be some DNA under her nails," he said aloud to the technician who stood silently next to him.

Turning his head upward toward the technician, he asked, "Rape kit?"

"No, sir. The coroner will do that."

"Make sure she is aware that I want to see the results as soon as possible."

"Yes, sir."

Mason returned his gaze toward Adina then nodded to the technician to cover her again. He rose to his feet.

He looked around him. There were forensic technicians dusting for fingerprints; police officers gathering evidence from every nook and cranny of Adina's home. The place was in a shambles.

"Adina, what have you gotten yourself into?" he asked aloud.

Chapter 2
A Birth: December 12, 1962

Looking out onto the street through the window of his first floor tenement apartment, a man holds a cigarette as he sips on a highball glass of Don Q. He drowns his thoughts in amber, his nightly ritual. It is a wickedly cold night and the wind is blowing the snow, thrashing street signs and rocking lampposts. There have been electrical outages in some areas of the city due to the storm. The streets are mostly devoid of walkers and all public transportation has slowed to a crawl.

Yet he's feeling grateful. He not only has a job, but a beautiful, dutiful wife who is about to give birth to his child. Though not completely sure he's ready for such a life-changing event, he is happily anticipating his child's birth nonetheless. He is hopeful for a boy to carry on the family name, but he would be happy with a healthy baby girl just the same.

New York City is his city. The city that never sleeps is now his home and it's all he can do to keep from jumping up and down. Jesús Rosario emigrated to New York City's "El Barrio" from Puerto Rico just five years earlier. It was the first time he had ever flown on a plane. He prayed during the whole flight and begged God to get him to his new home safely. Relieved when he finally arrived at the airport alive and in one piece, he tried taking it all in at once. Overwhelmed with its beauty, he recalled how he naïvely expected to see the streets paved in gold. They weren't. He and his wife had to work hard for what little they had and now they were about to have a child.

"God, please help me do right by my family," he prayed aloud as he took a full swallow and continued to gaze out the window.

In the bathroom down the hall, his wife, Cruzita has just finished her bath. While toweling off, she felt a sharp pain–no, it was more like a flaming sword–cut across her pelvis. Bending over slightly and inhaling deeply several times, she waited for it to pass. When it did, she takes another deep breath and straightens up. As she pulls on her robe, she shuffles to the bedroom she shares with her husband, takes a seat at her make-up vanity and begins to slowly rub cocoa butter on her belly. Once her belly is soft and smooth, she anoints the rest of her body with rose-scented lotion. When this indulgent ritual is complete, she reaches for her hairbrush and her mind begins to wander. Her scalp responds to the brushing with an exhilarating tingle.

Cruzita had been married once before, but never had any children. Now pregnant with Jesús' child, she prays that it's a boy because she thinks this is what he wants. She's been in New York seven years now. It took her two years to get the money together to send for her husband so he could join her. She's afraid that if she has a girl, Jesús will leave her. This fear is real only to her and it is because of her age–she's a decade older than he is.

Cruzita grew up in a culture where she learned that it is the wife's duty to present her husband with a son. As a youth in old world Puerto Rico, she was taught that as the "man of the household," Jesús could only be accepted as a "real" man if he had a son to carry on his surname. Cruzita also believed that this may very well be the last pregnancy her body would be capable of enduring. She has had five pregnancies before this one, all ending spontaneously at various stages.

"God, please let this baby be a healthy boy," she prayed, tears stinging the corners of her eyes.

The only child of a woman who died during childbirth, Cruzita has no memories of her mother. Now the yearning in her heart had come full circle, with the pending birth of her own child.

As a youngster, she blamed herself for her mother's death. In her childlike logic, Cruzita thought her mother died from deep disappointment because she wasn't born a boy. Intellectually, she knew her desire for a son stemmed from the old wives' tale she heard while growing up, but there was still a small part of her that thought this pregnancy was her last shot at happiness. If it was, she wanted to gift Jesús with a male child.

On the other hand, if having a boy was something that would matter to Jesús, and she ended up giving birth to a girl, she didn't know what she was going to do.

๛

Cruzita rose from her vanity just as Jesús walked into the room. When he reached her, he playfully grabbed her from behind and rubbed her belly like a Buddha statue. When she turned around to face him and return the embrace, it happened.

Her water broke.

She doubled over in pain so unbearable she didn't think she could withstand it. It was so bad that she thought it would be merciful if she died.

She looked up at her husband and told him that she loved him.

Then she collapsed.

Catching her swiftly, Jesús laid her on the floor and began to lightly tap her on the cheek as he called her name. She regained consciousness quickly so he helped her back into her vanity chair, urging her to stay put. He hurried to the kitchen and returned with a glass of ice water. Once he was sure Cruzita was all right, he dialed her doctor's office, thinking the wall phone's rotator dial surely took an hour for every rotation. He got an operator at the doctor's service who advised him that an ambulance would be dispatched right away.

When Jesús expressed concern the ambulance may be delayed due to the snow, he was reassured and simply told to wait. He was promised the doctor would meet them at the hospital. Feeling uncertain, he thanked the operator nonetheless and hung up. He was in a complete panic.

"Cruzita, can you walk? Do you think you can make it to the living room? An ambulance is on its way."

"Yes, I think so," she replied.

"Good. Let's go get your coat ready. Everything will be ok. Don't worry. I won't leave you until you're with the doctor."

Nodding, she rose slowly. Before she was completely out of the chair, she had another contraction, causing her to bend over and cry out. A panicked Jesús decided they could not wait for an ambulance.

As soon as she recovered from this contraction, he left the room to grab her coat and quickly returned with it in hand.

After helping her into it, he walked her out the door. He rattled on like the typical nervous husband about not wanting to wait and said they should try and hail a cab. Over and over, he kept repeating that he didn't feel comfortable waiting for an ambulance.

As they reached the curb, they were almost knocked to the ground. The wind was blowing hard and the snow had already piled up several inches. There wasn't a soul to be seen anywhere. Waiting for a cab with his laboring, pained wife made him impatient. Mr. Hernandez, the neighbor from across the street had been watching the storm through his window. When he noticed them standing at the curb for so long, he became alarmed and hurried out to see what the matter was.

"Hola! What are you doing out here in this weather?"

"Hola, Señor Hernandez. Cruzita has broken her water and she's in labor. I was hoping to hail a cab to the hospital," Jesús explained.

"Well, I can drive you. Let me bring my car around. Wait inside. I'll honk."

"Oh! Thank you, Señor Hernandez! That would be greatly appreciated!"

The neighbor navigated gently over frozen roads to the hospital and within thirty minutes, they were rushing into the emergency room of Metro Region.

Since they were expected, Cruzita was rushed into a wheelchair and then into the delivery room. Jesús was handed a clipboard with a bunch of forms on it. He turned in her direction as she was being taken away and mouthed the words "I love you."

His wife responded in kind.

Jesús watched as she disappeared through swinging doors. He stared at those doors long after they had stopped swinging. Mr. Hernandez then gently took a hold of Jesús' elbow and led him to a chair where he set about filling out the forms he was handed.

Once Cruzita was registered, Jesús was told to wait there until he was called. Though feeling dejected and concerned for his wife and child, he did as he was told.

சின்

Cruzita didn't think she could bear the pain any longer. It was now past eleven o'clock at night and there was no sign of relief. Dr. Cohen kept coming over to touch and gently press on her belly.

"Cruzita, the baby is in a breech position. If I can't turn it around, we may have to perform a C-section," he explained in Spanish.

Frightened, Cruzita nodded and responded that as long as the baby was not presently at risk, she did not see any point in waiting for it to turn around on its own.

"In order to successfully do this, it will require anesthesia. At this stage of your labor, manually turning the baby around is going to be extremely painful."

He paused for a moment over his clipboard to watch her.

Hearing this, Cruzita quickly made a decision.

"If I have to be anesthetized, we might as well do the C-section. I don't want to take any chances with the baby."

Dr. Cohen agreed and summoned his nurse, Barbara. In quiet tones, he asked her to go to the waiting area and apprise Jesús of the situation.

Barbara found Jesús leaning against the wall and headed in his direction.

"Mr. Rosario, the baby is currently in a breech position. Mrs. Rosario has opted for a caesarean section, meaning we will take the baby from her surgically. She is about to be moved to an operating room and the procedure may be a while. May I suggest that you go home and wait for news?"

She paused, waiting for his reaction.

"You do look like you could use some rest."

Jesús did not react. He just stared at her, dumbfounded.

Overhearing this conversation and seeing his neighbor's non-reaction, Mr. Hernandez, who had patiently waited with Jesús, thanked the nurse and led Jesús from the hospital, through the parking lot and to the car. They rode in silence all the way home.

Back in the operating room, a team was quickly assembled and preparations began for the surgery.

"When you wake up, you will be the mother of a beautiful, healthy baby, Cruzita, I assure you," said the doctor kindly.

Cruzita nodded, secretly praying for a boy once again while being administered anesthetizing gas. The mask descended. Asked to count backwards from ten to one, she was out cold by the time she reached six.

అ∽ఆ

As soon as she was unconscious, the members of the operating team began their specific tasks. One placed a catheter in her bladder to drain her urine during the surgery. Her lower abdomen was bathed with iodine then covered with sterile sheets by another member. Her vital statistics were taken, noted and closely monitored by yet another. The anesthesiologist stood by at the ready in case there was an emergency requiring an additional dose of anesthesia. Once all the preparations were complete, and everyone was in their places, the doctor was ready to begin the procedure.

Gloves and mask on, he leaned over Cruzita's belly and made a long horizontal incision, cutting to her pubis, and spread the flesh apart with special clamps to access her uterus. He then made another incision and clamped it as well. When the incision in her uterus had been completed and clamped, everyone in the room was taken by surprise. It was now obvious that there were two babies, each in independent placental sacs—one baby over the other. The doctor called out for a second neo-natal team and almost immediately it arrived.

At 11:35 p.m., Dr. Cohen delivered the first child: a beautiful, healthy baby girl with strong lungs, skin the color of caramel, and a head full of soft, curly, dark hair. Her umbilical cord was cut and she was handed over to a nurse who weighed her, put her into an incubator and began performing preliminary treatment. By this time, the second team was in place and all anticipated a second healthy baby.

Extracted at 11:36 p.m., this child was announced as "BOY." The baby was smaller and a bit darker than its sister but appeared healthy with the same head full of dark, curly hair. Once the umbilical cord was cut, it too was handed over to a team of nurses who followed the same protocol as the first.

Upon delivery of the second child, the doctor set about carefully removing both placentas and administering medication that would help the uterus contract and prevent serious bleeding. He then proceeded to close the incision in the uterus first, then the abdomen. He used very small, closely placed self-dissolving stitches so as to ensure faster healing and little scarring. In the midst of this very intense process, he was interrupted.

"Doctor?" Barbara sounded befuddled.

"Yes, what's the matter?" he asked as he continued suturing.

"I called it wrong. This child's sex is indiscernible. The genitalia on this child are visually ambiguous. You need to make a final determination," she responded.

"Are all vital signs normal?"

"Yes, doctor."

"Good. Then I will have a look as soon as I am done with these sutures. Keep the child in the incubator here until then."

ᔢᔡ

Learning of the breech position of his baby caused Jesús' head to swim all the way home. He dreaded the possibilities and he was extremely worried. Over and over, he asked himself why.

Why did I let her convince me to try and have a baby? he asked himself.

He would've been happy living his life out with her; just the two of them. And now, because he was weak when it came to her desires, both she and his child were in danger of losing their lives.

Once he arrived home, Jesús bid his neighbor good night and promised to call him as soon as he got word from the hospital. He paced in his living room, full of anxiety as he awaited news from the hospital. It felt like so much time had elapsed since he returned home. He wondered when he would receive word of their condition and time ticked off on his living room clock like punishment. Of course, he was fully aware that it could be too soon for any news, but it seemed to him he should have heard something by now.

Walking over to the cabinet where he kept his spirits, he forcefully opened its doors. His eyes searched for his bottle of Don Q. Frustrated, he turned and ran his hand through his hair when he happened to glance over in the general direction where the bottle sat, finally spotting it. He grabbed a glass and poured himself a drink. He swallowed it in one gulp then poured himself another.

His mind raced with unanswered questions and concern for his wife and child. He wandered over to the window and stared out, feeling tormented. From the very beginning, he knew there was a chance that this pregnancy could be dangerous for Cruzita. But, she had insisted on trying. Now full term, they were hoping that everything would be ok. He was desperate to believe, and his fingers knotted into fists at his sides. Uneasiness and confusion took turns rolling in his gut.

What are you worried about? The voice in his head asked again.

He could not come up with an answer. Again. So he prayed, whispering to himself that everything would work out.

He headed to the bedroom to try and get some rest. Dizzy with anxiety and fatigue, Jesús stretched out on the bed and gripped the pillow, finally punched into fitful sleep.

༄ ༄

Jesús struggled for air. He was drowning. His lungs burned from the effort he was making to capture a little bit of oxygen. Someone was holding his head underwater!

What the hell is going on? How did I get here? Who is this person? What do they want? Forlorn confusion filled Jesús' soul. Someone was trying to kill him and he didn't know who or why.

Continuing to fight for air, Jesús desperately tried to grab a hold of the hand pushing his head further down, deeper into the well filled to the rim with ice-cold water. He finally broke free, gasping for air.

His lungs ached.

His heart raced and he could feel blood pumping through his body; pounding at his temples as he shook his head free of the icy water.

Taking a quick glance around the room, he could see that he was in some sort of basement. He found himself surrounded by machinery and tools he had never seen before. Still trying to catch his breath, he stared into the eyes of an unknown, yet familiar man. He didn't know who he was, but somehow, Jesús thought he recognized the stranger. He wondered how he knew him and why he seemed so familiar to him.

"Who are you? Why are you doing this to me?"

"It didn't have to be this way, you know," was the strange man's response.

Then bells went off, long and loud.

ॐ—ॐ

Jesús awoke with a start, gasping for air. As he fought the fog of sleep, he reached for the black receiver on the nightstand.

"Halloh?"

His deep accent curdled from sleep.

"Yes. Jesús Rosario?"

"Yes, this is Jesús."

"This is Dr. Cohen. I'm calling about Mrs. Rosario."

"Yes?" He held his breath.

"Congratulations! I am happy to report that the procedure went smoothly and she is in recovery. You are now the parents of a beautiful, healthy baby girl. You may come visit your wife and your daughter anytime you like."

"Thank God! Thank you! I will be there as soon as I can."

"Perfect. She should be ready to be moved into her room shortly. Since it is past visiting hours, please ask for me when you arrive at the main desk here at the hospital. I will have to escort you to her room personally."

"That is very kind of you, Doctor. I will be there as soon as possible and I will do as you have directed," he said, then fumbled the heavy handset of the phone into its cradle.

Jesús looked at his watch. It was 1 a.m. He was still disturbed by the strange dream he just had. He shook his head and rubbed the side of his face as he walked toward the window to look and see about the weather. The streets had been plowed and he could see that buses were running again.

Good, he thought.

That meant there would be no need to wake Mr. Hernandez. He would take the bus.

Walking away from the window, he headed to the bathroom to shave and wash up in preparation for his visit with his family. A baby girl! He not only had a queen in his life, but now, he also had a princess.

Adina.

The name came to him like the wind that buffeted his apartment windows, unavoidable and demanding.

He would name her Adina Cruz Rosario if Cruzita were agreeable. He could not wait to see them and hold his newborn princess in his arms.

Chapter 3
A New Life; A New Family

"Mrs. Rosario? Cruzita? Cruzita!"

Her name echoed in a tunnel. Blinking, she regained some consciousness. She smelled something odd, typical after anesthesia. Grimacing, she swallowed. She tasted metal in the back of her throat; another remnant. A chill coursed through her body and she shivered. It was then that nausea overcame over her in a wave forcing her into complete awareness. Only then did she remember where she was and why.

She gagged and exploded a second time. A nurse quickly put a bedpan under her chin just as she expelled a clear, sour liquid. It was nasty. The vomiting caused her abdomen to contract, causing her so much pain it made her dizzy and her eyes watered.

While reassuring her, the same nurse who had been calling her name also wiped her chin. Cruzita's bed was raised to a forty-five degree angle and pillows were placed behind her. She was in pain and she was miserable, but she tried–albeit unsuccessfully–to ignore it. It was much worse than when she first awoke from the anesthesia and it now threatened to incapacitate her.

While the nurse put away the messy bedpan, Cruzita slowly pushed away the covers and lifted her robe so she could have a look at her abdomen. There were bandages along the length of her pelvic area, stretching from hip to hip. The area surrounding the bandage looked tender; it was swollen and very irritated. A small amount of blood had seeped through the dressing and this made her frown. She put her hand over the affected area and winced.

"Don't hurt yourself now, Cruzita," Doctor Cohen reprimanded as he walked through the double doors toward her.

"You must be careful. How are you feeling?" the doctor asked as he continued walking toward her.

"Hello, Doctor. I'm feeling strange ... down there ... and I'm hoping the nausea lets up soon. I don't like this feeling."

"Well, I can understand that. All of your concerns will soon pass, especially the nausea, as everything you are experiencing is due to the side effects of the anesthesia. The downside is that once those side effects go away, the pain will intensify for a bit. But, don't worry; I'll prescribe something for you to help alleviate your discomfort.

"On the positive side, once you're all healed, there will be little noticeable scarring and I don't anticipate the appearance of keloids in the affected area. I used very small stitches, spacing them very closely together specifically to deter their development. You should try to walk with a little bit of assistance in the morning. In fact, I insist. The sooner you are up and around, the sooner you will heal."

"Thank you, Doctor." She shifted a bit and winced.

"So, how's my baby? Did I have a boy or a girl?"

Dr. Cohen beamed. "You have a beautiful, healthy baby girl."

Hearing and understanding the news that she had given birth to a female child, an extremely disappointed Cruzita hung her head. The doctor could see she was not happy.

"What's wrong, Cruzita? You had a healthy baby! Aren't you happy about that?"

"I'm happy the baby was born healthy, but I'm disappointed because I wanted to gift Jesús with a son."

"Oh, Cruzita! Surely he will be just as happy with a daughter! Don't you worry your pretty little head about any of that nonsense! I've called your husband to give him the good news and he was ecstatic! He will be here soon to visit with you both.

"Now, let me have a look at your bandages."

Cruzita nodded, eyes downcast with shame. She was ashamed by the way she reacted when the doctor told her she had given birth to a baby girl. Yet she couldn't shake the disappointment.

Satisfied that the wound was properly bandaged, the doctor pulled the blanket up around Cruzita's waist.

"Everything looks fine. Soon you will be moved to your room and then I'll let you have a short visit with your baby. When your husband arrives, I will personally escort him so you can all visit together for a while as a family. But for now, just relax and get some rest."

The new mother leaned back against the pillows and slowly closed her eyes as the nurses began preparing to move her. The doctor turned and headed out of the recovery room. His nurse met him just outside the room and handed him a clipboard with forms for his signature as they walked away together.

❦

By law, Doctor Cohen had an obligation to complete a form for each child born live in his care. After completing the forms, he signed them and passed the clipboard back to his assistant. They continued walking down the hall.

"Have you had any contact with the preacher?" she asked.

"Yes, I spoke with him right after the birth. We will meet on Sunday immediately following the sermon."

"And, you're sure that this is the right couple for this baby?"

"Yes. Please stop worrying, my dear. They very badly want a child and they are fully aware of this particular child's circumstances. I promise you, it will all work out. Don't you worry about a thing, sweetheart."

"Fine."

Barbara held the clipboard to her chest, turned on her heel and walked off toward the administrative offices of the hospital. Dr. Cohen admired his wife as she walked away.

❦

In 1943, two years before Dr. Cohen and Barbara first laid eyes on each other, Gualberto Villarroel, came into power in Bolivia. The fascist anti-Semitic ruler was at the helm of the coup that overthrew the former President, Enrique Peñaranda.

President Peñaranda was known to have a full medical staff on call twenty-four hours a day. Prior to the coup, Dr. Cohen was employed as the President's personal physician. At the time, the good doctor was known by his given name: Rogelio Lopez-Barril. Villarroel retained him as his personal physician, after the previous government's overthrow.

World War II had just ended in Asia when Japan agreed to surrender. Barbara Gomez-Larralde was a young, childless widow looking for work as a nurse when she and Rogelio first encountered one another. He assisted Villarroel as he interviewed candidates for a staff nursing position when they first met. As he called out to a roomful of candidates, he spotted her—it was love at first sight for the two of them.

Less than three years later, another coup, and they fled Bolivia for America with brand new identities. Marrying immediately upon arrival in New York City, Roger and Barbara Cohen promptly set up an ob/gyn practice and called it Esperanza Family Clinic. Its purpose: to offer hope and medical services to the poor, specifically the city's immigrant Spanish-speaking community of El Barrio. The couple needed to blend in unnoticed in a community where the military of their country wouldn't be looking for them. They were convinced that this was the perfect place to hide—in plain sight.

Seeing the most destitute among these immigrants, they wanted to save as many children as possible born into this misery. Their initial intention may have been noble, but eventually, in their twisted, entitled thinking, they chose who was most deserving.

When the couple wasn't offering free services to this community, they supplied infants born of these circumstances to childless couples that were better equipped financially to adequately provide for them. At the same time, Dr. Cohen and Barbara saw an opportunity to exact financial gain for themselves.

Most of the children sold were born in their homes, not a hospital. Sometimes, these children were unwanted by parents who were merely resigned to having them; resigned because their religious beliefs wouldn't allow for any other options. If the doctor had any inkling that this was the situation with the expectant parents, they were lied to and told that their child died during childbirth; making it much easier for the doctor and his wife to supply these babies to other families. This was accomplished by surreptitiously sending the husband out to fetch some forgotten item in another room, or at the local pharmacy. If the baby they were selling cried, the parents were told the baby did not live but a few minutes or that the baby died during post-natal examination.

At the time of Adina's birth, Dr. Cohen and Barbara were in search of a baby who could be sold to a couple living in Pennsylvania. This was a difficult task as the adoptive parents had specifically requested a child that came from biological parents resembling themselves. In discussions with the doctor, the couple pointedly stated that they were committed to providing a loving home in which to raise any child found for them.

The husband in this case, a black man, was the pastor of a small Baptist church in Lebanon, Pennsylvania. This family had lived in the same town for generations. He was the latest pastor in a long line of men from his family who held the same post.

The pastor met his light-skinned wife, a former prostitute, whom he saved from a near-fatal beating courtesy of a customer.

Everyone who saw the pastor and his wife together remarked how blessed she was to have been rescued by him and how much happier he now seemed since they married. However, after ten years of marriage, they desperately wanted a child but were unable to conceive naturally.

While helping a parishioner with a move, the pastor's wife commented on her young child and how much she wanted a baby of her own. Several clandestine meetings and anonymous phone calls later, a meeting was set up and arrangements for a baby were made without preference for the child's sex. The pastor and his wife just wanted a healthy baby.

Dr. Cohen thought this couple would be perfect parents for this newborn with the ambiguous genitalia. He figured it was better than the alternative—a lonely, desolate life in a foundling hospital awaiting adoption indefinitely. He believed he was doing the right thing. While working with the Rosarios during Cruzita's pregnancy, he learned that they still lived by old-world standards—especially Cruzita. A hermaphrodite child would not be fully accepted in this particular household. This couple was too ignorant and traditional to understand that this was not an act of God but a biological phenomenon; and not particularly rare, at that. They were also not wealthy. Surgery was well beyond their means and no hospital would do it for them gratis.

Barbara, on the other hand, had a bad feeling about this match and had no problems expressing her concern. Dr. Cohen dismissed her feelings. He could see no other alternative. Presenting this Pennsylvania couple with this otherwise healthy child would serve two purposes: the couple would get what they wanted, which was a child to call their own; and the doctor would get what he wanted–which was to get paid. He would be paid a nice chunk of change that would inevitably be shared with her.

What's she worried about?

As the doctor walked back to his office, he pulled out a little black book from his breast pocket where he kept notes and wrote:

Otherwise healthy hermaphrodite child; Hispanic, dark caramel complexion; fraternal twin of healthy baby girl. (Surname Rosario); born Dec 12, 1962; Metro Region Hosp.; New York, NY/Lebanon, PA; $10,000.

Chapter 4
The Rosario Family Is Now Complete—or Is It?

Jesús walked through the doors of the main entrance of the lobby of Metro Region Hospital. As he approached the reception desk, the security guard on duty did not look up from his newspaper. Realizing the guard was fast asleep behind it, Jesús coughed, startling him. The newspaper rustled then fell as the guard found mental purchase.

"Good morning."

Jesús looked sheepish.

"Yes! Good morning."

The guard sputtered a bit, embarrassed.

"What can I do for you?"

"My name is Jesús Rosario. My wife, Cruzita, had a baby tonight. Dr. Cohen is her doctor. He called to tell me that I could visit with them tonight. He also said I should have him paged when I arrive."

The fifty-something guard blinked at him, while shifting his considerable weight in the squeaking chair.

"I'll call the maternity ward. They'll page him."

The guard gestured in the direction of the waiting area. Jesús thanked him and took a seat facing him. He was tense and displaced as he listened to the guard ask for a page.

තිත

Cruzita was just arriving in her room. Sensation was returning to the lower part of her body and she was starting to feel some tingling in her legs along with a slight ache in the area of the incision. Feeling extremely grateful that Dr. Cohen had made it possible for her to have a private room, she absentmindedly glanced at the IV hooked to her arm while the attending nurse took extreme care to make sure that she was comfortable. A few minutes after the nurse was done with all her fussing, Dr. Cohen arrived.

"Cruzita, I have good news for you! Jesús is here. He is anxious to see you and meet your baby girl. Are you ready for me to bring him in?"

"Is he? Yes, please do. Thank you."

"Good. I'll be back shortly."

Though she didn't think it showed, seeing Jesús made her extremely anxious. She wasn't ready to face her husband. She knew she had to apologize for giving birth to a female child and felt she had no choice but to promise him she'd try again.

But Dr. Cohen could not be fooled. He heard the anxiety in Cruzita's voice. He patted her hand in an attempt to reassure her.

"Everything's going to be fine! I'm sure he's going to be very happy. Don't you worry about a thing, Cruzita."

Cruzita nodded somberly, unconvinced.

"Again, thank you, doctor."

With that, the doctor left her room and headed toward the elevators.

࿇

"Hello, Mr. Rosario! Congratulations!" Dr. Cohen exclaimed as he stepped off of the elevator.

"Thank you, Dr. Cohen," said Jesús, accepting the doctor's outstretched hand.

"Thank you so much for all that you have done! You have no idea how grateful I am to you, especially given Cruzita's history."

"This is what I do, Mr. Rosario. I do the best I can for my patients. Now, please follow me."

Nodding, Jesús noticed the doctor was leading him through doors marked "Hospital Personnel Only" toward a service elevator. He wondered why they didn't take the public elevators, but brushed his concerns away because it made him feel important to be using a passageway reserved for hospital employees. He and the doctor chatted about how well the surgery went and how beautiful the baby was. Within moments, he was getting off on the twelfth floor and walking into Cruzita's room expectantly.

Though happy to see her, his brow furrowed a bit–he thought the baby would be in the room with her. No matter. Once at her side, he reached out to his wife, lovingly cupped her face in his hands and kissed her. Satisfied that she was ok, he looked into her brimming eyes as his began to well with tears.

"Why are you crying? Are those tears of joy?"

"She's just tired," interjected Dr. Cohen before Cruzita could answer.

Turning to the nurse sitting in the chair next to Cruzita's bed, Dr. Cohen asked her to please leave the room and wait for him in the hallway. He then turned his attention back to the new parents and began discussing the details of the surgery, omitting the fact that fraternal twins had been born. He answered their questions about what to do once they were home with the baby and how to clean and re-dress Cruzita's wound. They also discussed follow-up appointments for the new mom and the vaccination schedule for the infant. When they were done with their discussions, the doctor stepped out of the room saying that he would have someone bring in their daughter for a visit.

On the other side of the door to Cruzita's room, Dr. Cohen approached the nurse he had previously asked to leave.

"Mr. and Mrs. Rosario have been advised of the physical abnormalities of their child. They are devastated and wish to place the child up for adoption. However, they are ready to see the female twin and have requested that she be brought into the room for a visit. You are to bring the female child to them. Be aware that I am ordering you not to mention the abnormal child–the other twin–to them. They are grieving and we must respect their privacy. I want you to prepare all of the necessary paperwork for the transition of custody from the parents to The Foundling Network. I will obtain and witness the parents' signatures and present the paperwork to the hospital tomorrow morning."

He looked over the top of his glasses at her.

"Do you understand?"

"Yes, Doctor," said the nurse and off she went to get the female newborn.

Dr. Cohen leaned against the wall and waited for the nurse to return because he didn't want to take a chance that she might come back with the wrong child.

࿇

"I owe you an apology," announced Cruzita, the tears threatening once again to break the dam.

"You owe me an apology? What for? Why do you think you owe me an apology?" asked Jesús.

"I wanted to present you with a son. I wanted the world to know that you had an heir to carry on your name. You deserve to have a son to be your legacy in this world. But, I have failed you miserably and for that I apologize."

Her expectant eyes wavered under tears.

"Cruzita, you don't owe me an apology. Having a son did not matter to me. It was more of an issue for you than it ever was for me. Our baby was born healthy. My daughter and my wife–the two most important people in the world to me–you are thriving. As far as I'm concerned, nothing else matters. You will both be going home with me soon and I promise you, the three of us will have a wonderful life together."

Cruzita smiled and nodded in appreciation. Although she was still feeling a little bit embarrassed, she also felt blessed to have such a wonderfully understanding husband who would love her no matter what. She looked up into his eyes tenderly as they made plans for the future.

They were in the midst of discussing names when the same nurse navigated a rolling bassinet into the room. In it lay their newborn baby girl. She was wrapped tightly in a white blanket for their first visit as a family. Jesús stopped talking and looked over at the nurse from afar, his face beaming, then lowered his eyes toward the bassinet and caught a glimpse of his princess. He was so delighted that he was unable to move. The nurse reached in and took the baby out of the bassinet then carefully placed the child in its mother's arms. Cruzita accepted her daughter, gently kissing her head with Jesús still at her side. In a very emotional state, he gazed down upon them both as a single tear of happiness slowly slid down his cheek. He haphazardly wiped it away placing one hand on Cruzita's shoulder and the other over his baby. He felt connected, bonded by the love for these two very important people in his life.

Looking down upon them, he murmured: "She's so beautiful, so perfect. Her skin is so pink, so soft. And, look at all that hair!"

He bent down to kiss the baby's cheek then inhaled deeply.

"She smells so sweet! Cruzita, what do you think of the name 'Adina Cruz Rosario'? Isn't that a great name for her? This way she carries both our names just like she would in the old country, hmm?"

"I like it," Cruzita said, breaking out in a weary smile. "Adina Cruz Rosario. Yes. I like the sound of that!"

"Oh, Cruzita!" he exclaimed.

He stood, cradling the baby, his eyes shining.

"I will do everything in my power to make sure that she has every opportunity to become whatever she wants to be. She will go to the best schools and she will reach all of her goals. I will take her to museums and libraries and maybe even learn a few things myself! This child is going to be somebody one day; even if it takes every last breath I have in me to help her realize all of her dreams!"

"Yes, she will. I'm sure she will!" replied Cruzita.

That was the only immediate response she could give as she looked down at her daughter and began to accept the fact that she too had fallen in love with her.

"She will make us proud! I am so happy, Jesús. I promise you here and now, that I will be the best mother to her and the best wife to you that I can possibly be."

"Of that I have no doubt," said Jesús as he bent down to kiss her.

҈

Looking in through the small window in the door, Dr. Cohen watched this portrait of perfect familial bliss before heading back to the nursery where Adina's twin lay in its bassinet. He wanted to check in on the child before heading home for the night to make sure the newborn's vital signs were stable.

Once that task was complete, the doctor headed back to his office. A pile of paperwork needed to be prepared and presented to the hospital authorizing the transfer of custody to The Foundling Network. He had forged both parents' signatures on the form and had already advised his contact at The Foundling Network, that he had a new intake for him to authorize. His signature would make the paperwork appear legitimate. The doctor had taken every precaution in case there was ever an audit.

Chapter 5
The Church of Everlasting Glory, Lebanon, Pennsylvania

"Glory to God Almighty! On this magnificent day, I welcome you to The Church of Everlasting Glory! Hallelujah!"

"Hallelujah!" the crowd bellowed in return.

"It is a blessing to be here with you all today! Glory be to Almighty God!" The pastor raised an open palm toward the congregation's echoes of "amen."

"Yes, indeed! It is a blessing! Take a look around you. What do you see? I don't know about you, but I see God's glory in this church! I see it in all of your beautiful faces! Yes, I do! I see love! This place is a sanctuary of peace! And that is what I want to talk to you about today."

He stepped from the pulpit, scanning for eye contact from the crowd.

"There are many, many evils outside this room. There may even be some evil lurking around in your own homes. We all know that the Devil is tireless in his work; that an idle mind is the Devil's playground. But, we must abide by the law of God! We must be strong against the Devil's will. We must show him that it is hard work to take over the soul of God's people. We must prove to the Devil that the benevolent light of God's love is stronger than he, for we are the children of a king, not spawn of an evil prince!"

A chorus of "amen" and "hallelujah" accompanied by the scat of tambourines erupted throughout the small but crowded church. Parishioners noisily rose to their feet. Their arms raised up high in unison, waving to and fro as they called upon their collective spirit in passionate reverence to God.

The mass of bodies shifted left and right, a rhythmic undulation for a long while until finally, the man in the pulpit signaled for silence.

"I will continue. I have one question for you, my brothers and sisters, just one question:

"Where has the love gone? Please tell me."

His words were punctuated with pauses.

"I want to know where the love has gone!

"Today there is unbelievable violence everywhere. There is horrible death, pestilence and pain all around us. There is distrust among men; there is dishonesty. Nothing but hatred in the words we speak! All this hatred and all this negativity is not what God intended for his children! It absolutely is not! All you need to do to verify what I am saying is look in the Bible as it is so plainly written in black in white. We were meant to love one another in the name of God!"

"Amen!" cried out an elderly member of the congregation. A heightened tension of spiritual upheaval seized the room, nearly causing the people to jump up with the Holy Ghost once again. The preacher signaled for her to sit, which she did.

"We are all of one God. Whether a person's philosophies or religious beliefs lie in Christianity, Judaism or Islam, everyone shares the belief that we are all of one God! You'd better believe it! It is our responsibility to love one another, as that is how we show our love for God!

"As is so clearly dictated in the Bible; specifically, John 4:19-21, I want to remind you of the following:

We love because he first loved us. Whosoever claims to love God yet hates a brother or sister is a liar. For whoever does not love their brother and sister, whom they have seen, cannot love God whom they have not seen. And he has given us this command: Anyone who loves God must also love their brother and sister.'

Another "hallelujah" rang out as the preacher bowed his head. Someone started shaking a tambourine. Another began playing the organ as the pastor came down from his pulpit to joyously celebrate the word of God and be amongst his beloved parishioners. At that moment, he was a man full of love for his people.

Chapter 6
Pastor James Ezekiel, Margaret and RJ: The Prestons

Margaret's Story

Margaret Preston was barely awake when she walked back into her brightly lit kitchen. A shrieking ambulance tearing past her house interrupted the white noise of brewing coffee, slamming her back to a reality she no longer wanted to remember. Images floated up in her memory: her half naked body, the dark, dank room she had been confined in on that day so long ago.

The bra and torn panties she was wearing offered no protection for her fragile body as the kicks came again and again–furious and unrelenting. She tried to cover her face in an attempt to prevent the blows from connecting, but it was no use. She had no defense.

Her right eye felt warm to the touch. Soon, it was swollen shut. The muffled grunts that came with each blow were followed by a pull of her matted hair. She had been hit on the head so many times all she could hear was muffled buzzing. The blood from her nose ran over her split lip burning her raw skin. Just when she thought she would die there at the hands of her attacker, the police miraculously busted through the door. They swarmed all around him, saving her life in the process. Someone grabbed her by the arm and brought her up to her feet. Even while being held up, she could barely stand. A coat was thrown over her bruised body and she let her savior half carry her out to the waiting ambulance.

When she was safely in the care of the medical technician, her savior disappeared like the invisible guardian angel she knew everyone had. She truly believed he was her guardian angel, sent down from heaven by God to protect his charge.

While being strapped into the gurney, she moved her head from side to side, searching for him. She was too stunned and ashamed to be in the predicament she was in to even look at him directly when he first appeared. She didn't make eye contact with her savior, but she wanted to thank him for saving her life nonetheless.

"Who was that man? Where did he go?" she asked the paramedic who wore a tag that read "Smith."

"Please, just calm down, ma'am. I need you to calm down."

"Who was he? Where did he go?"

She insisted on knowing who the man was.

"Who?" asked the paramedic.

"The man who carried me out of there; who was he?"

"You mean Preston? Don't you know who he is? Everyone knows him. He's the one who alerted the police. I'm guessing you're not from here."

"No. I'm from Reading. I was brought here by a client."

"A client?"

"Yes."

"May I ask you a question?"

The rescued woman nodded.

"What kind of work are you in?" the paramedic asked as he examined the woman's face then shone the light of a small flashlight in his patient's eye.

"I am a prostitute. I get paid by strange men to perform sexual acts their wives won't perform."

Stunned, Smith stopped examining her. The matter-of-fact way in which the woman responded surprised him. This badly hurt woman didn't show pride or shame. In fact, she showed no emotion at all. He could tell that this was just a way of life for her; a way of surviving.

"At the end of the night another man comes along and takes the money I've earned before taking me home. I'm not proud of that, but it is the truth. I didn't plan on becoming a prostitute, but it was the only way out of the hell I was living in. I went from one nightmare to another when I believed my pimp could provide a life I dreamed about as a little girl. Everything he told me was nothing but lies."

The paramedic wanted to put his arms around this sad woman and tell her everything would be all right. But, he knew that wouldn't help. The light in her eye was gone.

Margaret was secretly ashamed of the position she was in, but there was nothing she could do about it now. She promised herself that she would heal and build a righteous life for herself even if it killed her.

She shuddered as she remembered this major event in her life. She recalled the look of pity on the face of the kind paramedic who sat slightly above her in the ambulance. Sitting at her kitchen table, she recalled how she didn't want to show shame in front of this stranger who was so compassionate toward her.

Why?

Was it because of the compassion he had shown her? Did she not feel worthy of his compassion?

It was sitting at that table, that she realized the answers to all her questions were "yes."

Margaret covered her mouth with that realization and stood up to look out the window. She pulled the curtain back and crossed her arms in front of her. She caught sight of two little birds sitting on a branch; one grooming the other and she wondered:

Why didn't she feel deserving of that kind of attention?

Why did the paramedic even care?

Finally, Margaret looked away and she began to cry. All she wanted was for the pain to stop. She went back to that horrible day in her memory.

The paramedic gently placed his hand on his patient's shoulder.

"I'm sorry to hear it's been so hard for you. Are you going to be all right after this? Do you have somewhere to go? Do you have any family around?"

"I have nowhere to go and I have no family left."

"Well, don't you worry about a thing, pretty lady. We're going to fix you right up. Once we arrive at the hospital, I'll have someone come and talk with you. Don't you worry, ok? Everything's going to be all right, I promise."

The woman thought about what paramedic Smith said and nodded. Then her eyebrows wrinkled with something that stuck with her.

"But, I still don't understand. How did this man know to call the police? The next house is so far away."

"This is a small town, Miss, and just like any small town, everybody knows everybody else. When a strange face comes into town, that face gets noticed. To top it off, your attacker wasn't friendly to the old ladies of this town, and that's a very bad way to start if you're looking to put down roots around here. He was a loner and he was anti-social. People quickly noticed that about him, so they kept an eye on him.

"One of the ladies noticed that whenever he left the barn where we found you, he always seemed angry and out of sorts. He often looked disheveled, as if he had been in a fight. This piqued her curiosity and so yesterday, she followed him here. She said she could hear him shuffling about but didn't think anything of it. Still, she was either just a nosy woman or something seemed wrong enough to her that today, she followed him again. She peered through the window but saw nothing, so she started to walk away and that was when she heard you screaming. So she contacted Preston. He called the police, and here we are. Thank goodness for nosy neighbors, huh?"

Nodding, the rescued woman seemed to relax a little bit. She was dizzy now. The medication given to her was taking effect and she blacked out, awaking in a hospital bed.

࿔࿔

Margaret recalled how sure the paramedic sounded when he said things would work out. He was so convincing Margaret believed him. And things did work out, for a while anyway.

James Ezekiel Preston was the name of the man Margaret considered, at the time, to be her invisible angel. He was the man who saved her life that day so long ago.

Shaking off the memory of that awful day, she started thinking about the first time she spoke with James and the memory brought a smile to her face.

But things were so different now.

"Are you daydreaming again, woman?"

Startled back into reality by the sound of her husband's voice, the first thing that hit her was the smell of freshly brewed coffee.

"There is so much work to be done around here! How is it even possible you could think it would be alright to sit around like a zombie all day?"

"Good morning, dear. I'm sorry. I just got lost in my thoughts."

Margaret tried with every fiber of her being not to be affected by his tone. He was obviously not in a good mood and she didn't want to make it worse.

"Well, would it be too much trouble to ask you to snap back to reality, please? Are you going to the sermon today?"

"No, dear. I hope you understand. I plan to stay home and get started with all the work that has to be done before the baby arrives. Would that be ok with you?"

Surprised by her tone, he responded: "No, it is not ok with me, but you can't be in two places at once, now can you?"

Mrs. Preston rose from her chair and gave her husband a kiss on the cheek. He did not reciprocate.

"I'll be there for tomorrow's sermon. I promise."

"Fine, but don't forget that the doctor will be here today to discuss the final details. Make sure you look presentable. We don't want him to think you're still 'in the life,' now do we?"

"No. I'll be presentable. Would you like your coffee now?"

"Yes, but hurry. I have to get going."

☙◦᙭

James Ezekiel Preston: A Brief Background

On his way out the door, James Ezekiel Preston stood before the hallway mirror and straightened his collar just before leaving for church. He was the forty-five-year old pastor of The Church of Everlasting Glory, a small congregation in an even smaller town with its own idiosyncrasies.

A native of Lebanon, Pennsylvania, he was considered to be a pillar of the community. But in reality, he was a tortured man; a victim of the tyranny under which his father ran the household he grew up in. He was also the third in his family to become the pastor of the Church of Everlasting Glory.

Married for almost ten often-turbulent years to the much younger Margaret Brown, he thought that by now they would be proud parents. However, it wasn't in God's plan for them to conceive naturally. He knew God was punishing him for not finding it in his heart to forgive his father for real transgressions, or his wife for that matter, for imagined ones.

୶∾ ∾୶

Rhys John Preston

The child obtained from Dr. Cohen by Pastor James Ezekiel and Margaret was named Rhys John, and quickly nicknamed "RJ." When RJ was twelve years old, he stumbled upon his father committing an act of sodomy against one of his classmates. RJ was unable to shake the horrible image from his mind of the young boy, bent in front of the father he thought he knew.

At the time, James Ezekiel was the deacon of The Church of Everlasting Glory.

RJ happened to be walking in the hallway leading to the rectory when he heard grunting and a boy sobbing from within. The door was ajar, so he slowly opened it further to discover that the animalistic sounds were coming from his father as he pummeled into his classmate; sweat dripping from his face onto his friend's backside. When the Pastor's son cried out to him, James tossed the boy aside and stood before his son with his own pants around his ankles, organ erect. It was an image the young boy could not and would never erase from his memory.

Decades later, he still shuddered when the image came to mind. Father and son never spoke of that incident again, but this sick man tortured young RJ for the rest of his life.

As a young boy and into early adulthood, RJ was regularly beaten and unduly punished by his father for something that was out of his control. The Pastor often threatened to do the same to his son as he had done to his classmate if he ever told anyone about what he had seen. Paralyzed by fear, RJ kept his secret sheathed in a deadly hatred deep in his heart for his father, and increasing self-hatred for his arousal at the scene–his body's betrayal.

Years later, in a media blitz, a list of names caught up in a prostitution raid had been released. RJ's grandfather, Adam, who at the time was the pastor of The Church of Everlasting Glory, found himself in the middle of a scandal as his name was on a list of targeted "johns."

While attending a conference at the Hotel Hershey in the famed town of Hershey, Pennsylvania, Pastor Adam had been invited to participate in some extracurricular activities. It soon became apparent that this was not the first time he had purchased the services of a professional as he had a propensity for what could be called "deviant tastes" just like RJ's father had.

The elder Pastor was later diagnosed with late-stage syphilis and died from the disease two years later after repeatedly refusing treatment. Pastor Adam felt the disease was God's way of smiting him for the mortal sins he had been committing over a lifetime and he believed the disease was his penance. He made peace with his sentence and accepted it.

For two years after the scandal, the congregation got by with temporary leaders but none of them ever really made a connection with its members. After having also served as a minister of the church under his father, James was tasked with being a liaison between the parade of pastors that came and went, and with members of the congregation as well as the church's elders. Examining the matter more closely, a vote was taken and the elders unanimously agreed to elevate James as the new pastor of The Church of Everlasting Glory as soon as possible. He was just thirty years old, the youngest pastor in the history of the Church.

At the time, he swore to his parishioners that he was not like his father. He promised them that rather than being the oppressor of women who had taken wrong turns in life, he would make it his life's work to offer them a safe haven in the community and an opportunity for a new path toward a life of promise. He would be a protector to all women–particularly those who had sinned against the word of God and lead them toward the light. This is what he believed he was doing the day he saved Margaret's life.

He would fail.

Pastor James Ezekiel first laid eyes on Margaret, ten years his junior, when he helped rescue her after having been held captive by a man her pimp sold her to.

Brushing his lapel, Pastor Preston headed out the door without saying a word to his wife.

Chapter 7
Adina Goes Home

At the exact moment that Pastor Preston left home for his church, Dr. Cohen exited his office. The last four days had been exhausting. He'd previously met with hospital administrators as planned and presented the successfully forged adoption papers. He went through the motions of processing the transfer of custody of the hermaphrodite child from the hospital to The Foundling Network. Though this was a legitimate vehicle for adoptions, as co-administrator of the organization, Dr. Cohen had access to all files and forms. He sometimes used the network as a funnel through which he processed those children born at the hospital and later sold on the black market.

When asked about the child's transport to the network, he offered to transfer the child himself saying there was no one available to do it. When questioned further, he added that he felt it was better to remove the child from the hospital premises as soon as possible because the sooner that it was done, the better it would be for the grieving parents. His argument was that he did not want to have the parents accidentally see the child in the nursery and cause them further pain. He had a strong argument and as a respected doctor, the hospital readily agreed. He was allowed to break with the rules and transport the child.

The fact of the matter was that he had no intention of transporting this child. Instead he was going to pay a little visit to the Prestons and hand over the child to them as per their agreement. His delivery of the baby today was to be a surprise for them. The Prestons did expect him today to go over final details, but he decided to present them with the baby as well in order to finalize the deal as quickly as possible.

Dr. Cohen knew he would certainly encounter morning rush hour traffic getting out of the city as well as truckers on the turnpike, so he needed to get as early a start as possible. He wanted to arrive at the home of the adoptive parents by early afternoon.

∂∽⌀

After spending almost a week at the hospital, Cruzita has finally been released. She and Jesús have completed the paperwork for her release and were now waiting for Adina to be brought to them. Ecstatic to be going home, Jesús made arrangements to take some time off from work so he could help Cruzita with their newborn daughter.

Although Cruzita was healing wonderfully, she was nervous about being alone with the child and Jesús could sense her apprehension. She tried to keep a poker face while waiting, but the excitement and the fear she felt inside competed for control. She breathed deeply and prayed for the strength to be the kind of mother and wife her family deserved.

Jesús was anxious as well, but he too did his best not to show it. The full impact of the responsibility he now had over his family was taking a firm hold over him but he was excited about what the future held for them as a family. He was really looking forward to his new life.

Chapter 8
Adina: A Life-Changing Event (1979/1980)

As expected, the next sixteen years were blissful, with Adina at its center, until *it* happened. They didn't see it coming. Adina had become a teenager and though Jesús and Cruzita wanted to believe they were doing all the right things, it was indeed an authoritarian household. It was one where Adina was the child and she had little say about anything. She was raised the way her mother was raised–isolated from other children her age. Education was emphasized. Like it or not, Adina personified the American Dream to her parents. But, maintaining and following the ways of raising children the way it was done in the old world did not work in late-1970s New York City. That was their downfall.

In early 1980, when Adina was one year away from graduating from high school, an event would occur that would blast right through the center of their perfect little world.

❧❧

"You are ruining your life! You know you can't get a decent job these days unless you have a college education! Besides, where else but college would you find a good man, one of fine quality? Don't you want a good man? A good life?

"C'mon, Adina! You really could have it all, you know. Get your degree, find yourself a good husband, have a family and if you have to work outside of the home, it will be easier for you to find a good paying job if you had a degree. I know you can do it all! Why is it so important for you to go so far away from home to study?"

"Ma! Don't you understand? I'm not saying that I don't want to go to college. I do. What I'm saying is that I want to go *away* to college. I want to *live in a dorm* with girls my age! Why do I have to go to a municipal university and live at home? Going away to study is supposed to shape me into an adult. How can that happen if I'm still living at home with you guys?

"Pa! Help me make her understand! Please?"

Her body language matched her father's: hands balled into fists, a fighter's stance.

"Adina, honey, I fully understand what you are saying. We just want to protect you. There are so many evils in the world. Men–both young and old–cannot be trusted. They want what they want, and they will stop at nothing to get it. You are a beautiful, but naïve young woman. As a man, I know what I'm talking about. As your father, I must side with your mother."

"You don't want to protect me so much as you want to protect my cherry! You think that I'm going to turn into some irresponsible sex fiend, don't you? Why won't you just trust me? Haven't I done everything that you've asked me to do? I've maintained my grades. I work part time. I am respectful and obedient. What more do I have to do to get you guys to trust me?"

"We do trust you, honey. It's everybody else, especially men, who we don't trust. Your father and I just want you to be happy. You will never find happiness if you give up your virginity before you marry. Nobody's going to want to buy the cow if you give away the milk for free, now will they?"

"I can't believe you just said that! How backward are the two of you! This is the twentieth century! There's been a revolution! A sexual revolution! Didn't anyone tell you? People don't think like that anymore!"

Frustrated, Adina shook her head and rolled her eyes. She sucked her teeth then glanced first at her father then her mother.

"Ugh! This is useless! I'm late for work. I've got to go. Bye."

Grabbing her pocketbook, the angry teenager flew through the door, slamming it shut behind her.

∂∘⟨

Though she had said she was going to work and her parents believed her, Adina's job as a sales clerk at a popular downtown clothing store was the last thing on her mind as she stormed out. In fact, her thoughts and daydreams involved her boyfriend who she would be spending the day with.

Less than a month before that agitated exchange about college with her parents, she had celebrated her seventeenth birthday. She had begun dating her older boyfriend the previous summer.

Benny had his own apartment just a few blocks from her job. He was an extremely handsome bad boy with a kind heart, a dropout who sold drugs. And, he was her first love.

Walking off the street and into Adina's store that beautiful summer day, he caught her off guard, as she tidied up the table where the end-of-the-season items were laid out. He so impressed her, everything seemed suspended in time to her. For Adina's part, her heart seemed to want to jump out of her chest. Her throat dried, making it extremely difficult for her to breathe. He strode toward her slowly, and she thought she was dreaming. She watched as he, much like a graceful gazelle, glided toward her. He waited to speak until he was close enough for her to hear his whisper and then, the seduction was complete.

The melody of his words spilled out of his mouth like a song. She couldn't help her physical reaction to the sound of his voice. Her pants became wet and it took her a second to remember she wasn't dreaming.

He was in fact talking to *her* when he said "Hello." Still, she was slow in responding. He repeated himself and asked if she would help him put together an outfit for his sister. Robotically, she simply nodded. He smiled with a twinkle in his eye and then she melted.

She set about helping him and she knew she was a little too eager. So she asked how old his sister was and then took the time to consciously become human again as he responded to her question. While she helped him decide, they spoke of end-of-summer events; in particular, an upcoming free concert, which was scheduled two days later featuring a local act, Amor. Her eyes sparkled and her hands moved slowly at these now-strange tasks. Her entire being was now focused on his presence.

As she bagged his purchases, he paused while putting away his wallet and asked if she would be interested in joining him at the concert they had been discussing. Adina agreed, a Rolodex of emotions passing over her face—shock, pleasure, shyness, coy reservation. It's the first time someone so handsome had taken any kind of interest in her. She was trying to grab on to every delicious moment.

During the next two days she floated like lilies on a pond. When the day finally arrived, it was all she could do to stay in control of her emotions.

On the day of their date, Adina worked her full shift. She told her parents she would be going to the concert with a girlfriend, so she only half lied. She knew her parents loved her. She knew they did the best they could for her with what little they had, but she put those thoughts out of her mind and allowed herself to be carried away by the music; to be enveloped by the vibe, and more importantly the feelings she felt being in such close proximity to Benny. They laughed heartily; they danced demurely, and afterward, they started out of the arena to a diner, more than eager to extend the evening.

Her stomach somersaulted and fluttered when he took her hand. It was official. She was in love for the first time.

During that summer, they slowly got to know each other. Initially, it was just a pure, platonic friendship. Adina spent every free moment she had with him.

A few weeks after that concert, they went to a movie downtown. Benny held her hand all through the two-hour long movie. He also kissed her for the first time that day.

As they were leaving the theatre, Benny suggested they get ice cream and she agreed. They sat in the ice cream parlor talking and telling one another jokes. She reached to clear a smear of ice cream from his chin. He would steal spoons of her sundae and she would mock chastise him. There was relentless joyful tension between them. The parlor held only the two of them even as it overflowed with teenagers. After a long while, they rose from the table to leave. Benny offered his hand to help her out of her seat. When she was up, he slowly drew her to him, the slowest tango in the world, and he never took his eyes off hers. Her lower lip trembled. Adina couldn't stop blinking her eyes.

As he closed in on her, she could smell his breath, sweetened by vanilla. She licked her lips and as he licked his, she, focused on the tip of his tongue sliding over his mouth. Her breath caught in her throat. She thought she would faint when he lowered his mouth to hers. A spark sprang from his mouth as it made contact with her lips.

He gently, tentatively tapped her lips with his at first, then lowered himself toward her a second time and repeated the gentle tap but lingered on her lips just a second longer. The third time he met her lips, she opened her mouth to breathe and he inserted his tongue. It wrestled with hers.

Oh, my God! I hope I'm doing this right! She thought at the moment, unsure what to do.

When they finally pulled apart, they gazed into each other's eyes. Her heart was a racing rabbit in her chest. He cupped her face in his hands and gently kissed her on one hot cheek as he pulled her closer still. Adina's hands slowly slid up to his chest and as she did, she could feel every perfectly defined muscle under his shirt. This was all very new to her. She debated whether to push him away, but it felt so good to feel secure in his arms. She hoped he would never stop holding her, loving her the way he did. She couldn't stop touching him. She ran her hands down his chest and under his arms putting her hands on his shoulder blades and pulled him in closer.

She knew people were looking at them but she didn't care. They were one in their universe. That is, until he broke the spell with real words–he said he had to get her home before they both spiraled out of control. Reality rushed in. They walked out of the ice cream shop in silence and remained so while she battled the urge to touch her lips that still tingled with his kisses.

Alone in her room that night, she replayed that scene in her head–critiquing her technique. She never forgot that first kiss and for the rest of her life, with every man she kissed, she sought to feel what she felt with Benny that night. As she got older and had other first kisses, she realized none would ever measure up to that one.

It wasn't just Adina who was head over heels. Benny was also very much taken by this woman-child. Like Adina, he himself never forgot that first kiss. She was nervous, he could tell. But she liked it, he knew that too. He wanted to teach her everything he could about love, being in love, and how to show that love to your partner. He wanted to protect her, and he catered to her every whim.

The first time they made love, Benny made sure to be gentle with Adina. He was in full awareness of her virginity. Adina, in turn, was a quick and eager study. Benny made her a woman, *his* woman, and having that status made her the happiest she had ever been in her short life. Benny introduced Adina to lovemaking as an art. They experimented. She eventually blossomed from the shy, only child of overprotective parents into a headstrong woman who knew what she wanted. She quickly recognized she had *POP*—power of the panties— and she wielded that power over him unabashedly.

Besides teaching Adina the secrets of a passionate lover, he also taught her how to be a woman who could take care of herself; turning her into the complete package any man would want.

They spent many days together with Benny gently pushing and supporting her in everything she did. He constantly stressed the importance of using her brain. He pushed her to question everything about herself in an attempt to get her to know who she was outside the boundaries of her sheltered upbringing. He wanted her to be a stronger, more independent woman. He didn't want her to merely coast through life. He wanted her to take charge of her own destiny, embrace schooling. He held himself up as an example of what not to become. He was always on her case. In the process, he shaped her into a self-confident, street smart, intelligent and powerful woman, a force to be reckoned with.

They carried on in this blissful state for almost a year. They were madly in love with each other. However, she realized that he was honest when he told her he was everything she was not.

Benny came from a broken home.

His father was killed in prison when he was just a boy and soon after his murder, his mother left him with relatives, abandoning him forever. When he became too difficult to handle, he was placed in foster care hopping from one foster home to another. As a teenager, he was a truant and for a short time lived on the streets after running away from the last home where he had been placed.

He fended for himself by taking odd jobs until finally he became a courier for a numbers runner who also dealt pot in large quantities. Once Benny proved that he was trustworthy, he was given small amounts of marijuana to sell at a 70/30 split. He got the bigger split because the man he worked with took a liking to him and admired his strong street ethics.

Benny did well with sales, saving all that he could while steadily rising up the ranks. He began securing larger and larger amounts of weed as his territory grew. With the growth of his territory, he realized that marijuana was small potatoes in comparison to other, harder drugs. This made him even more ambitious. So he got the money together to buy a kilo of cocaine and broke off from his criminal sponsor.

Benny built a solid reputation for himself in the cocaine trade and he was not surprised to find success there. The more successful he became, the greedier he got until he was arrested for a murder during a drug deal gone wrong. The buyer was an up and coming dealer himself whose intention was to rip Benny off.

The day before Benny was arrested, Adina received confirmation from her gynecologist that she was pregnant. Not only was she scared, but also devastated. She was on her way to share the unexpected news with him when she saw a handcuffed male figure being put into a police car near his home. A crowd had gathered to watch the events. Adina turned to the woman standing next to her and asked what was going on.

"They say the guy in handcuffs killed a man," the woman told her.

Shocked, Adina stared at the woman silently. She turned and walked away with tears in her eyes. The man in handcuffs was Benny.

Chapter 9
Cruzita's Manipulating Ways

In the years since Adina's birth, Cruzita slowly resolved her feelings about not giving birth to a son. Jesús was instrumental in helping her even though he was completely unaware. He doted on both his daughter and wife, and Cruzita realized he would never leave her. She became less and less the meek, subservient wife. She tested how far she would go finally realizing that she can pretty much get what she wanted from Jesús whenever she wanted it but she remained loving and loyal to him. He didn't even notice the change in her much and allowed her to make all decisions when it came to Adina's upbringing.

Cruzita's power over Adina was her Damocles sword. She kept a close eye on her daughter. She wasn't allowed to visit her friends at their home; but Cruzita wouldn't allow her to have friends over and she wasn't allowed to spend the night away from home. Adina was raised among adults with very little interaction with children her age outside of school. At home, she spent all her time reading and she was a voracious reader. Saturday afternoons were her "Daddy and Me" days and she never wanted to go anywhere but the library.

When she was old enough to work a part-time job, Cruzita ordered that Adina "donate" seventy-five percent of her pay to go toward household expenses after demanding to see her paystubs. When Adina began to notice boys, Cruzita would snoop through her things looking for clues that would prove her daughter was behaving like the loose girls she saw in the neighborhood.

Adina never complained. She always did as she was told but she kept her feelings bottled up inside not wanting to disappoint her parents. But that was before she met Benny and though she didn't want to disillusion her parents or be disrespectful to them, she was in love and no one could change that.

Eventually, the volcano would erupt.

❧

"You're pregnant?! How could you do this to me?"

Adina squirmed in her chair. The dining room table immediately seemed to shrink and she felt like she was Alice in Wonderland. The furniture was suddenly humongous. They had eaten many meals at this table and even as a little girl, she never felt as swallowed up by this table as she did right now.

This was not going to be fun. She looked at her parents sitting across from her. Her mother's appearance startled her. Cruzita seemed to age right before Adina's eyes. Lines of worry and concern mapped her mother's face like the Sahara during summer months.

Adina continued staring at them in utter defiance. She couldn't believe Cruzita's reaction. What kind of reaction was that? It was Adina who was pregnant. It was Adina's body. How could her mother accuse her of having done something to her?

"How dare you? How dare you bring this kind of shame upon this family?! Just the other day I was talking with Diane, the neighbor from upstairs, about how some people believe that they can cover the sky with the palm of their hand. Now how will this make us look?"

"Why are you so concerned about what people think? What did anyone outside of this household ever do for you? You weren't just talking with Diane! You were gossiping and this is what happens when you gossip about other people, Ma! What goes around comes around! Ever remember telling me that? Those aren't just words! There really is such a thing as karma, you know!"

"You better find your respect for your mother, girl, or I will have to slap it on you!" interjected Jesús in a rarely raised tone.

Jesús trembled. The chair he had been sitting in scraped the floor when he pushed it back in barely managed anger. Once on his feet, his hand shook as he pointed a finger at Adina and the spittle escaped his mouth as he spoke.

"I demand you apologize to your mother right now! And once you do, we will sit down and discuss this before I completely lose control. Go on now; apologize immediately! And, you had better mean it, young lady!"

Adina hung her head. She had tears in her eyes. They weren't tears of shame. They were tears of rage, but she refused to let them see her cry. She was red-hot angry to be treated this way.

Through a tight jaw and averted eyes came the words.

"I'm sorry."

Cruzita looked down at her lap, numb.

"Who is he?" she asked her daughter in an eerily calm voice.

"His name is Benny. I met him at work."

Jesús' nose flared as he struggled not to go hunt the bastard down. Sighing loudly, he closed his eyes and rubbed his forehead. Then in a deadly calm voice he asked:

"Does he work with you or was he a customer?"

"He was a customer."

"A customer? All right.

"Tell us about him. What's his name? What does he do for a living? Do you plan on marrying him? What are you two going to do about this situation?"

One by one, Jesús fired questions at his daughter.

"His name is Benny ..." Adina interrupted, her voice rising. "... and he has his own place and a job. Well, he had a job, until last week."

She didn't respond to the question about whether they would marry.

"Whoa! Not so fast! He lost his job last week? What happened? This is not the way to do this, Adina. How can I, in good conscience, hand you over to a man who can't provide for you?"

"'Hand me over'? What do you mean?"

"You'll have to get married, Adina. That is the way it should be."

"Even if I wanted to marry him, I can't. I don't want to get married."

She raised her head to look off in the distance.

"I won't!"

"Well, do you love him? Because obviously you thought you did when you opened your legs for him!" Cruzita angrily retorted.

Adina narrowed her eyes at her mother.

"I do love him, but I will not marry him in jail!"

Cruzita's bottom lip trembled as her hands tangled with each other in her lap.

Jesús who had been pacing, stopped mid-pace, his hands balled into fists.

"He's in jail, Adina? Why is he in jail?"

"They say he killed a man."

"Murder!? Adina!"

The words crumbled in her mother's mouth.

"That's it then! If you insist on having this baby, you will have it in Puerto Rico then put it up for adoption! I demand it! You will not talk to him. You will NOT SEE HIM. That is final!" commanded Cruzita.

Adina watched her mother sob heavily into Jesús' shoulder, un-believing. She looked over at her father who had put his arm around her mother's shoulder in unity. It was a silent but powerful show of support.

So, she was supposed to go into hiding, have this baby then just give it away? No fucking way she was going to do that!

"I'm sorry. This is my body and it is my baby. You may be ashamed, but I am not. I refuse to go into hiding. If I decide to have it, I'm keeping it. I will raise it on my own."

"What do you mean 'if you decide to have it'? Are you consider-ing an abortion?"

"Yes, as a matter of fact, I am, Ma."

Cruzita started crying again and Jesús held her tighter as he spoke.

"You absolutely will not have an abortion! I forbid you! Abor-tion is the murder of an innocent child! It is a mortal sin!"

"Everything's a mortal sin, Pa! To hear you tell it, breathing is a mortal sin! Hell, living is a mortal sin! I wish I were dead!!"

Adina's whole body twitched as she vaulted to a stand. The chair she had been sitting in crashed to the ground and she stalked off to her room. Cruzita and Jesús looked at each other in disbelief.

Finally, Cruzita spoke.

"What are we going to do, Jesús? What are we going to do?"

"Don't worry. We'll figure it out. It's all going to work out, I promise."

Cruzita nodded. Jesús held her face in his hands, and she seemed different to him somehow.

"Ok. I'll get dinner started. It's getting late."

"Yes, do that. I'm going to take a shower then read for a little while; take my mind off things for a bit. Call me when dinner is ready."

"I will," responded Cruzita and headed to the kitchen.

It was a good thing a whole chicken had been thawing and it was ready to be seasoned. She opened the cupboard where her spices were and pulled down jars of spices: basil, cayenne pepper, cumin, oregano, parsley, rosemary and sage. Then she boiled a large pot of water adding copious amounts of the spices and made a broth. She would use the broth to marinate the chicken and boil the beans.

ॐॐ

A few hours later, there was a knock at Adina's bedroom door. Cruzita was on the other side and through the door asked if she could come in. Adina replied "yes" and when her mother strode in, she saw that she was carrying a tray of food.

"You must be hungry," Cruzita tentatively stated.

"Not really," replied Adina, even though she was and dismissively began to flip through a magazine.

"How are you feeling? Are you nauseous?"

"No."

"Well, I'll just leave this here for you. You should try to eat something."

As Cruzita placed the tray on the edge of the bed, she lovingly looked over at her daughter, but there was sadness in her eyes. She recalled the night Adina was born. She remembered how afraid she was that Jesús would leave her if she didn't have a baby boy and how wrong she was to think that way. Cruzita loved her daughter deeply, but she was torn up deep inside at the sight of her child's willingness to throw away the best years of her life.

"Adina, can we talk?"

"Talk? Us talk? You mean, you talk–I listen *and* obey, right?"

"Adina, please! Just hear me out. I know you think you're in love and I also know you're hurting, but you can't be thinking of going through with this pregnancy and keeping this child. You are just too young to have a baby right now. To keep it is to drastically alter your life forever. Doors will close and no one wants a woman with that kind of baggage, especially not one of our kind. No Puerto Rican man is ever going to want to marry you."

"*Our kind?* Ma! Would you listen to yourself? What about all the speeches I heard my whole life about how equal we all are, huh? Whatever happened to: 'you can be whatever you want, Adina.' Or 'we are all one race, Adina. Human. We all bleed red.' And, what about 'I would be happy with whomever you choose to marry as long as you're happy'?

"What happened to all of that? Was it all bullshit? What changed? Something must have changed, because now you're singing a different tune! Could you please explain this change of heart to me?" Adina fumed.

"I see that you are very upset. I'm going to leave now and give you some time alone to think. I pray you are able to peel back your pain and see the reality of what your life will become if you insist on having this baby.

Adina looked away from her mother, the rebellious, teenage anger evident. Cruzita ached to hold her baby in her arms, make everything better as she fought the tears welling up in her own eyes and stepped over the threshold of Adina's room into the hallway. Slowly she closed the door behind her. Jesús, who had been waiting just outside Adina's bedroom, drew her into his arms where she sobbed and silently asked God to heed her prayers.

ॐ∽

As soon as her mother was out the door, Adina pulled the tray closer and peered at the food on it. She could not believe how ravenous she was but she could not give her mother the satisfaction of being right when she correctly assumed that Adina would be hungry. She lifted the lid that was put over the plate holding her meal.

The aroma from the still hot dinner made her swoon. Her mouth watered when she saw that her mom had made her favorite meal: white rice, red beans with fresh corn over a bed of greens sprinkled with oil and vinegar; fried plantains and baked chicken breast. It smelled divine! Not bothering with any utensils, she tore off a piece of chicken, put it in her mouth, and slowly chewed it, savoring the buttery/spicy taste. Then she picked up the fork and knife and began to mix the beans in with the rice.

❧❦

At the end of her meal, Adina's cramped stomach hurt but she crawled back into bed, pulling the blanket all the way up to her chin. Lying there and breathing heavily, she stared at the ceiling, focused on trying to figure out why she felt so sick so suddenly. Could it have been morning sickness? She knew that even though it was called "morning" sickness, it didn't necessarily mean she would only get sick in the morning.

Maybe she ate too much food too fast? She hadn't really eaten all day but she couldn't figure it out. Finally, she fell asleep and right into a nightmare.

❧❦

It was as though she were watching a movie. Adina could see herself lying on her stomach on a raft floating in choppy waters. Frantically, she looked around; land was nowhere to be seen. Fear of losing her grip and drowning in this body of water took a strong hold over her. She could not swim and she felt hopeless. She gave in to the realization that no one would come and rescue her.

Still, soaked to the bone, she cried uncontrollably. All of a sudden, a huge wave washed over her, tossing her to and fro, threatening to sweep her under water. She gasped, taking in quite a bit of saltwater and began to struggle to

catch her breath. Her eyes, throat and chest burned. Clinging to the raft she
fought to stay on.

It was then that she shot up in her bed still gulping air, chest heaving.

Relieved it was just a dream; she pulled the covers away from her body with one hand, while she wiped her brow with the other. She was sweating profusely and her thighs felt wet. It upset her that she wet the bed. She hadn't done that since she was a child.

She felt around on the mattress confirming that it was soaked. In the darkness of her room, she pulled a couple of tissues out of the box on the nightstand, wiped her hand, bunched up the used tissue and swung her legs over the side of the bed. She pulled on the cord to the lamp on the nightstand. Her intention was to change the sheets and started to pull them off her bed.

It was then that she saw the blood. She hadn't peed the bed; she was bleeding! She lifted her nightgown and saw the blood sliding down her thighs leaving red streaks behind.

"Noooo!" She cried out and folded to her knees on the floor.

∿•∿

Adina's blood curdling screams awoke her parents. They were fast asleep and completely startled. What could have happened?

Jesús sat up in bed with the thought that someone must have broken in.

Shaken, he yelled at Cruzita to stay where she was while he went to investigate. Grabbing his robe he tore out of their bedroom and barged into Adina's room, only to find her in a heap on the floor by the bed. She was curled up in the fetal position, crying.

He peered over at her bed and spotted the large red bloodstain that centered her white fitted sheet. Bending down so that he was eye level to her, he embraced her and held her close.

"What's happened? Is that your blood, Princess? Honey? What's happened?"

She sobbed and sat up; knees to her chest and looked up at her father, blood smears on her hands, her nightshirt.

Had she tried to kill herself? He glanced at Adina's wrists and was relieved to see he was wrong. She had not attempted the unthinkable. But, he still could not figure out what had happened. Where did all that blood come from?

"I was having a bad dream," Adina said.

"I thought I had an accident in my sleep. When I turned on the light, I saw it. My baby is dead! I've had a miscarriage!" she cried.

Jesús yelled for his wife.

"Cruzita! Cruzita! Come here, quickly!"

Cruzita dashed into Adina's room and stopped short when she saw the blood blooming on the bed. She was stunned when she entered the room, but upon coming to terms with what she saw, she felt a sense of relief in full understanding of the situation. Her daughter didn't have to throw her life away! She had lost the baby. Cruzita offered a prayer of thanks to God that her spicy marinade worked.

Chapter 10
RJ Takes a Life to Save a Life (1979)

Coincidently, just as this event was unfolding in Adina's life, a similar life-changing situation was taking place at a home in Lebanon, Pennsylvania.

A young man awoke from his restless slumber. Though the images that filled his vision of evil creatures in a sea of blood didn't bother him much, the din of the hushed but intense sounds coming from the next room did. The whimpering that followed the rhythmic strikes he heard kept him from surrendering to the extremely vivid images that excited him. He wished he were as powerful as the demons he encountered in his mind's eye. They seemed powerful over all things. He preferred those dream-creatures and other animals in his visions to real living beings. In fact, there was no one he cared about more than himself–the woman he called *Mother* and it was her whimpering he was hearing once again. He had been listening to those sounds for as long as he could remember, but tonight would be the last time she would have to make them; the last time he would have to helplessly listen to them.

He was fed up and finally ready, willing *and* able, he thought, to do something about it. He knew he would put an end to it on this night. He could no longer remain silent as she suffered the inhumane treatment she was subjected to.

༚·ઝ

As a young boy, Rhys John Preston was nicknamed RJ by his beloved mother. Now seventeen years old, he has big brown eyes and curly dark hair. Slight for his age but a little pudgy, he is obsessed with his appearance as he is sometimes mistaken for a girl. He didn't like that. Even his father teased him. However, his appearance is deceiving. Underneath his slightly effeminate ways and small build, he is very strong. He exercised and lifted weights constantly in an attempt to whip his body into a more masculine shape, but it wasn't working and he knew why. The doctors said the only option he had was surgery but his parents–rather, his father–refused to give consent saying he was exactly the way that God intended him to be.

He despised his father with a passion. He was extremely unhappy at home and he hated himself. The only reason he hadn't killed himself was because he couldn't bear to leave his mother alone to live out her life with the monster who called himself a man of God.

The Pastor verbally abused him. He challenged him to be more masculine. He called him a sissy in public; a little fag at home. Frustrated with a son he considered to be less than a man, the Pastor took his frustration out on RJ's mother. He slapped her around and blamed her for his son's deformity even though she had nothing to do with it. The Pastor said he knew it was his penance to learn to love him in order to make amends for his father's sins, but he couldn't find it in his heart to do so. He only kept him around because he needed to maintain his image as a devoted father and husband in the eyes of his congregation.

RJ sat upright in his bed, ears sharp. He knew immediately what was going on. He heard the familiar sounds and he knew that son of a bitch was at it again. It was time to make him stop. In a blur, he was out of his bed and running toward his parents' bedroom. As he burst in, he yelled maniacally.

"Stop it!"

Margaret's head snapped toward the bedroom door and RJ could not believe what he saw. His mother, Margaret Preston, was tied naked and spread-eagled to her bed; a ball and gag in her mouth. The welts across her stomach were red, angry and rising. Some were bleeding.

Standing at the edge of the bed, dressed only in his underwear, was Pastor James Ezekiel, a small cat o'nine tails in his hand; his penis erect.

The Pastor glared with disdain at his son. He was spitting mad.

"Or what? What are you going to do? Kick my ass? You couldn't if you tried, you little pussy!"

RJ's nostrils flared.

"I'm warning you. Leave her alone!"

The Pastor sneered at his son.

"I'm only doing what the whore likes. Did I ever tell you the story of how we met? Huh? Your 'mother' is nothing but a cheap whore. She used to get paid for doing things like this. She enjoys these games. Did you know that?"

RJ shook his head, unbelieving.

"I don't believe you. You're lying."

RJ turned toward his mother, and walked in her direction. She was now crying so profusely, her nose ran and she shook her head back and forth. When he reached her side, turning his back on his father he pulled a sheet over her naked body and began to undo the gag.

"Step away from her, you fucking freak!"

Again, RJ ignored his father and focused on making sure his mother was covered.

And then it happened. The world spun out of control. The Pastor took a hard swing at his son when he ignored his command to move away, connecting the whip with his bare back, breaking the skin with just one blow. The boy did not scream. He did not visibly react except for the trembling lower lip only his mother saw. His back stung from the impact of hard leather on soft skin.

Margaret's eyes grew big and wild with fear. Then something took over. The ever-growing rage possessed RJ, overwhelming his sense of civility. The object of his rage was at his back and all he could see was red.

"You see? One swing and I draw blood. You ain't shit!"

Looking into his mother's eyes, he undid her right hand and calmly, he asked her a question.

"Can you undo the rest of these ties, Mom?"

Margaret was shaking but she nodded.

"Good. Set yourself free and leave the room. Can you do that for me?"

Mute with fear, all Margaret could do was nod again and set about releasing herself, but she did not immediately leave the room.

"Oh, so you want to chit-chat now?" said the Pastor and swung the whip once more, striking his son a second time across his torso.

An angry, wide, red welt rose instantly. The cat o' nine tails had narrowly missed his mother and the sting of this blow was worse than the first.

"Stop it! Do whatever you want with me but leave him alone!" she screamed.

Between clenched teeth, RJ pleaded with his mother.

"Mom, please? Please leave! I want you to leave the room right now! Please!"

Margaret's son had now completely lost control and his voice rose with every single word that came out of his mouth. She ran out of the room into the hallway.

With his mother out of the room–he couldn't let her witness what he was about to do–RJ turned to completely face his father. The fury was now evident in his eyes. He seemed possessed by some otherworldly creature, just like the ones in his dreams. He could see nothing else but his mother's offender–his father–and now the object of his fury. All he knew was that he had a need to retaliate for what was done to him, to her.

He tackled his father head first, bringing him off his feet and slamming him into the wall, knocking the wind out of him. The older man was not expecting such a force coming from his "sissy" son. He was shocked as he hit the wall–hard–the whip flying from his fist. He was completely surprised by his son's inhuman strength and amazed by how easily he was taken off balance. The realization paralyzed him. Inhaling deeply, he looked into RJ's eyes and it was then that he saw murder there.

Silently, he began to pray.

RJ spotted the small whip on the floor and grabbed it. Wrapping the strap around his hand and pulling it taut, he swung it once, twice at his father's chest, then at his face. He swung it over and around his head and brought it down swiftly to strike his father again and again with satisfying cracking sounds; inflicting blow after blow all over his body until he was near unconsciousness. He took great pleasure in his father's weak mewling.

When he tired of beating him, RJ picked up his broken father's body and easily tossed him over his shoulder. He was disgusted with the man. This was the same man townspeople revered as godly and untouchable. Everyone in the neighborhood and the parish was completely unaware of his hatred and ugliness.

RJ headed toward the bathroom, purposely slamming his father's head and limbs against the walls and doorways with every step. Haphazardly tossing the monster that had haunted him all throughout his childhood into the tub, he opened the cold-water spigot and waited for his father to rouse. RJ thought about slapping him but didn't want to touch him.

Moaning, his father came to, baptized in brutal ice water. This was a new reality: not being in control, feeling hurt and terrified. He watched his son, now a stranger, without speaking.

RJ could not get the words, the questions, out of his mouth fast enough.

"How does it feel to be the one bullied? How does it feel to be the one on the receiving end of your bullshit? For years I listened to you fuck around with my mother. The noises gave me nightmares! I'd wake up pissed off at you, but I didn't say or do anything to keep you from fucking with her some more.

"You didn't fight me back. Why? Why didn't you fight me back? You fucking punk!" RJ ranted on.

"I guess I'm not the pussy you thought I was, am I? Motherfucker!"

Stunned into silence, the pastor could not respond.

Ignoring the shocked look on his father's face, RJ suddenly reached in and pulled his father out of the tub and dragged him through the house and out the door. He then forced him into the car, got behind the wheel and with tires screeching, he drove toward the woods, leaving his mother behind.

Chapter 11
RJ Returns Home and Margaret Remembers

RJ was the only person in the world who Margaret could count on in times of trouble, though he himself was indeed tormented. As she waited for her son and husband to return, she read the Bible. She would stop intermittently to pray for their safe return. She knew full well that her prayers were futile. She'd been here before.

Finally, the front door opened. It had to be the two of them and she headed to the stairs. Midway, she stopped, shocked by the sight before her. RJ was stepping over the threshold and into the house but he was alone. He was drenched in sweat and blood was smeared on his shirt and hands.

"What's happened to you?"

"It's over. He won't ever hurt us again."

"What do you mean? Where is your father?"

"He was not my father!"

"RJ, what do you mean '*was*'? What's happened? My God! What have you done?"

Margaret knew the answer to that question. She knew something terrible had happened. It was evident in the familiar stone-cold blank stare her son gave her in response. Looking into her son's empty eyes brought Margaret back in a flash to a day she would never forget.

Brenda, a woman she had known in her past life as a prostitute, appeared at Margaret's front door two years before this night. Margaret wished Brenda had never darkened her doorstep.

Apparently, their old pimp, "Jack the Mack," had been up to his old tricks right up until the day he died. He was known for regularly replacing older girls in his stable with younger ones he fancied.

Three months before Brenda showed up on Margaret's doorstep, while "having a taste of new meat," he died of a heart attack. Natural causes! It was inconceivable to anyone who knew him that such an evil man would end up not dying of a gunshot, a drug overdose, or the electric chair.

After Jack's death, Brenda tried to go it alone, "managing" the remaining girls herself. But after just a couple of months of doing that, she decided she didn't want to be their pimp. It was "too much trouble trying to keep them all in line." Besides, Brenda felt that she was the one who needed to be taken care of, not her taking care of a "bunch of bitchy, whiny women who were always complaining about the johns and their share of the evening's take."

In explanation for her unannounced visit, Brenda said that she remembered a rumor that Margaret had married a Pastor in Lebanon Valley. So, when things didn't go her way, Brenda decided she would head to Pennsylvania and find her friend. What she didn't tell Margaret outright was that she planned on hunkering down at her place until she could figure out what to do with the rest of her life. Margaret's old friend definitely did not want to end up alone in old age or dead in the same manner as Jack the Mack. She felt this was the right time to do something different with her life and Brenda had a plan.

First thing she was going to do was visit The Church of Everlasting Glory. It was the only church in the area so that had to be the church the good pastor and therefore, Margaret, were affiliated with.

The day Brenda arrived the handsome Pastor was in the midst of a passionate sermon about unconditional love.

"I bring your attention now to 1-Corinthians 13:4-7:

'Love is patient, love is kind and is not jealous; love does not brag and is not arrogant, does not act unbecomingly; it does not seek its own, is not provoked, does not take into account a wrong suffered, does not rejoice in unrighteousness, but rejoices with the truth; bears all things, hopes all things, endures all things. Love never fails ... but now faith, hope, love, abide these three; but the greatest of these is love.'

"Brothers and sisters, I say unto you–love is the greatest gift God has given us; the greatest gift we can give one another. Judge not others, but love them. Can I get an 'Amen'?"

"Amen!"

"Hallelujah!"

A rousing song and round of applause followed and the sermon was over.

Sitting in her pew and taking in the surroundings, Brenda thought about how she was going to get Margaret to show her some love and agree to let her move in for a while. She wouldn't mind living in a quaint little town like this. She might even get lucky, just as Margaret did. She slid from her seat, and slithered over in the direction where the Pastor stood talking with parishioners.

Brenda really couldn't help the way she moved. This was who she was–a wanton snake. But, she never got a chance to speak to the Pastor because he was gone in the blink of an eye. Frustrated, she walked over to a group of women who were standing around chatting.

"Hello, ladies. Beautiful sermon, wasn't it?"

The women turned to face her. There was no love in their eyes for her; so much for the sermon about unconditional love for your brethren.

They scanned her up and down in obvious disapproval, scorn and judgment. Her petite frame was squeezed into the short dress she wore and this is what bothered them the most. Surely she was a temptress sent there by the Devil himself to fetch their husbands! It was unmistakable that the frumpy older ladies all felt threatened by this seductive woman standing before them.

"Welcome," one stated flatly.

"Glad you enjoyed it," another simpered.

"You look new. How can we help you?" said the one who appeared to be the leader of the pack.

"Well, I hope you can. You're right. I'm new around these parts and I was hoping to find an old friend."

"Oh? And who might that be?" said another woman in the pack, fully believing no one in their midst might be friends with someone who looked like she did.

To be fair, Brenda was overly made up. Her dress was too short; it was definitely too tight, and she wore perfume in abundance. Her overall look was quite provocative.

"I'm looking for Margaret Brown. I understand that she has settled in these parts."

"Oh! You must mean Preston, Margaret Preston, Pastor James' wife?"

Brenda could not believe her luck! So it was true! Margaret did marry a Pastor. She just never imagined it would be the very handsome Pastor of The Church of Everlasting Glory! Good for her! It was a good thing she didn't get a chance to talk with him. If these ladies' reaction to her was outwardly judgmental, she could imagine how he would have reacted to her. She was left with no choice but to pour on the charm.

"Preston, yes! She goes by her married name now. How silly of me!

"Well, you see, Margaret and I used to work together. Seeing as I was in town, I thought I might surprise her. You know, pay her a visit and catch up a bit. Might you know where I could find her? Do you know where she lives?"

"Yes. She and the Pastor live just down the road–with their son; the fourth house on the left."

"The white one," chimed in a third woman.

"Why, thank you, ladies. I'll be on my way then. You all have a blessed day!"

And with that, she walked away, turning up the volume on her catwalk sashay as the women looked on.

Later that Sunday, Brenda arrived at Margaret's door. She peeked through the windowpane but didn't see anyone. She decided she would take a chance and knock. She smoothed her dress, wiped her teeth free of any lipstick and rapped quickly on the door. Margaret opened the door and blanched, jaw dropping, when she saw Brenda standing there smiling at her.

"Brenda! What in Heaven's name are you doing here? It's great to see you!"

"Oh! Margaret! I found you!"

She pulled Margaret into an awkward embrace.

Against her better judgment, Margaret invited her in for coffee. But, she couldn't leave Brenda standing there for the entire world to see. Margaret's old "friend" walked in and immediately began ooh'ing and ahh'ing about how beautiful Margaret's home was. Once she was done admiring the place, they sat together at the dinette in Margaret's kitchen alcove. They drank coffee and Brenda smoked cigarettes as they reminisced about a past they both shared. It was a life that Margaret wanted to forget.

As Brenda rambled on, talking about nothing, Margaret shifted anxiously in her chair.

What if James came home early? Then she snapped back to reality when Brenda hit her with the bombshell about what had happened to their pimp. At first, Margaret was stunned that Jack had met his end that way. But then she caught up with Brenda's train of thought and the real reason for her visit.

"... So I was wondering if I could stay here for a while."

"Oh, Brenda, I would invite you to stay with us if that would help you, but it is just impossible. I haven't the room. You would be uncomfortable here. But there's a motel just a mile from here, maybe you could go there? I could give you a ride."

And just as Margaret was saying that, the front door opened. Her heart stopped but began beating again when she saw that it was just RJ.

"Well, who do we have here?"

Brenda went into work mode.

"Brenda, this is my son, RJ. RJ, this is Brenda."

Margaret sat primly, ready to end the visit.

"Hello."

RJ ignored her.

Brenda's eyes ravaged him. A skill taught on the street, part of the come-on. It took years for Margaret to unlearn this behavior and she resented it now, here in her kitchen, directed at her son.

"My, my, my! What a handsome young man you are! Your mom and I were just catching up. I was in the neighborhood and thought

I'd pop in and see how she was doing. I'm so impressed she's done so well for herself. How old are you?"

"I'll be seventeen soon."

"So tender, but almost a man. Do you have a girlfriend? I'm willing to bet the young ladies are all over you!"

"No. I don't have a girlfriend," RJ replied. He narrowed his eyes in suspicion.

"Mom, I'm going fishing now. See you later?"

"Aren't you hungry? Let me fix you something to eat before you go," said Margaret as she rose to prepare a snack for her son.

"No, I'll be back in time for dinner. I'm going into the shed so I can get my things together, but I'll stop in again before I go."

Turning to Brenda, RJ coolly said: "Nice to meet you, ma'am."

"Oh! Call me Brenda! No need for formalities; your Mom and I go way back!"

RJ half smiled, nodded then turned to leave.

"You have a fine, young man on your hands, Margaret. He is so well mannered!"

"Yes. He is a fine, young man."

"Well, I'd best be going now. I should stop in at that motel you mentioned before it gets dark and check it out.

"Oh, it was so nice to see you! I hope we can do this again soon!"

"Will you be going to the motel I mentioned?" Margaret asked.

"Yes. I think I'll just walk and take in the sights."

"Well, it was nice to see you, too, Brenda. Thanks for the visit," a visibly relieved Margaret hugged her old "friend" good-bye.

Margaret couldn't be happier that her past was getting ready to walk out the door before her husband came back. She sent up a silent prayer that this would be the last she would see of her and that Brenda's plans to stick around didn't stick! She didn't want Brenda making it a habit of "popping in" on her either.

"Do you mind if I walk around your property and see what you've done with it?" Brenda asked.

"Sure. Let me show you around."

"Oh, no need to do that. I'll just see myself off when I'm done. Again, Margaret, it was good to see you after all these years! Thanks for the coffee and the chitchat. It really was great! I'll see you soon!"

And with that, Brenda walked out the front door, and around to the back where the shed was. She could see from afar that the door was open and she could see RJ packing a knapsack, presumably to take with him to the lake.

Margaret watched through her window as Brenda headed around the back toward the shed. It didn't seem completely right but she disregarded her instincts. Besides, Brenda just wanted to walk around the property. What harm could there be in that?

ॐॐ

"What have you got there, young man?" said Brenda as she entered the shed.

RJ was startled, but did his best not to show it.

"Um, just stuff I need for fishing. Can I help you with something?"

"You sure can. RJ, is it?"

"Yes, ma'am."

"Oh, RJ, I told you! There is no need to be so formal. Like I said, your Mom and I, we go way back. We used to work together, remember?"

RJ remained silent. He couldn't think of anything to say. He was getting nervous, feeling warm and everything about this woman was making him uncomfortable. He got that feeling in his groin. It was that feeling of tightness that was becoming all too familiar to him. Only now he hadn't killed anything. The only time he ever felt that tightness, really, was when the thrill of killing something engulfed him. He was beginning to panic about it when the next thing he knew, this woman was all in his space.

Catching him unaware, Brenda stood very close to RJ and her hand caressed his arm. He looked at her hand then raised his eyes to look at her. There was lust there. He could see it. She lusted after him. The boys at school talked about sex all the time. He never participated in those conversations for two reasons. One was because he really wasn't friendly with them, and second, because he'd never been with a girl. They would talk about the girls everyone knew were easy as if it were some sort of joke. Some of them got woodies. He didn't. He never did when it came to girls. But girls did sometimes make his groin feel funny, warm-like. He only got a woody, or at least he thought it was a hard-on, when he killed animals. He also leaked when that happened, like he was starting to piss and then only drops came out.

Brenda was the first female to ever approach him in that way.

"Please stop."

"Why? What's wrong?"

"Nothing's wrong. I just want you to stop. Please."

"Oh, I get it. You've never been with a girl, right?"

RJ was really nervous now and embarrassed. He wondered what she was going to do, and why he couldn't just step away from her.

She smelled good and the way she looked at him excited him. No one ever looked at him like that because they were too busy calling him names. The images of what it might be like to be with a woman like her and not one of those girls from school raced through his mind. To be with her, then delete her.

Now, he was really confused. How could he even think of her like that? This was his mom's friend! What was wrong with him? His breathing grew faster and his armpits became moist. His heart was about to beat right out of his chest. Small beads of perspiration broke out on his upper lip.

"Come on now, RJ. Relax. Would you like me to help you relax, hmm? Brenda's here and she can take care of you; good care. You'll never forget Brenda once she's done with you. How about a kiss to help you relax? Just a small kiss, huh? How about it?"

"My mom ..."

"Don't worry about her. She's in the house and she thinks I'm gone. I just had to come by and see you. When I first laid eyes on you, you took my breath away.

"So, what do you say? How about a kiss? All I want is just one small kiss, right here."

Brenda tapped a glossy fingernail on her full red lips. RJ looked at them and licked his own lips then bent down to meet hers. He laid a quick peck on her lips and jumped back as though he had touched a live wire. This made Brenda chuckle at his inexperience.

But Brenda was not so innocent. She jumped on this opportunity, taking a fistful of the young boy's hair, pulling him to her and kissing him full on the mouth; pushing her tongue between his teeth. Once she felt his mouth give way, she darted her tongue in and out of his mouth, working his head like a meat slicer. He grunted and pushed her back while pulling away, wiping his mouth with the back of his hand.

All he could do was stare at her mouth in abrupt dismay. He wanted her to do it again. And yet he was torn.

Is this sex? Is it ... something else?

Mostly, he wanted to get her close enough again to feel her buckle beneath him, to feel life slip from her body. He wanted to hear her gasp as she took her last breath. He wanted to wrap his hands around her throat in search of the elusive final release. He was very aroused and at the same time, confused. He just wanted her to die in his arms. He snapped back to the present and noticed her wounded look.

He responded, sheepish: "I'm sorry. I didn't mean to do that. It's just that ..."

"You've never French kissed, right?" she interrupted. "It's ok. I'm not offended. But you're going to have to learn sometime. Come closer."

Obeying her command, RJ approached. The nerves in his stomach felt like a volcano ready to erupt. The sensations he was feeling in his groin were getting more and more intense. He had to find a way to get her out of there but the throbbing, the twitching and the heat made him want more.

"Go to the lake with me. There's privacy."

His skin glowed. His eyes were alight. She mistook his physical response with lust and she grinned widely. Another win!

"Well now; the man has spoken! But, how can I possibly go in this get-up?" she responded brightly.

Brenda caressed her own breasts lightly, then her thighs, stopping at her crotch, a smirk curling her lips.

"Wear these."

He reached for a pair of sweats from a hook in the shed.

"You can change at a camp restroom when we get there."

RJ was desperate for her to agree. He wanted to reveal seductive lust, not murder lust. He wasn't sure if he was being successful. Painfully excited now, he had to do something soon to relieve the ache.

Brenda seemed unaware of the difference.

"What if your mom sees me getting into your truck?"

"I'll tell her I'm giving you a ride somewhere."

"Great idea."

"Good. I'm going to let her know I'm on my way out like I said I would. I'll be right back."

Chapter 12
A Day of Firsts for RJ

It was hard for Brenda to comport herself like a woman of experience and class. It had been a long time since she had seen any action and it had certainly been years since she'd been with a newbie. She rather enjoyed boy virgins. They made her feel powerful and worthy of their admiration.

That swagger was nothing more than armor that she wore to protect her insecurities, her vulnerabilities and most of all, her self-hatred. Sometimes a john would bring his son to her and she would be paid quite handsomely to "turn him into a man." So as far as she was concerned, there was nothing better than breaking in a young stud.

But RJ was different. There was something about him that resonated with her. She certainly wouldn't mind teaching him a few tricks for free. Feeling like a virginal teenager and fantasizing like one about a first love, she began to squirm in her seat as she waited for him to return, wondering all the while what was taking him so long.

Regularly sexually abused by both men and women in her youth, Brenda learned early in life how to use sex and the promise of sex as a gilded sword she could wield in order to get what she wanted. Sometimes her desires involved material things, but mostly it was just for the adulation she got from her targets–whether they were johns or casual partners. She was adept and merciless at getting what she wanted in this way. However, this time, there was nothing she wanted in return. It was just pure, raw lust. The anticipation within her to feel what she equated to pure, untainted love was becoming more and more unattainable as she aged, and she couldn't wait to get started with RJ.

This day had turned out better than she thought. Her intention was to wiggle into Margaret's house until she figured out what to do.

That didn't work out but she was presented with an opportunity that did not come along very often for someone like her.

RJ busted into the house, startling his mother.

"Mom! I'm leaving now!"

"RJ! You scared me half to death!"

"I didn't know you were still down here. I'm sorry."

"Are you sure you don't want me to put together a basket for you to bring along?"

"No, don't bother. Besides, I've got your friend in the car. I'm giving her a ride to the motel on Main Street. Do you need anything before I head out?"

RJ hoped she would say no.

Margaret's heart stopped, but somehow she calmly responded to her son.

"No, honey; thank you. And, RJ? She's not my friend, all right? She's someone I used to know. Now, you go on. Please drive carefully and be sure to get back home before dark. You know the rules."

"Yes, mother," responded RJ, exasperated but amused.

"See you later."

Margaret smiled at her son then gave him a kiss and off he went. She walked over to the window to watch him as he slid into the car. She couldn't help but naively hope Brenda would keep her paws to herself and that she would not expect anything more than to be dropped off at the motel. She worried for Rhys, but he was growing and she had to let him find his own way.

RJ left and walked toward the vehicle. His heart was thumping and the palms of his hands were sweaty. He knew that Brenda was trying to be discreet while she watched him as he approached. He was excited. This would be the first time that he would do the deed. He hoped he would know what to do, but he knew full well that if he didn't, Brenda would show him.

He finally reached it and hopped in.

"All set?" she asked as he slammed the door shut and settled into the driver's seat.

"All set," he responded.

He looked out the driver's side mirror for oncoming traffic and pulled out onto the road.

"Strap in," he ordered.

Brenda turned her head in surprise at his abruptness but she did as she was told. If this was the attitude this kid was bringing with him, she certainly had her work cut out for her. They rode in silence. She fidgeted then looked at herself in her compact mirror and re-applied her lipstick. Internally, she felt a mixture of excitement and apprehension.

The purr of the car's engine and the birds chirping in the sky were the only sounds that could be heard while RJ drove. The sun's rays beat down on their faces. His imagination wandered. He en-visioned what it would be like being with a real woman. His brow creased as he tried to remember if he ever had sexual desire for an-other human being. He imagined it to be sweet and warm. In his imagination he had proved himself a man with a woman over and over.

Today he wondered if it would feel like he had finished first in a race, a race to masculinity? If it did, then maybe his father would stop harping on his perceived lack of testosterone-fueled aggression.

He stole a peek over at Brenda and quickly turned his eyes back on the road.

He chided himself. What the hell was he thinking? Wasn't this woman a friend of his mother's? Hell, she could've *been* his mother. And then a thought crossed his mind that shook him to his core. What if she *was* his mother? What if, sitting here beside him was the woman who had given birth to him, then gave him up? It was entirely possible. This woman came out of nowhere; appearing at his house unannounced. He noticed that his mom certainly didn't seem too comfortable around her. She didn't seem happy at all. Did she know? Did the woman he knew as his mother his whole life know if Brenda was his *real* mother?

No. That was impossible because in his heart of hearts he knew that no other woman could be his mother. No one could take that away. No one!

He was angry now, angry with himself for having these thoughts. He couldn't understand why they came rushing to him at this moment in time. He *never* thought of his birth mother. What was wrong with him? Here was an obviously experienced woman who took an interest in him. It's not like he ever had to see her again. She was just going to the motel. She said she was just passing through.

Then he had other thoughts: *Why* was she interested in him? What did she *really* want from him? Did he misread this woman?

But she had kissed him. His birth mother wouldn't do that, would she? If she even was his birth mother. Maybe she didn't know he was her son. If this indeed was his biological mother, what does it say about *him* that he had sexual thoughts about her? What does it say about *her* that she would behave the way she did toward him? These questions nagged at him.

He took another look at her. No, she couldn't possibly be his biological mother. He looked nothing like her. But he wondered nonetheless what kind of woman would behave in such a seductive manner toward a young boy like him.

Brenda was the first to speak. She spoke in a sultry tone, her hand at her throat.

"So, RJ, what do you do for fun?"

"Nothing."

"Nothing? Oh, I find that hard to believe. There must be something you're interested in."

"Yeah, but it's not something I like to talk about."

"Really? Why?"

"Because it will upset people."

Silence was thick in the car. Brenda wondered what he could possibly be involved in that he didn't feel comfortable talking about. She briefly wondered if this thing he wouldn't talk about was illegal. She considered asking him about it, probing him a little more. She just wanted to get him talking in the hopes that doing so would put them both a little more at ease. But she re-considered and remained quiet.

RJ interrupted her thoughts.

"We're almost there now. I'll drop you off by the changing station then pick you up after I park."

"Oh, I won't be long changing," she said as she reached over and touched his cheek.

RJ flinched. He hated when his face was touched. His father always touched his face right before he called him a pretty boy then slapped him. His first instinct was to slap her hand away but he kept it together.

Brenda got out of the car and sashayed toward the ladies changing station, knowing he would be watching her. Halfway there, she turned to see if she was right. She was disappointed he wasn't and that he was already driving away.

Aw, well. I'm going to have his full attention soon, she surmised.

҂

This is where Margaret took RJ hiking as a young boy. He learned to fish and swim in its lakes under his mother's guidance. RJ developed a love for the outdoors in those woods and it was all because of the memories he and his mother created there. Now that he was older, he would sometimes go alone because he found peace in the place he considered his oasis. He would often sit in those woods and watch the birds and other small animals in their natural habitat. This was the only place where he felt whole and it was at Memorial Lake State Park that his mother taught him to be patient when hunting for his kills.

When RJ was just a child, he noticed that his body looked different from his father's and he asked him questions about it. There was no way he could address his concerns with his mother. Only a man could explain to him what he needed to understand.

One day, tired of his son asking the same question over and over, James Ezekiel told his son that he was different. When RJ pressed him to explain what he meant, his father said that RJ was the "personification of God's punishment for his sins as well as the sins of his father and his father before him."

Ever since then, this statement rang in RJ's head.

His father never joined them on these trips and RJ knew this was the reason why. He would use the excuse that he needed to tend to someone or do something church related, but RJ knew better. Margaret used to say it was better that way because the pastor couldn't or wouldn't understand their bond. The park was their special place and RJ always looked forward to their time together there.

RJ had just turned fifteen when he began escaping to the park, when his father's belittling and teasing about every little thing he did became a regular pastime for the Pastor. He knew the park like the back of his hand and though there were uniforms everywhere—meaning park officials—he knew how to find places within the woods where he could go unseen, undetected if the elements were right. Since it wasn't gated, it was easy for him to sneak out of his house at night to hike in the woods alone.

RJ enjoyed chasing and torturing small animals and birds. He used a slingshot, but he didn't consider what he was doing torture. After he tired of doing just that, he would kill them just for the thrill of it. He imagined his father's face in the eyes of every creature he slaughtered.

Margaret didn't like that he did that, but RJ was her son and she loved him. She prayed for God's forgiveness on his behalf. It was her duty to help her son cope with his feelings and the only way to do that was to teach him to keep from getting caught.

According to Margaret, if torturing and killing animals was the only way to work through the rage he felt for his father, then he had to be smart about covering his tracks. Therefore, she instructed him never to leave the animals behind. He was to bag up the remains and get rid of them. It was RJ's idea to hold the opened bag out his window while driving so that he could toss the animal's carcass on the road. This way there was no hint of what he had done and the remains of the animal he killed would just be run over and no one would be the wiser.

It was here that he took Brenda.

ॐ◌ॐ

Upon entering the changing station, Brenda began to unabashedly strip naked. An exhibitionist, she liked prancing about in the nude. She particularly liked to do that in public places where the shock value was immeasurable. She found it very validating to do such things when others around her were out of shape, old, or their body language suggested they had a negative self-image. She had a knack for picking those people out in a crowd.

She then slowly slipped into RJ's sweats and tied his shirt high at her midriff. Sitting on the bench, she put on a pair of old work boots that also belonged to RJ and were ill fitting. When she looked in the mirror, she was pleased that she was able to pull off the outfit and thought she looked decent enough, but she was uncomfortable in the work boots. All of her clothes would soon be lying in a heap anyway, so she didn't give it a second thought. She gathered up her belongings and stepped out into the late afternoon sun to find that RJ had returned. She headed in his direction.

Brenda twirled.

"How do I look?"

"You look fine. I know a spot where we could have some privacy," responded RJ, quickly changing the subject.

"Oh," a dejected Brenda responded.

She wondered what was going on. RJ was sullen and she was unsuccessful in cheering him up with her playful antics. She worried because that ploy usually worked. Each time she tried to show him any affection, he rejected her by moving away or being cold toward her. This confused her because this was not the way he responded to her kiss back at the shed. It seemed to her that he was trying to avoid any physical contact.

She kept trying to get close to him. She even pretended to trip in the hopes that he would reach out to her and break the invisible barrier he had put up between them. She pretended to be the helpless woman who needed to hold on to him in order to traverse the rugged path. But he didn't reach out or offer his arm to her. Instead, he nonchalantly stated she should be more careful. He instructed her to watch for uneven terrain then closed that avenue of conversation by stating that they were close to the spot he wanted to go to.

Deeper and deeper into the woods they went. The further away from the normally trafficked areas they got, the louder the alarms in her head sounded, but she chose to ignore them. Her eye was on the prize of a virgin boy and she was not about to pass that up at this point in her life. The thoughts running through her mind elicited visions of what could happen between her and this man-child. Those visions gave her the strength to shore up and proceed with her plan to make a man out of him. She was a pro at this kind of thing. He would always remember her fondly after she de-virginized him, she was sure of it.

Now excited, Brenda yearned to feel his skin against hers. She had a desire to experience the innocence of his kisses. But most of all, she needed him to fuck her. She wanted to answer to the curiosities of his desires.

It was while in the midst of these thoughts that they came upon an area near a lake that was thick with vegetation.

"This is the spot," RJ announced.

"Oh, this is perfect," sighed Brenda.

To her this meant this was the place where they would finally begin their adventure. To him, it meant something else entirely. Her skin tingled with anticipation.

"This is a good spot. No one will find us here. Help me pitch a tent," he said as he pulled his camping bag from his shoulder, put it on the ground, opened it and pulled out the green tarp.

Sidling up to RJ, and using a soft, purring voice, Brenda cocked her head to the side and said:

"Pitch a tent? RJ that doesn't make sense, now does it? Why can't we just go down by the water? You said yourself no one would find us here. Come on!"

She grinned playfully, seductively.

"Besides, wouldn't it be nice to make love for the very first time out in the open, with the sun going down behind us? Wouldn't that be a really nice memory to have for the rest of your life?"

Brenda hoped she was convincing.

RJ hesitated, finally nodding in feigned agreement. He just wanted to fulfill his fantasy.

"You're right, but I'll still bring this with me. We'll need something to lie on."

"Fine, bring it with you," Brenda responded and stepped up to RJ to place a soft kiss on his cheek.

৵৶

Settling on a spot near the edge of a stream, they sat together tossing pebbles. They watched the ripples form outward. Brenda attempted to get him to relax by chatting.

"Do you come here often, RJ?" she asked.

To her, he seemed lost in thought and she wanted him to be present.

"Sometimes. Often enough, I guess."

"Well, it's very beautiful. What do you do when you come here?"

"Not much really. I used to come here with my mom. We used to camp here a lot."

"Really? Just you and your mom?"

"Yeah, my dad never came. It was just as well. I don't really like him much."

RJ chewed on his lower lip and ran his hand through his hair.

Sensing RJ's disturbance, Brenda put her hand on his shoulder. She figured this had to be why he was so sullen. He gave the impression that the pastor was not actively involved with his son and she inwardly wondered why.

Maybe the good Pastor is abusing him.

But that didn't stop her from moving forward to achieve her goal. She patted RJ on the back then rubbed his shoulder for a few moments before taking advantage of the situation. She moved upward toward the back of his neck and began to caress him there.

"Well, I'm sure your father loves you very much and I'm sure you love him. All teenagers go through this. It'll be ok. You're just trying to find your way in this world and sometimes parents aren't helpful. Everything will work out. You'll see."

RJ didn't respond; he didn't even look at her. Instead, he continued tossing little pebbles into the water.

She sighed deeply, frustrated that she was getting nowhere with him. But, she had one last trick up her sleeve. If that didn't work, she would just give up and ask him to take her back into town. She would find her way to the motel if she had to once she got back on the main street.

"My, you feel tense. Why don't I give you a neck massage? I guarantee you'll feel much better when I'm done. The only thing is, you'll have to take off your shirt so I could get right up in there and dissolve this knot in your neck."

RJ looked at her, obviously confused. He wasn't sure if he should agree. He wanted to be close to her but he was nervous and remained silent.

RJ's silence frustrated Brenda even more than before. So she leaned up toward his face to give him a kiss on the cheek, but when he didn't lean down into her, she took matters in her own hands.

As Brenda gently pulled him down toward her, RJ's heart began to quicken. She placed her lips against his and slipped her tongue in his mouth. RJ liked that. He couldn't control his physical response. Brenda's kiss made his member throb and he noticed that it also hurt a little. He shyly kissed her back, but then pulled away to look into her eyes.

As he did, RJ felt a change come over him. Before the kiss he was just confused and slightly angry. Now he was excited. He thought he felt just like a real man might feel.

With eyes downcast, RJ pulled the tee shirt he was wearing over his head and turned around with his back to Brenda so she can begin her massage. Naked from the waist up and with his back to her, he didn't have to worry about anything. All he had to do was focus on what she was doing.

He concentrated on the sensations he was feeling–that someone was touching him. He focused and the little hairs on his arms stood up on end; the butterflies danced their fluttering little dance in his stomach. He stayed in the moment; basking in it without worrying about what would happen if he took off his pants and bared his lower body to this woman. He didn't want to ruin these feelings by thinking about what her reaction might be when she saw what was between his legs.

Kneeling behind RJ, Brenda licked her lips as she rubbed her hands together in order to warm her fingers. Even though it was late August, she didn't feel they were warm enough to make an impact on him. Her hands needed to be warm in order to penetrate the muscle and finally give him relief from the tension he carried around with him, a tension she could easily feel. She wished she hadn't locked her handbag in the locker back at the changing station. She had a small tube of hand lotion in it and it would have at least made her hands soft. Shrugging, she put her hands on RJ's shoulders and her heart beat faster, causing her to struggle in order to breathe evenly.

Slowly massaging RJ's neck in a circular motion, Brenda used only her thumbs. She took a deep breath and after a while, she began to squeeze the muscles in RJ's shoulders. Light kneading over his upper back and his shoulder blades followed the hard squeezing. Soon, she felt RJ begin to relax. He lowered his chin to his chest and closed his eyes. In a soft, soothing whisper, Brenda talked about how beautiful she thought he was; how soft his skin was and that it was important that he find a way to take time out for himself in his daily life.

RJ moaned. He wanted to turn around and toss her to the ground. Instead, he let her fingers do their magic. She continued talking and again praised the silkiness of his skin and how much she loved a man who took care of himself.

RJ wished she would just shut up and let him sink into comfort.

She breathed in his essence deeply and commented on that as well. She talked about how fresh and clean he smelled. She told him she wanted to taste him, to feel the velvet texture of his skin on her tongue.

RJ's eyes flew open and before he could react, she was nibbling on his ear, her breasts resting against his back. He could feel them rise and fall with every breath she took. Everything went quiet and the only thing he could hear was the thumping in his chest. Blood rushed to his member, the painful throbbing soon took root.

Brenda licked his earlobe then blew hot air on it immediately causing bumps to rise on his skin. He squirmed.

She stopped and told him to relax. She placed light kisses starting from his earlobe, down along his neck and finally across his shoulders then back to his neck. She began massaging him anew and gently squeezed his neck.

"Hmm! That feels good," he murmured.

RJ sighed. He had never experienced such intense feelings before. He moved his head back and slowly opened his eyes. He looked up in the sky and noticed the thin clouds floating up there for the first time all day. The sun was low and orange. He let himself go with the feelings he was experiencing for the first time in his life. He told himself he would never forget this day, because on this day he would become a man.

Silent for once, Brenda took notice of his reaction and began her assault on his senses. Again, she laid butterfly kisses all along his upper back then ran her tongue half way down the length of his spine stopping only to restart her manual assault on him.

After a little bit, she stopped and broke her silence.

"Why don't you lie face down so I could get to your lower back?"

Now in a haze, RJ didn't hesitate and nodded, succumbing.

Brenda was masterful. She sat on his ass and started her assault on his back muscles by first pounding them softly with the heel of her palms. Then she began kneading along his ribs and sides in a meticulous and systematic manner as she moved down to his waistline. She was adept at bringing his nerve endings alive in a symphony of sensations that caused RJ to quiver and drool. She could see the goose bumps rise on his flesh. And then the onslaught began again in earnest.

She ran her tongue at the base of his spine and his tailbone. She slowly ran her tongue back up along his spine, then across his shoulders. Upon reaching his ear, she slowly licked his earlobe, taking it in her mouth and gently sucking on it. She inserted her tongue in his ear and then used it to rim its contour.

RJ lost control and rolled on to his back, bringing her on top of him; kissing her deeply, roughly, crushing their mouths together. This time, he was the one who initiated the kiss. He was the man, triumphant!

They flipped again and with Brenda now on her back, he hovered above her. RJ kissed her a second time; this time hard and long on the mouth as though his life depended on this one kiss. He pulled her closer by putting one arm under her and around her waist. With his other hand, he took hold of the back of her head. She tried to bring her arms around his neck but he let go of her to grab them and pulled them over her head to hold them there. When he tired of kissing her on the mouth, he nibbled at her throat.

Taking his cues from what she had done to him, he licked her ears and kissed her décolletage, not really sure what he was doing but continuing to experience feelings that grew ever more intense. He felt like a powerful God about to give the order for the eruption of a dangerous volcano.

For her part, Brenda knew what she was doing. She *wanted* him to lose control. She *wanted* him to ravage her. So what if he got a little rough? She thought she could handle him because she believed she was stronger than he. He was just a boy, and today, she would turn him into a man.

Even though she loved his raw desire, she needed to stop him before he let loose and came all over himself. She freed herself from him. Grabbing a hold of his shoulders. She pushed him away.

Pulling up and away from her, a confused RJ stared at her. His nostrils flared. He couldn't believe she had just done that. He thought this was what she wanted.

"What? Did I do something wrong?"

"No, sweetheart. You did nothing wrong. In fact, you did everything right. We just have to take it a little slower. We need to pace ourselves, make it last so we can get to the grand finale. Don't you want to do it like real men do?"

Embarrassed, RJ could only nod, and climbed off Brenda; collapsing face up on the ground.

Brenda rolled over to her side and looked at him. She played with his hair and asked:

"Are you enjoying yourself?"

Reaching out to caress Brenda's face, RJ's eyes were moist. You might say there was a twinkle in his eye when he pulled her down toward him, kissing her lightly this time.

Taking the kiss as a yes, and without taking her eyes off of him, Brenda sat on top of RJ. She looked around and when she was sure no one was within view, she undid the buttons of the shirt she was wearing and exposed her bare, full breasts to him. RJ's eyes almost popped out of his head. He involuntarily licked his lips as Brenda positioned herself more comfortably over him, her voluminous breasts in his face.

Then something struck her. She couldn't feel his erection through his pants and she wondered if he had already climaxed. She decided she could and would definitely rectify that in no time.

"Do you like what you see?"

An almost imperceptible whisper escaped RJ's lips.

"Yes. Yes, I do."

"You can touch them but you must be gentle and you only get one touch for now."

Nodding, RJ tentatively reached out with the fingers of one hand just as a child would who was about to pet a dog he wasn't sure was friendly. In a trance, he circled the nipple of her right breast with his fingertip. He raised his other hand to do the same with her other breast. He explored the softness of Brenda's skin and appreciated how pliable her breasts were when he softly poked them. He liked the way her nipples came to life and stood erect when he brushed his thumb against them. A smile broke on his face.

It was now time. Brenda took hold of RJ's left hand and placed it on her right breast. Then she took a hold of his right hand and placed it on her left breast holding both hands steady. She moved both his thumbs simultaneously over her nipples. She watched his eyes as her nipples hardened and slowly licked her lips as she asked him how it felt to have the power to make her nipples rise at his command.

RJ's mouth opened slightly but no words came out; he could only take short gasps.

She leaned in and kissed him on the lips; just a peck and began to grind against him. RJ closed his eyes then slowly opened them again as he shifted under her to get the most friction he could against his most sensitive area.

He slid his hand down Brenda's belly having never felt the softness of a woman's flesh against his fingertips and relishing the feeling. Her skin was satiny. RJ fussed with the waistband of her pants and struggled to undo the tie but fumbled. He became frustrated.

Seeing this, Brenda undid it herself, lowered the sweats down a bit then guided his hand to her crotch. He was surprised she wasn't wearing any underwear but got over that really quickly and began caressing her. Her bare vagina was soft to the touch. With Brenda guiding him to her opening, he slipped his finger in and around the inner labia then removed his hand. Face slightly scrunched up, and incredulously, he looked at the moisture left behind as Brenda rose from him. She slowly slipped out of her pants to stand above him naked below the waist.

What was left of the setting sun's rays shone low behind her giving her silhouette an aura resembling a heavenly being descending with the sole purpose of blessing him. The shirt she wore hung loosely around her, flowing in the soft breeze. He rose to his elbows and found himself within inches of her vagina. She smelled powder fresh. He felt a quiver in his pants and the wetness he was becoming familiar with was back. He was glad he still wore his pants because he would be mortified if she found disgust in his moisture. He pushed the thought out of his mind choosing instead to admire the beauty before him.

As he straightened up further into a sitting position, Brenda widened her stance above him, spreading her vulva to give him a better view of what awaited him. She was extremely moist now and her opening glistened above him.

"Do you see that RJ? You excite me! I can't control myself. I'm so wet. RJ, I need you to help clean me up. Can you do that for me?"

"Umm. There are tissues in my bag," the unfinished thought hung in the air between them.

"No. Not with a tissue. Have you ever seen a pussycat clean itself—give itself a bath?"

"Mm hmm..."

"Well, my vagina is your pussycat, and right now she needs cleaning. If you use your tongue it will make me purr. Can you wipe me clean with your tongue? Lap at my pussy like a cat does? It would make me happy and I promise I will return the favor."

"I might hurt you. I'm not sure... My teeth... I'm not sure what to do."

RJ's palms were sweaty. But, most importantly, he knew he had lost control by admitting that he didn't know what to do and he hated that. It hit him hard how out of control he had become. The anger over that realization was now building up inside of him. It was strangely mixed with the excitement he felt experiencing this new thing he didn't have a name for; this mishmash of feelings he didn't understand.

"You're not going to hurt me. Just do what comes naturally," Brenda murmured.

She shifted her body over his face and slowly lowered herself with her legs spread wide, causing him to lie back down. She got on her knees and brought herself over his mouth.

The now lilac sky served as the background for what was right in front of RJ's face. He turned his vision from the sky to the opening before him and licked tentatively as though it was some forbidden candy. Brenda moaned affirmatively and gently guided him through the process, spreading herself wider and better positioning herself over him.

Encouraged by Brenda's soothing voice and continued purring of approval, he took another lick then another and soon he found a rhythm, grabbing a hold of Brenda's thighs and bringing her even closer to him so he could have his fill. They danced this way for a while as he lapped at her, trying not to miss a drop.

He wanted to wipe her clean of all her juices. In his mind, he was cleaning her up and the merciless, inexperienced teasing he applied to her button drove her wild. He wanted to make her legs tremble with pleasure and he succeeded in bringing her close to the overcoming wave he sought for himself.

For his part, RJ felt that if he continued this way, maybe by some miracle he too would reach a place where he could find his long desired release. He wanted them both to end this dance together, but he couldn't even get close. The intense throbbing in his pants was just a tease.

Chapter 13
RJ's First Kill

"You are nothing but a whore! All you wanted to do was tease me, didn't you? I was so close! I was almost there! Why didn't you touch me? Why didn't you help me come? Why did you let the moment pass? You promised you would do the same for me as I did for you!"

Brenda just stood in front of RJ shaking her head. What the hell just happened? She was stunned.

"No, RJ. You're wrong. I was enjoying what you were doing. I ..."

RJ interrupted Brenda with a hard slap to her face. He hit her so hard her teeth bit down on her lip, splitting it. Whimpering, Brenda brought her hand to her face then charged him, arms up, ready to strike.

RJ easily blocked Brenda, grabbing her by her wrists and bringing her close to his body in an effort to still her.

"I'm going to, just once, ask you nicely to calm down. Next time, I will not be so nice."

In that instant, RJ didn't sound nice at all. In fact, he was quite menacing.

Brenda felt the threat settle into her bones. She stopped thrashing about and stood still against him. She was surprised he was so strong. He seemed so slight and weak on the surface.

He kissed her roughly on her bruised lips then lapped at the blood on her lip.

Pulling away, she asked, "Why? Why are you doing this? Why are you behaving this way?"

"Shush. We are going to sit here quietly until the sun goes down. Then I'm going to take off my pants and you will do as I say. Got it?"

Now feeling in control and powerful over this woman, just as he did over the animals in the woods, RJ breathed easier. He was invincible in his element and as they sat there silently, they each sank into their thoughts.

Brenda could not figure out what went wrong. How could this man-child appear to be so naïve and yet so twisted at the same time? What was his problem? Was he mentally ill?

Something was terribly wrong and she didn't know how to handle the situation she found herself in. She had to get away from him, this place. Looking around her, she could find nothing to use as a weapon.

What could she do?

Nothing, there was nothing she could do. She could only go along with his demands until she found an opening to escape.

RJ was confused as well. He really didn't want to hurt Brenda. He just wanted to reach a climax. It wasn't much to ask, was it?

His thoughts and questions bounced around in his head. He didn't know what was wrong with him. Why couldn't he come?

He glanced over at Brenda but she just looked straight ahead. He couldn't see beyond reaching a climax and she just had to help him otherwise he would just go crazy.

&⚬&

It was finally dark. RJ looked over at Brenda who returned his gaze through tears in her eyes. When did she start crying? He hadn't noticed she had been crying.

"Don't cry, Brenda. Isn't this what you wanted? You asked me earlier why I was doing this. Well, *you* made me do this."

RJ stood up and extended his hand to her.

"Come with me," he said.

After hesitating a moment, Brenda thought she'd better do as he asked. She took his hand and rose. They walked silently over to the edge of the creek. Brenda spotted some rocks and considered what she would do. RJ swung her around to face him and grabbed a hold of a handful of hair and held her face close to his.

Oh, no! He noticed I was looking at the rocks!

Brenda tried not to show him fear.

RJ pulled her in closer and roughly tried to kiss her.

At first, she resisted but eventually gave in to him hoping that by appeasing him she could calm him down and escape. His hands began to roam about her body and found their way to her crotch. He caressed her there and though she tried to fight her urges, her body's reflexive response to his touch was unfaithful to her. As she tried to keep her wits about her, she embraced him and soon he came around, responding and breathing heavier. They continued this way for a while and finally, just as she was about to lose control, she pulled away.

Eyes dark, RJ stared at her. The situation was about to take a bad turn and she had to do something quickly.

"RJ, you're right. I do want this. I want you more now than ever. I like it when a man is rough with me. Please take your pants off. I very much would like to see your manhood, to hold it in my hands and feel it in my mouth."

Her eyes widened, her lower lip petulant.

"Would you do that for me?"

A panicked RJ was thrown. The time had come for him to show his real self to her, come what may. Still looking in her eyes, his hand went to his waistband.

He undid the button.

He took hold of the tab on his zipper and began its slow descent.

Brenda bit her lower lip.

RJ lowered his eyes.

Brenda gently pushed his hand away and finished the job for him. With his zipper now undone, she put her forefinger on his chin and lifted his face to hers.

RJ held his breath. With a smile and a wink, Brenda brought her attention back to the job at hand. She had planned to take him in her mouth then take a bite out of him. She prayed her plan would work. Tugging at RJ's pants, she slowly pulled them past his hips, and down his legs. RJ quickly stepped out of them. He was wearing boxer shorts. Brenda looked at his crotch and saw no discernible bulge.

Something wasn't right.

Looking back up at RJ, she slipped her fingers along the waistband of his underwear, readying to pull them down as well. RJ's hand went to hers, quickly putting an end to her actions and led her deeper into the water.

"Not here," he said.

Smiling, she nodded.

They walked together into the shallow water. It couldn't have been more than three feet high. Once in the water, RJ took off his shorts.

Brenda looked down. She couldn't hide her surprise and she gasped.

Standing before her was this sixteen-year-old boy whose manhood was beyond anything she had ever seen before in her experienced life. It looked like an overly fleshy vagina with a knob about the size of a large walnut resembling the head of a penis on a short, thick stem.

This is why she didn't feel an erection! He was underdeveloped!

She began to laugh hysterically. She couldn't help herself nor could she stop.

"Is this for real?" she hollered, turning her face up to look at him.

And then, everything went dark and she collapsed against him. In her fit of laughter she hadn't noticed RJ had bent down into the stream and pulled up a rock, swinging it with all of his might and bringing it down forcefully against the side of her head.

A furious RJ grabbed the back of her head, and thrust her face beneath the water with a loud splash. The impact of that action brought her back to consciousness and she began to thrash about. He held her down for a very long time. Her arms twitched, then stopped. He relished the rush he felt when she began to weaken and finally succumb to his power. He held her under water a while longer–steady, brazen–just to make sure he had total dominion over her.

He felt no remorse.

All the while, RJ played with his knob.

Finally, Brenda was still. He released her body. Sighing deeply, he watched her sink. When she was barely visible under water, he snatched up his underwear and put them back on, then walked back behind the tree.

He slouched against it and slipped his hand into his underwear to play with himself again. He alternated between plunging his forefinger into his opening and rubbing his mushroom knob, desperate to find relief. But try as he might, he couldn't reach his apex.

Frustrated, he put his pants back on, grabbed the tarp and quickly headed back to the truck.

His pounding head was nothing compared to the ache in his crotch.

How dare she laugh at me? She got what she deserved, that fucking bitch!

The angrier he got, the hornier he got. But he could only think of one thing and that was the elusive climax. He had never had an orgasm.

He didn't think about the fact that Brenda had left all of her belongings in the locker back at the changing station.

Chapter 14
There's Nothing a Mother Wouldn't Do for Her Son

Today, Margaret was sure RJ had done it again. She also knew it would take a miracle for him to get away with it this time. She had no choice but to do everything in her power to help her son leave town safely.

A few days after the incident with Brenda almost three years earlier, a camper discovered her body and an investigation was begun. When an attendant noticed one particular locker had not been opened in a while, she got her supervisor to open it. In it they found Brenda's belongings, but there was no evidence linking RJ to it. The contents included Brenda's driver's license and the authorities were notified.

A statement was taken from both the attendant and her supervisor. The locker was dusted for fingerprints confirming that the items contained within the locker did indeed belong to Brenda. Brenda's criminal record also became known. This information automatically put Brenda's murder low on the priority scale but a conversation with one of the women at church who saw Brenda pointed the police to Margaret and they paid her a visit.

Margaret was surprised to see the police at her door, but understood they had a job to do.

"Yes, sir. She was here but she said she was just passing through. Said she might stay at the motel up the road."

"We've checked, Mrs. Preston. She never checked in."

"Well, then. She must've changed her mind."

"Do you have any information on her next of kin? We'd like to reach out to them."

"Can't say that I do. I knew Brenda many years ago. She was an orphan; an only child. She was alone in the world."

"Well, thank you anyway, Ma'am. We apologize for any inconvenience."

"No inconvenience. Good-bye."

She never heard anything more about it again, proving to Margaret that not much was being done in the way of finding Brenda's killer.

Brenda was a stranger in a small town. She was a prostitute who had no roots in the community. She was just passing through and no one asked any further questions. So, the investigation just died as no witnesses came forward to claim the body or her belongings and there was no trace evidence. It was a lucky break for both Margaret as well as for RJ.

❧❧

RJ had always been an easy read for Margaret. When he returned the night Brenda disappeared, his eyes had a wild look about them. It took some cajoling, but RJ finally told Margaret that something bad had happened. She asked what was wrong—did he have a car accident? She hoped that was all it was. He had just gotten his license.

But RJ shook his head no.

Now really concerned, she asked if he was all right. Did something happen to him? Again, he shook his head no and replied that he was fine. However, Brenda was not.

Margaret didn't understand what he was trying to say. She pushed for an answer, begging her son to tell her everything, but all he would say was two things: he said that Brenda laughed at him and that she had drowned. He said nothing more. Margaret knew that the time had come. Brenda was a sex-starved woman and Margaret had a feeling she would try to seduce RJ just by the way she reacted when he arrived home that day. But she thought RJ would simply drop her off at the hotel and be on his way. In denial of the monster her son was, she never imagined that something like this could happen. She believed she had taught her son well and trusted him. It simply had to have been an accident.

The time had come for her to have the talk with RJ she had dreaded his whole life. It was time to explain why nothing was done when he was a baby, why his deformity was ignored. She had to take steps to avoid something like this happening again.

At the end of that conversation, though very angry, RJ did not blame his mother. She too was under the Pastor's ironclad household rule. His father was not to be defied; not to be questioned. He was to be obeyed! His word was golden! RJ knew Margaret did the best she could for him. She had little to offer him but a mother's love.

જ∾ৡ

Throughout his life, Margaret was RJ's sentry, ever watchful over him, protecting him from insensitivities directed at him by everyone he encountered, including his father. She always stood between her husband and her son.

RJ, in turn, consistently defended her against her husband's raging temper. On her son's behalf, she bore the brunt of all pain and suffering put upon him by all who knew or thought they knew of his deformity.

The time he spent in middle and high school was hell for her son. He failed physical education every year. It wasn't because he wasn't physically able. It was because he could not bear the thought of having to wear his gym clothes in public or shower in front of the other boys. He hoped he would contract some imagined disease that would keep him from his school's required physical activities.

He didn't go to his middle school prom because he wanted to ask one of the boys. He didn't because he knew that would only bring him trouble and, he believed, shame to his mother.

He didn't go to his senior high school prom because he knew that the girl he wanted to ask would reject him before the question was completely out of his mouth.

He found solace in his mother's company so he spent a lot of time with her doing things together that ultimately made them each fiercely loyal to one another. They couldn't have been any closer had she borne him herself. And now, once again, it was time to stand vehemently before her son as he had done for her the night before. She had to fight the fear that was rattling her senses in order to speak.

"RJ, you know I love you. You know I would do anything for you. But, this time, as much as I'd hate to see you go, I think it would be best if you left town. This one will not go unnoticed. Questions will be asked. I don't know if I will be able to save you.

"I have some money put away and I want you to have it. I want you to take it and go somewhere where you could start over again. Maybe you could go to New York? I have a terrible feeling that this time you will not get away with what you've done."

"I will not leave you here alone, Mother. It'll be ok."

"No! I insist! You must leave right away!"

"I can't just leave right now! If I do that, it will look suspicious. Who leaves their mother at a time when her husband, especially a well-known pastor, turns up dead?

"You know, once it comes out that you and he had a less than perfect marriage, first you, then I, will be viewed as suspects. I have no choice but to stick around. No one will think I did it. Trust me. In time, I will leave, I promise."

"You *are* my son, RJ. It doesn't matter that I did not bear you. You have enriched my life in ways no other person ever has. I cannot let you go to prison for this! I absolutely will not allow that to happen! The authorities will understand that you did it in my defense. Together we must decide how we're going to handle this."

"I know what we must do, Mother. When the sun rises, you will report your husband missing. The police will ask you a bunch of questions, and you will respond by telling them you argued with him. You will tell them that he roughed you up and that I argued with him as well in your defense.

"You'll tell them that you managed to calm us both down; that you asked him to leave and he did. You will tell them he said he was going for a walk and eventually, you fell asleep. When you awoke, you realized he hadn't returned from his walk.

"You'll explain that you were worried about him and called the police.

"Don't worry. It will all work out. Let them sort it out. It will undoubtedly be a while before they find him, if at all. Once things cool down, I'll leave for New York. I'll start a new life there. Everything will be all right. I promise."

By now, Margaret's brain felt like runny mashed potatoes. She always knew it would someday come to this. RJ could not be blamed for what he was. It was not his fault he had been born this way, and it was not his fault he'd turned into the person he was today.

She blamed her husband. She truly believed that if her husband had loved his son the way he publicly professed he did; if he had only supported him and sincerely shown him a father's love—one on one— RJ might not have turned into a monster. She did the best she could with him, but she would never betray her son.

In all honesty, Margaret knew that her husband was a tortured man as well. Given his own history, it was no surprise he behaved in the manner he did. He had his own demons to battle. She was left with no recourse but to be supportive of her son and help him get away.

She analyzed the situation they were in.

He would be eighteen soon, old enough to manage a small trust fund she set up for him when he first came to them. It was dirty money; money she had saved up when she was working the johns but it would have to do. That and whatever they could scrape together should be enough for him to start over somewhere else. There had to be somewhere he could go where his past would not hinder him.

"Sit down, RJ. I have something to tell you."

Over the course of a few hours, Margaret unabashedly told her son her whole life story through tears and sincere pronouncements of love. She answered all of his questions honestly, including what she did for a living before she met her husband, and omitted nothing. She detailed how the Pastor rescued her and how later, James Ezekiel would belittle her and use her past against her.

She told her son that she tolerated her husband's abuse because she had no place else to go. Besides, there was no way she would leave without her son. She stressed that as far as she was concerned there was no justification for leaving him behind with the hypocritical pastor, ending her tale by telling him that she had planned on leaving the Pastor anyway once RJ was on his own.

"He had the nerve to call you a whore, Mom?! How dare he? Even Mary Magdalene was forgiven and saved by Jesús Christ. That hypocritical asshole stood in his pulpit, day after day, preaching the love of God. He preached about God forgiving all of our sins and he himself did not live the word of God! He was not man enough to practice what he preached daily. He used the pretense of faith in God's word to lie to everybody in church! I feel no remorse for what I did. He deserved what he got."

With those harsh, final words, RJ walked out of the room leaving Margaret alone to take in everything he said. She peered through the window. It was now that time between dusk and dawn and the thinning rays of moonlight shone through the glass window.

Margaret crossed her arms on the dinette table, resting her head in the cradle formed by her forearms and cried until she dozed off.

Having gotten very little sleep, Margaret called the police when she awoke, and reported her husband missing. Within a few minutes, they arrived to take down the details. RJ stood by his mother's side, his hand resting reassuringly on her shoulder as she told the police the events of the previous night. When the initial questioning of them both was completed, mother and son were escorted to the station for further, separate interrogations.

The investigators thought that by separating them and moving them out of their element, something might come to light that would give them a hint as to what really transpired the previous evening. They persisted in trying to find out about any events that may have followed the argument and right before the Pastor vanished. Nothing stood out to the investigators. They actually thought that Margaret was telling the truth when she said that he told her he was going out to let off steam. They also wondered amongst themselves if the Pastor had a mistress he might have gone to for a little comfort and lost track of time.

This line of thinking did not deter the authorities from continuing to question RJ and Margaret in an attempt to figure out if they wavered from their explanations of what happened that night.

But, after spending that entire day at the police station, and unannounced visits at their home later during the rest of that week, the police could not glean anything more from them. No suspicious clues were brought to light.

In the end, both Margaret and RJ were warned sternly by the investigators not to plan any trips out of town while simultaneously being promised that if any other information turned up, the family would be the first to know.

There was no doubt in either of their minds that they were now both under suspicion. It would be hard for RJ to leave now because guilty or not, they would both remain under the watchful eye of the authorities.

In the meantime, flyers went up and newscasters reported round the clock on the popular pastor's disappearance. Reporters and photographers camped outside of the Preston home for weeks on end. Eventually, as no leads developed, the furor died down.

The case remained open, but RJ never discussed the incident with his mother again. This was a subject that they avoided entirely. For a year and a half, they simply continued living their lives and tried to build a future.

The gossipy ladies in the community speculated about what might have happened to the Pastor. Many of them knew of the elder Pastor Preston's scandal so many years earlier. A rumor started going around that maybe Pastor James Ezekiel had also contracted syphilis, just like his father had years before. They commented that rather than face his parish, the current Pastor Preston left without a trace to go off somewhere to die–not only from the disease but from embarrassment as well.

દ?∾ઌ

Once the cops backed off him and his mother, RJ felt it was safe to leave town. Margaret agreed with her son and sold the house that held so many memories for them both. She packed what she could take with her, sold whatever she could, tossed the rest and moved into a senior citizen community after splitting the sale proceeds with RJ.

Now almost twenty years old, he was long of the age where he could legally gain control of his trust fund.

RJ decided to use part of that fund to purchase a recreational vehicle. It would also serve as his new home until he found a place in which to settle down.

Chapter 15
RJ Leaves Lebanon

The day had finally come when RJ would leave Lebanon, Pennsylvania forever. He spent his last day with his mother at her new home. When it was time to leave, he bid her a tearful good-bye.

"Let me walk you out, RJ."

"No, Mom. Stay here. I can't bear to see you cry."

"I won't cry, RJ. I promise."

"Oh, man! I can't win with you, can I?"

"No! I'm the mother and you have to do as I say!"

RJ took his mother's face in his hands and looked into her glassy eyes. He held her that way for a long time. He was surprised to see that she had aged. Lines feathered her eyes and along the corners of her mouth.

"I love you, Mom. I love you with every fiber of my being," he said and drew her close.

Margaret fought a losing battle with her tears. What would happen to her son? Who would protect him? She hugged him a little bit tighter and inhaled deeply. She would never forget his scent as long as she lived. Somehow, she knew this would be the last time she would ever hold him like this; that this was the last time she would ever see him.

"I'd better go," RJ said, breaking the spell.

He looked at the ground.

"Don't cry, ok? You have a chance to do some living now. We both do. You should be happy. Promise me you'll be happy, Mom."

"I promise, son. Now you be careful. And remember all I've taught you. Remember what you will need to do to maintain control. If you ever feel like you might need someone to talk to, call me. Call me before you do anything rash. Promise me!"

"Ok, Mom. I promise."

RJ gave his mom one last kiss on the cheek and another long, tight hug. This time Margaret pulled away first. He caressed her face then turned toward the RV. Before he jumped in, he turned around and blew her a kiss and in that instant he felt homesick. He took a peek in the side mirror and saw his mother waving. She mouthed the words "I love you." He would never forget that image.

RJ blew the RV's air horn and pulled away from the curb. He decided to take a last-minute detour to his childhood home for one last glimpse of the house he had grown up in.

Margaret stared at the RV until it was out of sight as she prayed for her son's safety.

ॐॐ

RJ was heading for bright lights in the big city–New York City, The Big Apple. The ride would be a couple of hours long, so he decided he would use that time to think about things once more. He purposely took the scenic route even though it was late at night and there was really nothing to see. He didn't have a clue as to what he was going to do once he got there. At minimum, he figured he would find a place where he can park the RV and do day labor.

Soon, RJ was at the halfway point of his trip. He calculated he would be reaching NYC in a little over an hour–in no time, really. This was definitely a good time to take a break. He was going to need gas soon anyway and he also needed to use the bathroom. He decided to grab one of those taco and beef burrito meals while he was there.

After paying for his meal, RJ grabbed a handful of condiments, and sat at a rickety table near the window. He took a sip of his huge soda and unfurled the wrapping from around his taco. He polished it off in a handful of bites.

As he wiped his mouth clean, RJ glanced down at the greasy burrito sitting in front of him. He brought it closer and absentmindedly pulled at the ends of its wrapping. As he gazed down at it he lost any desire to eat it when he saw that the meat wrapped up with all the gook was still pink. Grimacing, he looked away from it and through the dirty glass window on his left.

Damn it!

He liked his meat well cooked.

I wonder if it's worth the trouble to ask the clerk to exchange it for something else. Maybe I should just throw it away? He groaned in defeat.

RJ was totally unaware that a life-changing event was about to happen. It was at this point that he encountered the one living being, other than his mother, that he would come to consider his companion, his best friend.

It was amazing to him. All he was doing was ruminating about whether or not to exchange the burrito for another when he happened to glance out the window. His mind filled with an idea. Grabbing the burrito, he hurriedly left the station. Once outside, he tentatively approached what would, outside of scientific parameters, be called a lost "soul." The closer RJ got, the less wary this "soul" appeared to behave, seemingly craving human contact. Upon closer examination, his new friend appeared to be severely undernourished. RJ glanced down at the haphazardly wrapped package containing the burrito with the raw meat and tentatively extended it in offering to this hapless creature. This seemed to be a much-appreciated gesture. The grateful soul took one whiff, snatched it out of RJ's hand and ate it.

Well, no. This generous and kind offer was inhaled, nearly swallowed whole.

At once, RJ felt a kinship with this creature. Except for his mother, he had never noticed that he was capable of having feelings such as the ones he was having right now. He certainly was not the empathetic type.

Once his new friend was done eating and appeared to be content, RJ led him to his vehicle where they retreated for a bit. He helped his companion get comfortable in its new surroundings then readied for their journey together.

RJ happily talked the whole rest of the way to New York City while his companion sat in the passenger seat, mute. He even gave his new friend a name. He called his new friend "God."

God was already showing signs of loyalty and love toward him, a love he had never known before except for the love he received from his mother. He, in turn, decided that he would return the favor and be a loyal friend to God. Once they came together, they were insepa-rable and they shared just about everything.

Chapter 16
Adina's Fractured Journey into Adulthood

It was a cheery, sun-filled day. The weather, though in the nineties, was low in humidity and the sun shone brightly through the lace window curtains in her bedroom. Sitting at her vanity, Adina leaned out of the sun's way to avoid squinting while applying her makeup. A light breeze played with the coppery wisps of hair that framed her face.

It was graduation day and she was not only relieved, but also extremely proud of herself for finally completing her grueling curriculum. She'd gotten through her studies half a semester late but managed to maintain a 3.5 average, earning a degree in marketing. Although she did well scholastically, it had been a hard road filled with dangerous emotional obstacles.

For a bit after the miscarriage, Adina's mental health was very precarious. Her emotions swung back and forth between altering cycles of deep-rooted depression and periods of high anxiety. When she was depressed, she spoke about death incessantly. She was obsessed with death and often wondered aloud what it might feel like to die. She weighed the various ways in which to commit suicide and debated the benefits.

She could do it non-violently by overdose or, she could hang herself or jump out a window. Her twisted logic had her believing that a potentially violent death like the ones she considered might not be the best way to go. She thought that if she survived jumping from a window, she might become a vegetable and have to live trapped in a body she did not want to be in with no opportunity to try again. That, to her, was a fate worse than life.

Jesús and Cruzita thought all this talk of death and dying was just the way she mourned her baby. Each time one of these dark periods passed, she would appear to make peace with her loss. But any peaceful time was short lived. Sometimes she didn't talk of death and suicide at all. Instead, she became difficult to live with.

She was argumentative, irrational and irritable during those periods. There were often nights when she didn't sleep; other times she couldn't get out of bed in the morning. Then she would awaken feeling drained and tired. Depression would set in again and the cycle would begin anew.

Alarmed, her parents decided to accompany her to one of her follow-up gynecological appointments even though she put up a fierce fight against the idea. But they insisted and went with her. While she dressed after the examination, they discussed their concerns to her doctor. Adina's doctor asked her a few questions and was dissatisfied with her answers. He found that her responses were illogical. When she stated that her parents killed her baby, the doctor expressed his concern for her and firmly advised that he would have no choice but to have her admitted to the hospital.

Adina felt completely defeated, but she grudgingly agreed to meet with whomever her doctor wanted her to meet. He had been her doctor for a long time but she trusted no one. She was immediately admitted to the psychiatric ward of the hospital her doctor was affiliated with and placed under observation with little input from her. Arrangements were made for her to meet with the psychiatrist first thing in the morning.

Early the next morning, nurses escorted Adina to her psychiatrist's office. Within a few minutes of their meeting, Dr. Christine Benjamin began jotting down notes in her notepad. When the session was over, she read back to herself what she had written:

"17 yo, Hispanic female, shows symptoms of psychotic depressive disorder w/ suicide ideation post spontaneous abortion. Recommended treatment—25 mg. Sinequan 3x/day w/ daily, in-house psychiatric treatment until stable + re-evaluation in 2 wks."

Dr. Benjamin put her pen down and rubbed her forehead. She could tell Adina was smart from the short, fleeting moments of lucidity she had during their session. Then a thought crossed her mind. *Sinequan.* That was Latin for the phrase: *an essential part.* She thought it ironic that a medication used to treat mental illness would be so aptly named as mental health *was* an essential part of overall good health.

℞∾

Cruzita and Jesús anticipated that once in the hospital's care, Adina would soon begin to feel better and be sent home, but that would not be the case. Initially, the medication made her symptoms worse. She was always drowsy because it produced insomnia, which made her extremely tired as a result. She was more often than not extremely irritable, hostile and easily agitated. It took over three months for her symptoms to level out. Adina remained at the hospital during that time, and upon her release, she attended weekly grief counseling sessions for an additional three months. These sessions were in addition to her thrice-weekly visits with Dr. Benjamin. Her medication was closely monitored during this time and her behavior was carefully recorded in an attempt to find stressors so they could be avoided. Due to noted fluctuations in her moods, she was reminded how important it was for her to take her medication every single day.

Showing steady signs of improvement, eventually her visits were reduced to weekly appointments. It was a year before she decided on her own to stop going so she began to slack off on her medication.

If she took her medication regularly, Adina worked hard and thrived. She graduated from high school with a certified diploma even though she had spent the better part of her senior year–six months– under psychiatric treatment. Seeing the improvement, her parents counseled her about college. After a few of these conversations, she finally gave in to their wishes and enrolled in the local university. It was a compromise, if only so that she could have some peace. The implicit understanding was that she would complete her studies, attain her degree then leave New York.

All through her college years, her moods remained stable. However she would sometimes miss a couple days of medication and her irritability would resurface. She had also become extremely reckless sexually, particularly when she drank too much. Her parents confronted her about her behavior numerous times, and the cycle to attempt to regulate her moods would begin yet again. These confrontations with her parents became more and more frequent, and they often culminated with Adina expressing remorse and realizing that she could be a lot worse off. When that light bulb went on, she always promised to re-focus on doing the right thing.

Around the time that she was released from the hospital, her old boyfriend Benny was going through his trial, after which he was sentenced to twenty-five years to life. He was charged with and found guilty of felonious murder because drugs were involved. He would become eligible for lifetime parole after he served a minimum of ten years. She visited him just two times before the trial and eventually stopped writing to him altogether after the sentencing. He in turn, had her image tattooed on his forearm with the word *Suki*, which loosely translated meant "I love you" in Swahili. She had broken his heart and her doing so left him feeling alone and somewhat angry. But deep down inside, he knew he could not expect that she would wait for him. If on the off chance that they did manage to get back together, he did not believe she would want to live out her life with a convicted felon. She was beautiful, smart and had a bright future. He didn't want to be the one to take that away from her.

One day, Adina ran into one of his old friends. He told her Benny had spent quite a bit of time in solitary after she broke up with him due to his constant mouthing off to the prison guards and that he was always involved in one fight or another. She couldn't believe it as she felt that was not the Benny that she had fallen in love with. When they were together, he was a different man. She wholeheartedly believed that.

Yes, she still thought of him—infrequently. It was more like a dream that you barely remember upon awakening. She remembered him in the way she remembered dreams that dogged her all day long, the details eluding her, until some piece of it floated up into memory. Dreams like that tended to linger long after the details were forgotten and the feelings they evoked randomly popped up at the most inopportune time.

For his part, Benny didn't know how much Adina had changed since the miscarriage. Hell, he never even found out she was pregnant. He was totally unaware that she was no longer the naïve young lady he once knew. He patted himself on the back for turning her into a woman.

☙❧

Over the past five years–the end of her senior year at high school and then her four years at college, Adina studied hard, worked part-time and fooled around ... a *lot*. As usual, her behavior was worse when she wasn't on her medication and she often had one-night stands.

She dabbled in drugs, but they didn't get her off. She didn't like being out of control, so she hardly ever indulged. Everyone around her seemed to be drinking all the time but she rarely did. To her, drinking was worse than anything else because the high you experienced if you had too much alcohol was a sloppy one, especially when combined with her medication. If she knew she was going to have more than a few drinks, she purposely didn't take them.

Adina's drug of choice was sex. She thought that if it were possible to be addicted to sex, then she was. She wasn't concerned about getting pregnant again because now she was on birth control pills. She contemplated how strange it was that when she fantasized about her future, she never saw a child in it; never even envisioned herself as a married woman. She had plenty of lovers and she was truly enjoying herself.

As a rule, she never talked to her parents about the activities she took part in within the walls of her private life. Her parents weren't naïve though. They figured she might be having sex outside of marriage and it was much to their chagrin but they looked the other way. Adina only talked about things she did with her girlfriends, school events she attended or her responsibilities at her internship and where she saw herself in her career.

"Career" talk only took place because her father insisted that she have a plan for her future. He was constantly challenging her on it, but it wasn't something she really had to think about. People liked her instantly and she was promoted regularly at her job. Adept at being charming, she knew how to get what she wanted. She was so good at manipulating people, they actually believed whatever they were doing for her was their idea all along because of her charm. She did this at home, she did this at school and she did this with men. She called it "getting over like a fat rat in a cheese factory" and she was a master at it.

But today, as the saying went, was the first day of the rest of her life. She didn't want to think about anything else but having fun.

After the graduation ceremony, she and her parents were planning to get a portrait done by a professional photographer, followed by a special graduation dinner early in the evening at the famed Benihana Restaurant. Benihana's was famous for their chefs who theatrically prepared meals on a grill around which you sat with strangers. Afterward, her friends Margie, Solymar and Tiffany were going to swing by and pick her up. They planned on going to a movie then heading over to The Red Parrot for a little dancing. Adina was very excited. Her boss was kind enough to give her tickets for this one-time affair as a graduation gift.

Chapter 17
Adina Celebrates Her Graduation (1985)

The Red Parrot was Adina's latest favorite hotspot. After handing over all their tickets to the cashier, she happily shuffled onto the dance floor, her heart beating in time with the bass of the intoxicating music. Its waves carried them to a spot directly under a speaker on the edge of the dance floor. The blinking lights together with the smoke in the air distorted her vision making it seem surreal. Bodies moved en masse, appearing to sway as a single organism manipulated by the hard-hitting beat and strobe lights. The floor was crowded and the dancers' movements seemed robotic, disjointed and slow but still keeping time with the music.

Starting with the mesmerizing sounds of Lisa Lisa and the Cult Jam singing about what would happen if they took you home; Adina, together with her friends, danced a string of similarly heart pounding songs. Each song rose in crescendo as they chased the always-elusive musical orgasm until the DJ turned to a mellower sound.

"That was so cool!" exclaimed an overly excited Solymar as the rest of the girls giggled at her awe.

Solymar was from Yonkers, a suburb of New York City in lower Westchester. She and Adina met during their freshman year at college. Soly, as she liked to be called, was new to city life. Margie and Tiffany were sisters, childhood acquaintances of Adina's. At the time, the four of them were extremely close.

"That was nothing, girl! You just wait 'til the band comes! It's live entertainment tonight! You're going to get a taste of what big city living is really like!"

The girls giggled in unison.

"Stop! Don't make me laugh! I've got to pee. Can one of you order me a drink?" asked Adina.

"Sure. I'll get this round. What do you want?" responded Margie.

"My regular–Absolut Screwdriver."

"I'll take one too, but don't let them give you anything other than Absolut. That other shit will give me a headache," demanded Tiffany.

"Ok. What about you, Soly?"

"Same!" she responded.

"Alrighty, then! Absolut Screwdrivers all around! All with cherries, 'cause we can use all the help we can get! Am I right, ladies?"

The girls broke out in hearty laughter.

"We'll meet you at the bar," Margie said to Adina, still giggling. "Go."

Smiling at her friends, Adina turned and walked toward the restroom.

As usual, there was a long line. Adina leaned back against the wall and looked around the club in order to take her mind off her full bladder. She took notice of all the beautiful people in the club and as she scanned the area, she stopped to feast her eyes upon a rather chiseled god of a man who immediately appealed to her.

Sporting well-muscled shoulders, a head full of shaggy dark hair and wearing what she called a gladiator beard, Adina immediately dubbed him "Gladiator Guy." If he wasn't so tall and broad up on top, he could pass for Al Pacino in "Serpico."

He was fine and she decided, right then and there, that he would be hers by the end of the night.

She stared at his reflection in the mirrors that lined the walls opposite where he stood chatting with a group of guys, a big smile on his face. While she stood there, she did not see any women approach him. That could mean one of three things: he was alone; his date was in line with Adina waiting to use the ladies' room as well; or the girlfriend hadn't yet arrived and was meeting him there. Adina was convinced that there was no way such a handsome guy would be at The Red Parrot without a date.

In all honesty, she really didn't care about any other women. If he was there with someone or was going to be meeting up with someone, whoever she was wouldn't even notice what was happening once Adina started to move in on him. She was sure of that.

Adina inched along in line, but she kept her eye on him. As she entered the alcove to the ladies' room, she chanced another glance. Based on what she had seen so far, she was fairly certain he was there alone.

Well, now. It looks like he's alone ... but not for long. Not if I have anything to do with it!

Adina smirked to herself.

᪣ᣭᢒ

She stepped out of the stall and quickly washed her hands. She rinsed her mouth with the mouthwash that was sitting on the tray in the vanity of the bathroom tossing the little bottle into the silver bin under the sink. Spying courtesy hair spray, she spritzed her hair then carefully applied another coat of her own lipstick. When she was done, she dropped a dollar bill into the attendant's tip jar and left.

She knew she looked good. One guy came up to her to tell her how beautiful he thought she was and asked her to save a dance for him. She didn't really like him–he was too short, but she said yes anyway. Adina was feeling good and she didn't even have a drink yet. She knew she had to watch it, though. She didn't want to get sloppy tonight.

Spotting her girlfriends at the far end of the bar, she approached. They were giggling about something or other when Soly suggested that since it was still early they get table service before it got crowded. Her thinking was that they shouldn't hang out at the bar or keep going back for drinks. The girls all agreed and were soon seated at a table on the far side of the club.

This was a great idea! This way, she could steer that beautiful man to her table, invite him to join them for a drink and then see what happens. Maybe he could bring some friends for the girls. She loved being a woman!

As they settled in, the waiter brought the bottle of Absolut and mixer they had ordered. She surreptitiously looked around for her Gladiator Guy but didn't see him. It was now really crowded and she figured he must be around somewhere.

Where is he?

She was hoping to bump into him accidentally on purpose when she next saw him.

Did he leave?

She doubted it. At least, she hoped he hadn't.

Lost in her quest, she was jangled back to reality when all of a sudden everything went quiet except for a tapping sound coming from a microphone and the feedback that followed. The MC/owner of the club was on stage.

"Ladies and gentlemen! Welcome to The Red Parrot!"

He waited for the applause to subside.

"Tonight we have a very special event for your entertainment! A rare live, exclusive appearance of one of the most popular Latino bands has been made possible courtesy of Mari Records! For just one night and for your dancing pleasure, we offer you the great musical talent of Salsa music pioneers.

"Without further ado, from the streets of El Barrio of New York City, please put your hands together and help me welcome Amor!"

Deafening, thunderous applause broke out. Aptly named "Amor" the quartet was the first Salsa group to sign on with an internationally known American record label. They were about to embark on a tour of six cities in the heartland of America to promote their first album, *Canciones de Amor/Love Songs*. Red hot and taking advantage of the momentum they'd created, the plan was to cross over into pop culture and make an impact musically on mainstream America.

Their debut album was filled with classic Spanish love ballads sung with English lyrics laid over a salsa beat. Just released, it was quickly rising up the charts all along the eastern seaboard. This was a phenomenon never before seen particularly in this musical genre. The undertaking was a huge risk.

Amor began as an underground group, playing mainly hole-in-the-wall nightclubs. Typically, they played weddings and quinceañeras. The band had been struggling to make a name for themselves for years. In the late '70s and early '80s, summer open-air concerts in El Barrio were all the rage. They were the opening act for many other struggling acts. The final concert of the season was to be headlined by a famous percussionist, Larry Colón. Larry was the most successful Latino solo artist on the record label.

While planning the last performance of the season, Larry personally requested that Amor perform with him after the son of a friend gave him a demo tape to listen to. He was so impressed that he crashed a party they were playing in order to check them out and see if they were any good in person.

He later brought the band to the attention of Matt Queler, owner of Mari Records, and the rest was history. In fact, it was Matt's idea to translate the lyrics of those classic Spanish ballads into English and pour them over those sensuous Afro-Cuban beats called Salsa.

Salsa was becoming extremely popular and it was genius on Matt's part to strike while the iron was hot. Now, less than a year later, Amor was about to go on tour.

As natives of New York's El Barrio, the quartet was home again to bid a fond adieu to its hometown in a one-night extravaganza. Before beginning their set, the lead singer announced that all proceeds from the event were to be donated to The Foundation for Emerging New Life.

Adina looked away from the stage. The announcement floored her! The Foundation for Emerging New Life was where she interned. It was where she would begin working full time next week! No wonder her boss so easily and eagerly handed over the tickets to her as a graduation gift! He said he was extremely proud of her and grateful for all the assistance she provided him and his patients.

Unbeknownst to Adina, this evening would set the stage for what path her career would take over the next fifteen years.

Immediately after the announcement, they began with their first song, "Qué Lío." This was a very popular song about a man in love with another man's wife. Hector Lavoe last recorded it in Spanish as a cha-cha years earlier. This new sound was infectious!

As soon as the first chord of the song was struck, the guy who asked her to dance earlier approached Adina. He was thoughtful enough to bring along friends for her friends, and happily, they all went out on to the dance floor and let loose.

The passion and sounds reverberating from the stage as the band performed this first song caused the rest of the club's patrons to join them on the dance floor at once. Everyone seemed to love it! If you looked down on the dance floor from the DJ booth, you could see the mass of frenzied bodies undulating and swaying to the music as one unit. Adina was in her heaven and was immediately wrapped up in the music. Being spun by her partner, the conga player caught her eye.

It's him! The guy with the gladiator beard!

She almost lost her step so hypnotized was she by the muscles roping his forearms. She admired the way his chest expanded with every beat. She licked her lips when he bit his lower lip, threw back his head and jutted out his jaw defiantly so impassioned was he by the music. He closed his eyes while he rhythmically and brutally beat the skins.

Adina was immediately turned on and her body responded in kind. She moistened then pulled herself away from her dance partner–who was bound and determined to hold her close. She had to get closer to Gladiator Guy ... and when she was close enough, she began a solo dance until she arrived front and center to the stage.

Like a puppy, her now non-essential partner followed. She ignored him until he gave up and went about searching for another partner to dance with. Adina continued dancing alone, focused on the conga player, telepathically willing him to look at her. She continued watching him; reveling in the passion that oozed from him. To her, it was obvious he was the kind of man who would be open-minded in the bedroom; the kind that would allow her to take the lead. This excited her immensely.

He finally looked her way and she made eye contact with him–a look that showed she meant business. The constant beat of the drum was the only sound she heard, and his eyes the only thing she saw.

She lingered, focused only on him as she danced.

Enthralled, he stared back.

When the song ended, she blew him a kiss, winked and seductively walked off blending in with the crowd.

He was completely blown away. He wanted to follow her, but the next song was about to begin. As each successive piece was performed, he scanned the crowds looking for her, even sometimes missing a beat.

What the fuck just happened? he thought.

At last, the set ended. All of the members of the quartet and back-up band members gathered at the bar for drinks. Slow songs played softly amid the chatter of the club's patrons. Gladiator Guy continued scanning the crowd and Adina watched him search for her from her seat at the table behind the crowd where he couldn't see her.

She'd won.

He was hooked and she seized upon the opportunity to move in. As she gazed at him, she thought about her interview for her first job.

Chapter 18
The Foundation for Emerging New Life

The Foundation for Emerging New Life is the non-profit organization where Adina had done her internship during her senior year of high school and remained as a part-time, paid employee throughout college as well. She stayed on for the credits that would go on her transcript, not because she was sensitive to the needs of its patients.

Just before graduation, Dr. Boulas, director of the Foundation, offered her a full time job. Knowing it was a really good opportunity and that it would serve a purpose for her, she jumped at the chance. It didn't pay much, but it was enough for her right now and the perks were outstanding. There were dinners, networking events and fundraisers to organize and attend, and there were men–lots of them–for her to meet. The mutually agreed upon date for her first day at work was coming up and she was ambivalent about working there.

Established in 1981 by general physician David Boulas, after he lost his long-time partner, the Foundation's mission was blossoming. It had come to serve as a beacon for sufferers of a disease that seemed to be appearing exclusively in the homosexual community: a disease that appeared to mimic a multitude of other diseases. Believed to attack and weaken the immune system, the scourge came to be known as The Monster. As time wore on, doctors throughout the city began to see more and more of an increase of skin cancers occurring in this sector of the homosexual population.

Already on the fringes of society, this very diverse, and until then, underground homosexual population had nowhere to turn. Historically scorned by its neighbors and especially as the illness sank its teeth into the lives of its inhabitants, this community of people had just one person they could go to in their time of need, and that person was Dr. Boulas.

Rumors sprouted and spread that the disease originated from a primate. These unconfirmed tales became so ridiculously outlandish that religious fanatics preached this was God's way of punishing homosexuals for going against the natural order of things. In addition, deaths from the effects of a strong and incurable form of pneumonia began to occur regularly.

An epidemic of this unknown disease was feared and again, the homosexual population was where this pattern was showing. Ultimately, the marked weight loss seen in all of these cases, as the victims wasted away, meant there was no hiding the illness. A trend in immune deficiency was becoming notable among the victims and rumblings of contagion amid an epidemic began to get louder. Everyone was scared and doctors began to turn patients away for fear of catching it as well. There was no clear process for dealing with the large crop of new patients that seemed to rise out of nowhere and none of the victims seemed to know how they became sick.

Dr. Boulas' long-time partner, a former teacher, was forced to quit the career he loved when his body began to waste away from the disease. He was one of the first known victims.

Except for a short break ten years earlier, David Boulas, M.D. and Harry Bosch lived happily together for twenty years in a three-story brownstone located in Central Harlem. The first floor had a reception/waiting area with a medical office, a small bathroom and an examination room located in the rear where David tended to his patients. The second floor was their living area and this was where most of their time together was spent. Their sleeping quarters and bathroom suite were on the top floor.

Harry was stricken about seven years after reuniting with David after a short affair. Each time he thought he was getting better something else would go haywire. The doctor looked after him not just as a partner but also as a patient and treated him with compassion until the day he died in his arms.

While mourning Harry's death alone in the home they shared, and noticing more and more similar cases, Dr. Boulas vowed to help as many victims as possible. As time went on he saw that other doctors still refused to see these patients. He soon became the rare medic in the city, and the only one in Harlem, who steadfastly continued to see victims on a regular basis, gathering information on the disease as he did so.

Eventually, as even their own families ostracized those stricken, he began to allow his patients to stay at his townhouse. He did the best he could by putting beds wherever they'd fit on the second floor of his townhouse. These patients were destitute, and David received no payment from them. He willingly and very often saw them gratis. However, by doing so, the doctor slowly depleted his savings, which was used to pay all expenses necessary in order to keep medication in stock and the clinic operational. He did this until he could no longer afford to do so and one day, he finally swallowed his pride and filed for "not for profit" status.

When the process was completed and he was officially named proprietor of a not-for-profit entity, he named the townhouse "The Foundation for Emerging New Life." As such, it proffered hope to his dying patients. Over time, he realized the Foundation was merely a full service hospice.

Dr. Boulas was always looking for support in the way of volunteers, clothing donations, bedding, towels, or flatware. Fundraisers were held in the hopes of capturing the attention of anyone who was willing and able to offer financial assistance. He was prepared to do anything to help prolong the lives of his patients, vowing to stop at nothing to help ease the suffering they endured while fighting this disease.

Five years after Harry's death, the disease that killed him was now known to be a virus. It was called Auto-Immune Deficiency Syndrome and became more commonly known as AIDS. Scientists were hard at work trying to find a way to eradicate what had now reached epidemic proportions–as predicted.

☙◦❧

It was Adina's senior year of high school when she first learned of the Foundation through her guidance counselor at school. The only reason she chose the Foundation was because she needed three community and/or life credits to fulfill her obligation for her elective curriculum. The Foundation was a bonanza. It offered four and a half credits. Doing an internship there would enable her to graduate and begin her college years with a surplus of credits which would, in turn, allow her to receive a Certified Diploma. This worked out perfectly for her since she was anxious to get on with her life.

On the morning of her interview, Adina carefully dressed in her nicest black slacks and white blouse with short, puffed sleeves. It was 1981 and her parents indulged her by helping her purchase all the latest fashion trends. Adina thought they did it out of the guilt they felt after the miscarriage.

Finally, she took a peek in the mirror and was pleased with what she saw. She wanted to look professional except her hair kept falling on her face. She reached for her hairbrush and brushed it back pulling it into a ponytail, then applied some lip-gloss and headed out.

It was such a nice day and since she had plenty of time, Adina decided to ride the bus uptown. It would give her an opportunity to think.

I hope he doesn't keep me waiting too long. I'm not even sure I want to be working at a hospice.

What if I catch something?

But what else am I going to do?

I'm just going to get my credits then figure it out after graduation. I'll find another job in the city while I'm in college.

Upon arriving, the doctor didn't keep her waiting long; maybe just five minutes and she was relieved that he was prompt. By the end of their meeting, she'd won him over with her winning charm. She had done her homework on him and the Foundation and impressed him with her knowledge on social issues; something she really didn't care about. She cared about graduating and finishing college so she could leave home. This was all just a means to an end for her.

After the interview, they chatted about mundane things for a bit. He took a genuine interest in her and saw great potential. He knew she was perfect for the job and made an offer to her on the spot. The fact that he immediately took such a liking to her didn't surprise

Adina–she knew she could definitely be charming when she wanted to be. What surprised her was that it didn't feel like an interview; it was more like friends chatting and catching up with each other. She was learning to be an extraordinary actress and stifled a self-satisfied grin.

Adina thought it ridiculous that one person who has suffered the loss of someone so close could still be so compassionate. She shuddered at the thought of his selflessness. She was not that person. She just didn't get it.

What she didn't know was how sharp Dr. Boulas was. He could see the pain she carried around with her. Her lips were turned upward in a smile, but her eyes told a much different story. He was thrilled when she agreed to start right away. For her part, Adina didn't care one way or the other. She would much rather work with these people than sit in a classroom all day. The fact of the matter was that since all of the good doctor's patients were dying at such an alarming rate, meant that she shouldn't and wouldn't have to form any bonds with any of them. She did, however, take care not to show her indifference.

๖๏๙

After she graduated from high school, Adina was asked to stay on during college. Dr. Boulas was very happy when she agreed to continue working with the Foundation and told her so. He explained that he could only pay minimum wage; it was the best offer he could make her and she accepted.

David had become dependent on her for assistance in the day-to-day operation of the Foundation, and during her internship, she became his backbone. He now reveled in teaching her everything there was to know about how to run such a facility, except for the medical aspects. He never allowed her to dispense any medications. She was, in essence, his apprentice and they worked together extremely well.

Eventually she became the Foundation's representative at various meetings and fundraising events. She found that she really enjoyed the kind of work she was doing in that area of fundraising, and she was inspired to pursue a degree in marketing so that she may better hone her skills.

Adina loved what she was doing, but it wasn't because of all of the good that was being done there for those helpless souls. She loved it because she met all kinds of people at functions who were willing to do all sorts of things sexually. She knew how to use her sexual prowess to secure funds for the Foundation, all of which were usually made anonymously.

Adina had a secret. She had turned into an extremely promiscuous young lady even though she'd come from a culturally traditional household. She did what she wanted with whomever she wanted and she didn't really care too much about anything or anybody but herself. Benny had created a voracious monster and Adina was hungry. She also had certain fetishes. She enjoyed role-playing games in and out of the bedroom and dressing up. She got a huge thrill from taking chances. She never considered the risks she took, especially the ones she took with her health.

Chapter 19
Adina Gets up Close to Gladiator Guy

This is too fucking easy, Adina thought to herself.

She leaned in close to her girlfriends and told them she'd be right back. Smoothing her skirt, she rose and headed in Gladiator Guy's direction. She'd just spotted him sitting at the bar talking to the lead singer.

He didn't notice her until she was right up on him, shouting in his ear because of the loud music.

"Should I call you Al or Serpico?"

The surprise in his eyes when he turned around to face the titillating voice was undeniable.

It's her! The dancing queen! He couldn't help but smile.

"Name's Carlos. And what, may I ask, is yours?"

His eyes twinkled beneath his long, dark, thick lashes as she held out her hand.

"Adina. Adina Cruz and believe me, the pleasure is all mine."

"Well, Adina," he said, as he brought her hand to his lips.

"I am extremely pleased to make your acquaintance. Let me introduce you to my friend Joon, here.

"Joon, this is Adina. Adina, meet Joon."

"Joon? What an interesting name. It's so nice to meet you!"

Joon was small-framed like a lot of Asian men. His straight hair hung long and smooth.

"It's very nice to meet you too, Adina. Care to join us?"

Adina saw her opening and she eased through it.

"Why, thank you. I think I will."

"I must say, that was a great set! You have a beautiful baritone voice, Joon," she purred.

"I thoroughly enjoyed myself." She centered her attention on Joon.

"Congratulations on being the first group from El Barrio to be signed by Mari Records! This must be a very exciting time for you and your band!"

"Thank you, Adina. Yes, we are very excited *and* very lucky," said Joon.

"I hear an accent. You're not from here, are you?"

"You're sharp!"

They all laughed and Adina let eye contact linger with Carlos for a bit before Joon continued. When she heard him speak, she turned her attention back to him.

"My parents are from South Korea and have lived in El Barrio since they arrived. I was born there. So, yes, I do have a slight accent. I thought it was a Puerto Rican accent and that no one could tell."

They all chuckled again a bit.

"But, like most children of immigrants, my accent does slip out when I'm angry or nervous," he said.

"Same here, we speak Spanish at home. So, which was it for you just now? You're not angry, are you?" Adina said with a giggle.

Adina was talking to Joon, but she was looking sideways at Carlos.

"No, I'm not angry. It's your beauty that makes me nervous."

"You flatter me. Thank you. So, why did your family choose El Barrio in which to settle?"

"What you're really wondering is why we didn't settle in Chinatown, right?"

"I'm sorry. That was rude of me to ask …"

"Not at all; I get asked that question all the time. The thing is that my parents wanted me to have a diverse cultural experience, so they decided to settle in here, among you beautiful brown people. They didn't know either language–Spanish or English–very well, but they knew how to cook, so they opened a takeout restaurant and everyone in the neighborhood bought our takeout. I had the best of all worlds because I learned both the language and your culture.

"I didn't have to work at the restaurant. My parents wanted me to make friends with the kids in the neighborhood. All they wanted from me was to do well in school and that I be the best at whatever I chose to do. I liked to sing and I fell in love with traditional Spanish music, so I started hanging out with a bunch of guys who played Salsa. That's how I met Carlos here."

"Wow! That's some story! What about you, Carlos? Were you one of those kids that spent all his time banging on his mother's pots once he could crawl?"

"You're very funny, Adina!" retorted Carlos.

"Well, I try."

"Carlos, how can you be so rude? Why don't you buy this lovely lady a drink? I'll go take a walk around this joint and see if I can't find another beautiful body to ogle since you never answered her question.

"Adina, you asked, 'Al or Serpico ...'; I'd say neither. He's not even close!"

Joon took Adina's hand, pulled her close to him and chastely kissed her on the cheek before walking away. As he did, he winked at Carlos.

Carlos turned to her.

"How about having a drink with me and we can discuss my skills as a percussion master?"

"I'd love to, Carlos."

"Wonderful! Bartender!"

"What's your poison, good sir?" quipped the bartender, wiping the area in front of them.

"Vodka on the rocks for me and whatever the lady is having, please."

The bartender smiled at Adina, then: "Ma'am?"

"How about a Screaming Orgasm? Substitute the Smirnoff with Absolut, please."

"Sure thing," Adina and the bartender winked at each other.

"Thank you."

Carlos squinted at Adina with a smirk. She mystified him.

"A Screaming Orgasm? What's in that?"

"It's vodka, Bailey's Irish Cream and Kahlua over crushed ice. It calls for Smirnoff, but I prefer Absolut. Cheap vodka can make the Irish Cream curdle and we don't want that to happen, now do we?"

"No. We don't," replied Carlos with a lingering smile before speaking again.

The DJ had switched music. It was getting louder at the club and this gave Adina the opportunity to scoot closer to Carlos. He moved closer as well and with elbows touching and heads together they continued chatting.

Carlos spoke first.

"That was some dance you did before."

"That was some conga playing!

"Listen, I want to thank you and your group for the donation you're making to the Foundation. I work there. As a matter of fact, I came tonight because my boss gifted my friends and me with tickets to this event. I wonder if he knew that you would be making such a generous gift."

"Is that right? Well, he probably knew. All's we wanted was to do something nice for our hometown. Our manager, Mr. Queler agreed. He was more than happy to support us and he was able to convince the owners here to showcase us live. Either way, it's good publicity all around. We knew of Dr. Boulas and we think he's an amazing man, doing really good work. We don't care that his patients are gay.

"What does it matter who loves whom or how? The bottom line is that these people are sick and they are dying and no one is willing to stand up for them. To ignore that they are suffering is just another form of prejudice, you dig?"

He paused to pull in the drink the bartender set down before them. He took a sip, then said soberly, "Ignorance is not bliss. It's blinding."

Not only was he easy on the eyes, but he was a genuinely nice guy as well. For a fleeting moment, Adina almost changed her mind about him. On the one hand, she was thoroughly impressed with him physically, but on the other hand, Adina thought Carlos might be too "vanilla" for her. His physicality won her over. She could have fun with him.

She stayed.

"So tell me Adina, what do you do at the Foundation?"

"Well, I began as an intern there about five years ago. I was so taken by the work Dr. Boulas was doing, that when he offered me a full time job a year later, I jumped at the opportunity."

Yeah, right! What a load of bullshit, Adina thought to herself as she sipped her cocktail.

She continued.

"In my new position, I'll be working on marketing and fundraising. The generosity you and your band have shown really inspires me! I can't wait to get started."

"Well, you know, I might be able to help connect you with some people who might be interested in working with you. I know of other artists who would be keen on maybe performing at fundraisers or marketing events you might be planning."

"That would be fantastic! Maybe we can talk about it a bit. Would it be possible, after you're done with your other sets tonight, for you to give me your number? I can call you when it's convenient."

"Well, how about both. Let's blow this joint after my last set then go somewhere quiet and talk; maybe have coffee or something. If we find that we are on the same page, we'll exchange numbers and brainstorm. How's that sound?"

"Perfect!"

Carlos had no idea how perfect that was. Adina was adept at getting what she wanted and once again, here was someone getting ready to do something for her and thinking they came up with the idea all on his or her own. She was very good at that.

᭞᭞᭞

After the band's last set, the DJ took over the music booth. He played "coming down" music–music that was mellow and slow. It was now close to closing and the crowd was thinning out. Carlos spotted Adina in a corner of the club in a huddle with her girlfriends.

One of them suggested they all go find a diner for breakfast but Adina declined and sent them along saying she was planning to hang out with the conga player. After merciless teasing, her friends left the club and promised to catch up with one another the next day.

Carlos was so intrigued by Adina he just wanted to hold her close. Once he saw that she was alone, he approached her with an outstretched hand. Upon accepting it, he led her to the dance floor and did just that while they danced. Slow songs played for a long time and with each song, Carlos held her tighter against his body, stealing kisses from her whenever he could.

"Let's blow this joint," he whispered in her ear, his voice thick with lust.

Adina dreamily looked up into his eyes and nodded. The next thing she knew they were on the sidewalk. It was four o'clock in the morning.

"Let's find an after-hours spot."

"No. Let's go somewhere quiet," she responded.

Carlos needed no encouragement and suggested they go to his place, on the Lower East Side. Adina readily agreed.

Carlos' one-bedroom apartment was surprisingly neat and well appointed. A framed picture caught her attention immediately–a woman wearing a pearl headdress and matching necklace; her invisible décolletage.

She held a candle and her torso faded into a dark background right where the pearls ended. She had big, vacant eyes. They seemed to follow every move she made.

"Beautiful place you have here. I'm particularly impressed by your choice of artwork," Adina commented as he approached her and gathered her up in his arms.

"You like what you see?" he asked.

"I like everything I see," she responded and wrapped her arms around his neck while rising on her toes to kiss him.

Carlos leaned down into her, swallowing her mouth as they kissed. Their tongues tangled and Adina could hardly breathe, but she didn't care. The hunger in this extremely passionate kiss told her everything she needed to know. She got in closer and ground her body against his. She could feel him respond as he inhaled deeply. He held her even tighter as he exhaled. She took a deep breath and swam in his essence.

The warmth that emanated from him, coupled with the desire they both shared made her lightheaded.

He held her cheek in his right hand tenderly. Then he grabbed a handful of hair with his left hand and gently pulled her head back, the right hand slid down her neck. He held it lightly as Adina's breath caught in her throat. She tasted the bittersweet liquor that lingered in his mouth. His tongue was hot and desperate. He was ripe for the picking.

She took a hold of his face with both hands and kissed him back just as passionately. Her tongue seemed to ignite him even more and he began to moan.

She took in his breath.

The deep, guttural sounds coming from him excited her. She moistened and trembled a bit, almost reaching a climax herself. The idea that a man could do this to her with just a kiss surprised her and Adina was first to break away.

"Mmm," Carlos moaned softly and folded against her as he held her tight.

"That was nice. I could kiss you like that forever. You don't know the effect you have on me woman ... I think I'm in love!"

Looking up at him she threw her head back and laughed derisively.

"Do you believe in love at first sight?" she asked.

"I believe everyone comes into your life for a reason. I believe in instant connection. That connection doesn't have to be love, though. Ever meet someone and instantly hate that person and then you wonder why? I think it's because of unfinished business we have from past lives. Crazy, huh?" responded Carlos.

"I don't think it's crazy. That's just what your belief is and we all have different beliefs. I think it's just a coping mechanism, a way to understand the unknown. Who knows why people do the things they do; why they feel the way they do? It's like trying to understand a psychopath, or a serial killer. It can't be done."

"What do you believe, Adina?"

"I believe I am exactly where I am supposed to be–right here, right now. This is where I was meant to be at this moment."

"You're fucking amazing!"

They kissed hungrily as they undressed. When they pulled apart, he picked her up and brought her to the bedroom and carefully placed her on the bed. Then he kissed her once more. Hard as it was, he tore himself away from her, and walked over to his stereo system. After turning it on to soft music, he lit candles that were already on the dresser.

As the music played in the background and Carlos prepared the atmosphere, Adina looked around the room. There was a short hall that she assumed led to the bathroom.

Good, that meant she could wash up pretty quickly and sneak out if she wanted to.

Just then, he turned to face her and slowly walked in her direction. She watched his muscled arms swing with each step he took. She admired the way his stomach muscles alternately tensed and relaxed as he approached the bed. She watched his slightly erect penis swing back and forth when he climbed in beside her. She thought that was a funny sight, but stifled a giggle. When he gathered her into his arms she felt its cool velvet skin against her thigh and she wrapped her arms around his neck. He pulled her leg over his and they cuddled. They kissed for a long time before participating in the dance that would ultimately end in a loud mating call.

Sex.

What they did couldn't be called lovemaking. It was pure, un-adulterated animal lust. When they finished, they lay in bed together, in each other's arms while they talked about their sexual fantasies. Carlos admitted that he sometimes liked to be toyed with and Adina shared that she liked to be in control.

This was getting better by the minute and Adina was thrilled.

෨෴

George Michael's "Careless Whisper" played softly as Adina laid the bowl with ice cubes on the nightstand next to the tiny bundle of feathers. They were tied in a small bunch with a thin leather strap and they lay alongside edible, candied talcum powder. Beside the powder was a small riding crop. Carlos was face up, spread eagle on the full sized, four-poster bed. His ankles were tied to the foot posts with neckties. His arms were stretched over his head and his wrists were tethered to the mahogany headboard above him with ties attached to fur lined handcuffs. The toys were a pleasant surprise. Adina was delighted he had a selection of sexual accoutrements.

She gazed down upon the marvel that was before her. Sweeping her eyes along his well-built body, she smiled. The flickering lights cast a yellow glow in the room. Topless, she leaned over Carlos to make sure he couldn't peek from behind the blindfold he was wearing. Once she was confident he couldn't see, she slowly leaned in and kissed him.

Her warm, wet lips startled him; he wasn't expecting a kiss from her. He really didn't know what to expect because she was so quiet. He was beyond excited. He couldn't keep from shivering and his skin rippled in anticipation of her touch. The bed sank on either side as Adina straddled him. His breath quickened; his heart raced and he stirred. She leaned in close. Her hair skimmed his forehead.

Feathers? Was that the feathers?

He couldn't tell. The sensation electrified his body and his mouth became dry.

Finally, her lips made contact with his. The shock that the one kiss produced made his penis quiver; bolting upright against his stomach and the excitement manifested itself in its tremble.

She bent down again and teased him with her hair.

He threw his head back with a loud moan. It sounded almost painful.

She slowly ran the strands of her curly hair along his neck and down to his chest, then back up again, stopping to place her lips on his. She lingered there for a millisecond in order to allow him to become fully aware of what was happening to his body. She wanted him to be in his most vulnerable, most heightened and most sensitive state. He lifted his head toward her mouth and hungrily sucked away at her tongue, her lips–anything he could get a grip on with his mouth and when she abruptly pulled away, a long string of saliva was their only connection.

"I wanna play a game. Do you want to play with me, Carlito?"

Carlos nodded. Words eluded him.

Adina eyed her ... well ... *his* toys. What would she use first?

"Lie still," she ordered.

She reached for the small riding crop and slapped it against her open hand near Carlos' ears so that he could hear it.

"Wha ..."

"Shush, don't you make a sound. No matter what I do to you, you will not speak unless I say you can or you lose. Got it?"

Carlos nodded and licked his lips in anticipation.

"What do I get if I win?" Carlos asked.

"Me," she responded.

His penis jerked in response.

Adina smiled wickedly and sat back on his thighs. His erect manhood was now throbbing, quivering, glistening. She traced his abs with the end of the riding crop and enjoyed watching them contract. Then she slowly dragged it along his rib cage and finally along his sides for a short time.

Although Carlos struggled not to audibly react, while his body contorted and twitched in response, sounds of pleasure escaped him. Upon hearing this, Adina slapped him hard on this thigh with the riding crop, causing him to cry out.

"I asked you nicely not to make a sound. Now we have to start all over."

Carlos licked his lips.

Adina rose from atop him and reached into the bowl containing the ice and pulled out a dripping cube.

"Your lips are dry. Would you like some ice?"

Still blindfolded, Carlos nodded, afraid to voice his need lest he displease her.

Adina rubbed his lips with the slightly melted ice cube. She then rubbed her own lips and slipped it in her mouth. She leaned in and kissed him. The contrast of the ice and the heat in their warm mouths almost completely melted it. The cool liquid slid down Carlos' parched throat as he licked his lips.

Satisfied with his reaction, Adina reached for the feathers.

"You may speak only to tell me what you feel when I touch you, understood?"

Carlos nodded. He knew not to speak.

"I'm going to touch you in a moment, so get ready."

Carlos nodded and licked his lips in pained expectation when Adina began speaking:

"You have a beautiful body. Your dick is a work of art."

Adina did not touch him there though he anticipated she would.

He panted and smiled, hoping she would read his mind: You're going for my dick! Oh my God. I'm going to fucking cum when you do. I'm going out of my mind. Just listening to your voice is driving me crazy. This feels so fucking good. Don't stop! I want to hear more!

Adina continued with her verbal assault.

"Your face is beautiful. The beard is striking. The long eyelashes–the envy of both men and women, I'm sure."

A still silent Carlos writhed.

I want to feel you caress my face. Please. Kiss me again. Come closer, please!

He was disappointed Adina did not touch his face.

"Your hair is so full and lustrous. You must spend a lot of time on it."

Are you going to grab a handful? Are you going to pull it hard? Jesus! I can't take this anymore! Please! Touch me, please!

Carlos shook with suspense. He was sure Adina would forcefully grab a handful of hair and begin the physical assault on him that will bring him relief. His engorged penis hurt.

"Do you want me to touch you now?"

Carlos furiously nodded his head in the affirmative, unable to respond verbally. The words just didn't come.

"Well, that's not going to happen! Not yet. I'm not done admiring you.

"Your hands are smooth and your fingernails are clean. They look like the kind of hand I would like massaging my body or the kind that glides over the keys of a piano effortlessly."

"Please untie me. I'll give you a massage. I want to; I have to touch you; I need to hold you ..."

He couldn't remain silent any longer and he began convulsing; trying to get loose.

"I know you want me to release you. But I'm not going to do that. Not yet."

Carlos groaned in agony.

Adina ran her fingers through the feathers and held them over Carlos' knees, then lowered them slowly. When they finally made contact with his skin, it was like a bolt of lightning running rampant through his body and his knee jerked uncontrollably. He gulped in an attempt to take in a deep breath. Adina continued running the feathers slowly up his outer, then inner thigh until she got to his crotch.

At this point, she mercilessly toyed with his scrotum, avoiding his penis, and he began to twitch uncontrollably. She switched to an ice cube, first running it the length of his torso then circling his belly going down near his groin.

Goose bumps rose up and down his body. Deep within his chest a moan rose until it became a growl. He frantically tossed his head to and fro, crazed by desire. He bit down on his lower lip, drawing blood.

Adina untied one arm before she mounted him.

Still blindfolded, Carlos thought about how sore his arm felt from being tied up that way for so long, but he was excited she was now sitting on him. When the pins and needles in his arm subsided, he grabbed at her thigh, scratching it. She took a hold of his free arm, and held it at his side while she lowered herself on him. Filled to her core with his penis, she didn't move a muscle. She just sat there with Carlos snug inside of her.

After torturing Carlos like this for a little bit, Adina slowly rose from him, then just as slowly lowered her body back down; filling herself with his staff. Carlos pulled the blindfold off his face. He had to look at her. Without taking his eyes of her, he slowly slid his now free hand up the length of the front of her torso and between her breasts. When he reached her neck, he stopped for just a second and suddenly wrapped his fingers around her neck. He squeezed and roughly pulled her down to him. Adina gasped and for half a second she was afraid he might squeeze tighter, but the excitement she felt with that one gesture was far greater than the fear she felt and it subsided. Her eroticism escalated.

Slowly, she bent down toward her quarry. Carlos' breath quickened as she did and he slid his hand around to the back of her neck to pull her down toward him. Impatient, he raised his head toward her. Adina pulled back and ground tiny circles on him with her hips. Carlos gasped as he closed his eyes and threw his head back then picked it up again to gaze in Adina's eyes. She lowered her lips toward his and kissed him long and hard.

He let go of her neck and grabbed a handful of hair pulling it slightly then let it go as Adina, again, rose slowly above him until he was almost released from the delightful prison between her legs. She then leisurely lowered herself on him once more, burrowing him deeply inside of her. She squeezed. Over and over, she performed this physical chant, increasing her rhythm until she herself could no longer stand it. She rode him for all it was worth and together they exploded in ecstasy, finally collapsing.

❧◈

Adina stayed the night. When the sun began its ascent and the morning light played peek-a-boo with her, she extricated herself from his hold and quietly slipped out of the bed. She grabbed her clothing and took a slow turn around the room taking it all in.

She also noticed a small refrigerator in a corner and opposite that was a chair sitting under a lamp alongside a small table. On the table sat several books all with bookmarks sticking out of them. Next to the books there was a pad and a pen.

There was no artwork on the walls in this room. She thought this was strange considering the eclectic artwork he had in the living room. She also noticed he didn't have any plants in this room either.

It was actually quite bare in comparison to the living room and she got the impression that most of Carlos' entertaining was done there.

She could see that the bedroom was his refuge; his haven and she thought she should feel something since he had brought her into this space, but she didn't feel a thing. All she knew when she first laid eyes on him was that she had to have him. She had to dominate and conquer him.

Without a glance at Carlos, she slipped into the bathroom, quickly washed up and dressed. She was gone before he awoke.

&⚹&

The first thing she did when she arrived home was jump into the shower. She leaned forward and rested her forehead on the tile. The hot water pounded her sore body as she relived the evening. It was thrilling for her and she was sated ... for now.

&⚹&

Adina and Carlos never saw each other again. He went on his tour and when he returned, he looked for her in the faces of women at venues around the city, wherever his gigs took him. He never forgot her and he never got over how she spoke of love then disappeared. Sometimes this made him sad, but mostly he was angry she left without saying a word. He never even got her phone number.

&⚹&

This became Adina's modus operandi and she perfected it. This one event gave birth to her ever-increasing taste for sexual games. Her peccadilloes over the next fifteen years would mold her into the foremost expert fundraiser ever known in New York City. The Big Apple was her playground and the rich men in it, her willing toys.

Chapter 20
RJ and Anthony: Memorial Day Weekend, 1990

Ten years have passed since RJ had taken up residence in New York and in that time God had become his most trusted companion. Going to New York was the best thing he could have done. He loved that he could live anonymously there.

RJ strolled along the crowded boardwalk at Coney Island. The festivities for the Memorial Day Weekend were in full bloom. The sounds of children surrounded him as they skipped ahead of their chaperones. It was a bright, beautiful day. He enjoyed the cool, damp sea breeze as it tickled his cheek. He squinted and turned his head upward while the hot sun beat down on him. He took a deep breath. At that moment, he was content within his place in the universe and he thought about his arrival in The Big Apple.

It wasn't long before he found work as a dishwasher at a popular restaurant.

He happened to stumble upon the eatery when he first arrived. After a few visits and chats with the proprietor, who he had come to know as Joe, they came to an agreement that allowed RJ to park his RV in the back alley for a small fee. This was a mutually beneficial arrangement. RJ was very handy and living on the premises made him accessible to Joe who was getting older.

And, so he set about making a life for himself. He was as comfortable as he could be given the circumstances.

Six months after arriving in New York, RJ's mom, Margaret, suffered a heart attack and passed away. After her estate was settled, he found himself with a sizable inheritance. Joe had been extremely kind to him and RJ wanted the old man to live out the rest of his years comfortably without the burden of the responsibility of such an establishment. RJ proposed purchasing the restaurant for an obscene amount of money, making it hard for the old man to refuse. As the new owner, RJ renamed it "Rhys' Pieces" and proceeded to update and remodel the establishment.

The restaurant re-opened with much fanfare and became very popular both for families as well as special events.

Along with the purchase of the restaurant came a new identity for RJ. He would no longer go by his childhood nickname. From now on, he would be known as Rhys.

☙❧

Thinking about his early days in New York made Rhys smile.

He was just a boy when he first arrived; barely even had any facial hair and wore his curly hair close cropped. Now boyishly handsome, and always clean-shaven, his fresh features were flawless. His caramel skin glowed as if he had just been sunbathing. Still slight, but deceptively strong–he was well dressed, well mannered and charming.

He was also extremely proud of himself, and not just with the restaurant.

He was now able to control his less attractive desires. Rhys knew his triggers. Thanks to his mother's help and the lessons she taught him when he was younger, he learned not to let anything upset him. Margaret would have been proud of him too, and that thought is what kept him on the straight and narrow ... most of the time.

While keeping all the lessons his mother taught him as his focus, he gained self-confidence as a bonus. But something still troubled him deep down inside.

The one thing that weighed heavily on his mind most recently was the feeling of loneliness that was building within him. He often thought about seeking companionship but struggled with his sexual frustrations. When meeting people, he often bargained with himself that if things didn't go well, he would just walk away. Surprising even himself, he was successful at keeping his yearnings at bay.

Rhys continued walking along the boardwalk. He thought about summers back home as he took in the sights. With Nathan's in his line of vision, he decided to stop and get a hot dog. He got in line and scanned the faces of the people around him–a young man caught his eye. Nervous, he looked away, thinking the lad was too good looking to be interested in someone like him.

"Next!" called the man behind the counter.

"I'll have one with everything and a large Coke, please."

"Coming right up!"

After thanking the counterman, Rhys paid for his food then stepped to his right toward the end of the counter. As he looked up toward the beachfront, he felt someone standing close to him on his left. Discreetly, he looked over. He was pleasantly surprised to find that the same young man he had been admiring earlier was now standing next to him, holding out cash to the counterman in exchange for his hot dog.

They made eye contact.

The man smiled then winked at him and proceeded to walk out. Excited, Rhys grabbed his order and followed. Once outside, he didn't immediately see his object of desire but soon spotted him standing at a railing. He walked over and casually began chatting.

"Beautiful day, isn't it?"

"Indeed," the stranger said with a smile. He had a twinkle in his blue eyes, which were shaded by long, light brown lashes. About thirty years old, this tanned, tall, muscular, handsome creature extended his hand to Rhys in greeting.

"Hi! I'm Anthony, Anthony Dennison. What's your name?"

"Rhys. Rhys John. Nice to meet you, Anthony."

"Pleasure's mine, Rhys. Are you from around here?"

"Actually, I'm a transplanted New Yorker; been here about ten years."

"I see. Well, I wonder if you could help me."

He tilted his head while he sipped from a straw.

"I'll see what I can do. What do you need?"

"I'm not from around here and this hot dog won't keep me satisfied for long. Do you know of a place where someone could get a decent meal; preferably not far from here?"

"Ah! An out-of-towner! You need an honorary homeboy to show you around! Sure, I know a great place. There's a really good home-style Italian restaurant just a few blocks from here. It's called Flo's Home Cookin'. The food is fantastic. They offer a great wine selection and you will find that the atmosphere is really laid back, comfortable. I think you'll enjoy it."

"Oh, that sounds great! If I may be so bold; may I ask if you have any plans the rest of this afternoon?"

Rhys became flustered and the heat rose in his neck toward his face. He thought Anthony was painfully attractive and it was obvious he felt the same about him. Buoyed by the prospect, he quickly decided he could handle the challenge and readily agreed.

"Well, you're in luck! The truth of the matter is that I don't have any plans for the rest of the day."

"Fantastic! How about you show me around this playground and we mosey on over to Flo's Home Cookin' together afterward?"

Rhys had no problem with either one of Anthony's ideas. He was elated!

The rest of the day was pure bliss for Rhys. He and Anthony walked around the amusement park, ate cotton candy and challenged each other at the various carny games.

A woman dressed as a gypsy read their fortunes in a booth. She foretold tragedy for them both and though taken aback by her prediction, they laughed at the ridiculousness of her psychic "talent."

"People can't tell the future," they agreed.

So they left her den and headed toward the Aquarium, another of Coney Island's attractions.

"Hey, how do you feel about roller coasters?" Rhys asked his new friend.

"Oh, I'm not a fan. They scare the hell out of me!"

"So, you're telling me that you won't join me on the Cyclone?"

"Well ... I don't know if I can stomach it."

"C'mon! It'll be fun and I promise to look out for you. Hell, I'll even hold your hand if it'll help make you feel better."

"Ugh! How about I think on it for a while?"

"I'll tell you what. The line is long and we can watch while we wait our turn and then you can decide. What do you think?"

"Well, I don't want you to think I'm a pussy. Hell, I don't even like pussy! And you do seem strong enough to take care of me if I need you to."

Anthony looked into Rhys's eyes, emphasizing the true meaning behind his flirty words.

"I'll probably regret this, but ok!"

Rhys could not contain himself. Excitedly, he grabbed a hold of Anthony's hand and led the way to the ticket kiosk.

When it was finally their turn to board, Rhys politely asked to be seated in the first car. With his request granted they sat calmly and waited for the rest of the passengers to board. This would be particularly exhilarating for him, and adrenaline rushed through his body in anticipation of what would come. With its steep inclines, deep drops and sharp turns, this was a ride for thrill seekers.

"You look nervous, Anthony. You know you don't have anything to worry about, don't you?"

"I am nervous, Rhys. I've heard a lot about this ride. It's one of the reasons why I wanted to come to New York. It's very famous, you know. But I never imagined I'd be sitting here. I never thought I'd actually be sitting here.

"So, yeah; I'm scared shitless!"

Rhys stared at Anthony and a familiar feeling began to come over him. He ran his hand through his hair and tried to tamp it down. He failed miserably. The recognizable throb in his groin was becoming hard to ignore. He tilted his head and in an attempt to be reassuring he squeezed Anthony's hand, smiled and told him to breathe.

Rhys glanced over his shoulder at the guy who would be at the controls of the ride when it rumbled to life. The Cyclone jerked and began its slow, steady glide over the tracks, climbing the first incline. When it reached the top, it tipped slightly and increased in speed, prepared for its first descent, picked up more speed along the way and began to drop.

Gripping the rail in front of him, Anthony shut his eyes tight and screamed for his life as his stomach rose to meet his throat. Sitting beside him, Rhys stared straight ahead, but couldn't help himself and he too screamed at the top of his lungs. He didn't scream for fear. It was excitement for what was to come that caused him to scream.

At the bottom of the drop, Rhys laughed maniacally. He looked over at Anthony and saw tears sliding down his cheeks. There wasn't time to react. The roller coaster sped up the next incline then twisted forcefully left to right causing them to slide into one another, banging their bodies against the cart they were sitting in.

Anthony took one hand off the rail, and squeezed his new friend's thigh tightly. Rhys covered Anthony's hand with his and caressed his knuckles as the roller coaster began to drop in a slant forcing Anthony into his ribs. He gasped, and his eyes rolled into the back of his head in agony. His member throbbed painfully. He could feel the moisture in his underwear.

That was the moment he knew what he had to do.

For two whole minutes Rhys endured the drops, the sharp twists and Anthony's screams. And for two whole minutes, he thought he was at the edge of ecstasy. He had to get Anthony away from there.

When it was finally over, Anthony clung to him. He shivered like a scared child in Rhys' arms and he was in heaven.

"Hey, hey! You did it! You should be proud of yourself!"

Anthony could not voice his relief at being on solid ground. He remained silent.

"Let's get out of here, ok?" Rhys suggested.

Anthony simply nodded and they began to walk away from the crowd.

ॐ╼✖

Flo's Home Cooking was just a short walk from the boardwalk. It was crowded and pretty noisy when they arrived. Rhys wanted some privacy and requested a quiet table near the back. The hostess graciously led them to the bar after explaining that it would take a few minutes to get a table ready for them and offered them their first drink on the house.

"That's great! Thank you. A drink is exactly what my friend here needs right now," responded Rhys to the waitress' offer.

"Perfect then! Follow me."

Once seated at the bar, Rhys turned to Anthony and asked him how he was feeling. The green pallor his face had been hiding under was starting to fade and his normal color was returning.

"I'm feeling better now that I'm on solid ground!" Anthony replied with a chuckle.

"I hope I didn't hurt you. I was squeezing your thigh pretty hard."

"Not to worry. We should have a drink. That should help you relax a bit more. Have you ever had a 'Bold Chieftain'?"

"Can't say that I have; what is that?"

"It's whiskey, Cointreau and Prosecco. It's my favorite celebratory drink and I think we should have one. You know, to celebrate your survival of your first Cyclone ride!"

Laughing, Anthony agreed.

"Well, since you're in a celebratory mood, how could I refuse? Yes, I'll join you."

"Fantastic!

Rhys caught the bartender's eye and yelled, "Two Bold Chieftains, please!" over the loud chatter.

He and Anthony sat at the bar drinking and talking for a while before taking their seats at a table for two in the back.

During dinner, they talked about all the tourist attractions the city had to offer while Anthony raved about the food. A walk along the shore after dinner was had in quiet satisfaction. Rhys recognized the end of the day was in sight and impulsively invited Anthony on a ride into Times Square to see the lights and some more drinking. A visibly thrilled Anthony agreed and together they walked to the parking lot where the RV was parked.

After a short twenty-minute ride into Times Square, they strolled along blending in with the crowd.

"Wow! Would you get a load of all these lights! And the people! I should have moved here long ago! I could very easily get lost in all of this action!"

"It's not so bad. The Big Apple really is just a melting pot. By the way, you never did tell me where you were from, Anthony."

"Nowhere special, really. I'm more of a vagabond than anything else. I don't like feeling bogged down. I don't have any roots."

"I take it you don't have a job right now either, correct?"

"Correct."

"Well, I recently purchased a small restaurant. If you're interested, I could use some help."

"That would be wonderful! I'll do anything and I can start right away."

"Fantastic. I think this is cause for celebration! How about we go to my place? We could keep the party going there."

"That sounds great!"

Chapter 21
What Happens at Rhys' Pieces Stays at Rhys' Pieces (1990)

Just off I-87, Rhys' Pieces is located in the affluent Northwest Bronx neighborhood of Riverdale. It regularly bustles with activity because of its roomy and comfortable atmosphere. An icon in the neighborhood, Rhys' Pieces caters to regular neighborhood folk as well as financially affluent clientele from the surrounding tri-state area. Rhys normally tended bar and kept two very creative chefs on staff. The regular menu features three types of cuisine: American or "Native Fare," Hispanic or "Variedades" and Italian or "The Godfather Special."

It was well past two a.m. when Rhys pulled the RV into the back alley where he usually parked. He and Anthony jumped out and headed onto the premises then up the stairs to his place, which was right above the restaurant.

As soon as he neared his door, the sounds of panting and sniffing could be heard from the other side. God had rushed to the door to happily greet his owner. When they entered, he wagged his tail eagerly, happy to have his master home. Rhys bent slightly to pet him.

"Welcome to my humble abode! What can I get you to drink?"

"Anything's good," responded Anthony.

God was at Anthony's feet, sniffing, but he couldn't bring himself to pet the dog for some reason.

"Interesting looking dog you have here, Rhys," Anthony said flatly.

"He's a stray. Picked him up on the turnpike. He was starving.

"I'll be right with you."

Rhys was a bit annoyed by Anthony's comment.

"This place is really bare. Did you just move in?" Anthony asked as he tried to get away from God.

He didn't wait for Rhys to come back from the kitchen and wound his way there. He reached for a stool at the kitchen island.

"No. I just haven't had time to do any decorating.

"Here you go."

Rhys handed Anthony a frosted bottle of Corona beer, a thin slice of lime decorating its rim. Anthony stood to face him.

"Thanks. A toast! To new beginnings."

"To new beginnings!"

They clinked bottles and each took a swallow while they looked in each other's eyes.

Anthony moved closer to his host and kissed him lightly on the mouth. Surprised, Rhys put his bottle of beer down and caressed Anthony's face, betraying his nerves, which had come alive. The rhythm of his heartbeat sped and his breath hitched. He took the bottle from Anthony's hand and placed it beside his. Anthony inched closer still and pulled Rhys into an embrace.

Their kiss was warm and tender. He sucked on his new friend's tongue and his member throbbed. Finally Anthony pulled away and planted a lingering kiss on his lips. The now familiar worm that crawled in his belly button, down to his groin was unnerving.

He shifted; his excitement undeniable. Anthony held him against his body tighter still and began to grind his groin against his. Rhys threw his head back and inhaled slowly; hissing sounds coming from his lips; his ecstasy interrupted by Anthony seductively grabbing a handful of hair. He pulled Rhys' head toward his lips. He licked the outer rim of Rhys's right ear then softly blew in it before he whispered.

"Why don't you give me the grand tour?"

Rhys struggled to answer. His head swam with delight.

"There's really just one room that I would like to show you."

Anthony smirked, impish.

Rhys smiled back at him then took his hand to lead him into the bedroom.

❦

Rhys paced back and forth, turning on his heel every four steps. He pulled on his hair with trembling hands. He always did that when he lost control of the situation. It was as if he had to cause himself pain in order to punish himself for messing up, and he had messed up again.

"What have I done?" He questioned the air.

Rhys glanced over at the naked body on his bed. Shoulders slumped, head down, he quickly turned away. The anguish prevented him from turning back to look once more, but he knew he had to. It had happened again.

"You motherfucker! Look what you made me do!" He yelled at the still body.

Reaching over, he carefully pulled the tie from around Anthony's neck. His tears slid onto the dead man's face. He gently wiped them away then tenderly lowered Anthony's eyelids. Looking down on him now, Rhys thought he looked like an angel frozen in time.

Slowly, he scanned Anthony's body lengthwise. Then he whispered:

"We were having such a good time! But it's ok. Look at you now."

When he was done admiring the corpse, he reached out and took Anthony's still stiff organ in his hand and marveled at it. It was the most beautiful penis he had ever seen. He softly placed a kiss on its tip.

This must be what they call 'Angel Lust' he thought to himself. He sighed heavily.

"You're not laughing now, are you? You'll never laugh at anyone else again."

He looked down at Anthony, almost tender with regret.

Desire rose in him again, overwhelming him again. He had to take advantage of the gift Anthony was offering him. Rhys scrambled onto Anthony's body, habitually looking around to make sure he was unseen, and positioned himself over the dead man's penis. He slowly lowered himself. It hurt, but it also felt good. Rising up then lowering himself over and over, he rode the staff slowly at first, then fast and hard. He threw his head back and began to feel a welcome throbbing. He gently rubbed his knob in a circular motion. The sensations tickled his whole body. Goose flesh rose on his arms. His nipples hardened, his breathing quickened and he began to moan.

Frantic now, his moaning grew louder and louder. He jerked up and lowered himself onto the dead man's penis over and over; hard and fast, slapping his ass against Anthony's thighs. He rubbed his own tiny penis furiously. He threw his head back.

"Yes! Yes!" he yelled.

He was close to reaching a peak he had never known before.

But his hand was becoming tired, his fingers stiffened and started to cramp. He bucked over and over and then nothing.

Nothing happened.

"No!!" he screamed, as he wrenched at his ball sack painfully.

So he switched hands, but got no response from his diminutive, reluctant organ. He was raw and there was no sensation. He felt nothing but frustration. Rhys collapsed in a heap on Anthony's outstretched thighs and sobbed.

With a grunt, he heaved himself up off Anthony and shuffled out of the room. He sat in a stool in the kitchen island and finished his beer. He needed to think. When he was done, he returned to the bedroom and proceeded to dress his newest victim. He didn't want to be seen carrying a huge bundle. If anyone were to be looking out his or her window, it would be better if he were to be seen helping his drunken friend into his RV.

Once he was done dressing him, Rhys put Anthony's arm over his shoulder and half dragged him down to the restaurant and through the back door leading to the alleyway where his RV was parked. He put the body in the vehicle over plastic he kept there for purchases at the butcher shop for the restaurant. He undressed Anthony again and placed his clothes in another bag then went back inside to get the butcher knife. When he re-entered the restaurant, he heard the soft tick of God's feet coming toward him.

"Hey there, friend!" he said.

"Sit tight. I'll be back shortly and if you're patient, I'll have a treat for you when I return," he said jauntily, and left.

⮞⮜

God looked up at RJ; panting in eager anticipation.

"Hungry, boy?"

God licked his lips and seemed to nod, snorting.

"Well, that's good because I have a treat for you. I hope you like it!"

Rhys unwrapped the brown paper bag he was holding and pulled out a bloody piece of meat wrapped in plastic. Unraveling the plastic over a cutting board, smiling, he reached for his mincing knife and began to chop. When he was done, he put it in a dish and mixed it with some of God's regular food then placed it before him.

God ate his master's offering in three bites, satisfied.

Chapter 22
Hide and Seek

"... Seven ... Eight ... Nine ... Ten! Ready or not! Here I come!" The unusually hot rays of a summer afternoon's sun beat down on Joey as he counted to ten in the latest game of hide and seek with his younger siblings in Brooklyn. Unaware of the thick, humid air that hung in the dirty, abandoned brownstone, Alex and Jennifer sought separate hideouts in the crevices of their favorite playground. Now just a shell of its former beauty, the building offered no overhead protection from the sun's unforgiving assault. As far as they were concerned, this was no different from any other free summer afternoon.

As usual, Joey didn't have a problem finding Jennifer. She was the youngest and had little, if any, imagination. She always chose the same spot in which to hide–a closet located just to the left of where the front door would be.

"Aw, Jennifer! There are so many places to hide in this building! Why do you always hide in the same spot?"

"I'm afraid you won't find me, Joey!"

She held back a sniffle.

"'*I'm afraid you won't find me, Joey!*'" he mocked his little sister. "Scaredy cat!"

"Stop! So what?" she unwound herself from the space and faced him.

"Fine. Let's just go find Alex, ok?" Joey said as he took his little sister's hand. He was suddenly hot and feeling impatient.

"Alex! Alex! Come out, come out wherever you are!" they yelled in unison.

Their voices fell flat. The air felt terribly wrong. Fear gripped Joey's heart and the little hairs on the back of his neck stood at attention. He shivered as he held his sister's hand a little tighter.

"Alex? Alex! Where are you?"

Still, there was no response from his little brother and this made Joey's heart quicken. There was a loud shuffling and then a crash could be heard coming from just ahead of them.

"Alex!!"

Joey tugged on Jennifer's small hand and dragged her along as he ran in the direction toward the sound. When he got to the door, there was no knob. He paused, and then burst through it with his shoulder only to be knocked back by the stench that rushed up to greet him. He gagged and fought the urge to vomit. Little Jennifer cried out at the smell and with a twitch brought her hands up to cover her nose and mouth.

In the corner of the room was an old stove that had been pulled away from the wall. Not far from it, stood Alex, frozen in silence. Joey followed his brother's line of vision and rested his eyes upon something no child should see.

Joey spied blood smeared all over the side of the stove and on the ground around it. Out from behind the stove he focused on what his brother was staring at—bare feet. With a shiver, he pulled his sister against his body, simultaneously covering her eyes. Jennifer shook in her big brother's protective embrace. As she squirmed in his hold, Joey took a few paces closer to the body and stood in front of Alex to purposely block his view.

The victim was on the ground, naked. His skin discolored and bruised. Stepping backward, his mouth an "O" of horror, Joey turned his head sideways and saw his own expression on his brother's face.

"Alex! Look at me. Come on! Look at me!! Alex?"

Alex turned toward him, his eyes lit with terror yet unseeing.

"Good. Good, now come to me, Alex! Come on! We have to get out of here!"

Joey anxiously reached for his brother with a thin, trembling hand.

☙❧

Lights ablaze, several police radio motor patrol cars surrounded the brownstone while one lone policeman stood guard. Other uniformed officers prowled the perimeter of the building searching for any clue that would tell them what took place there. Emergency Medical Technicians assigned to the three ambulances that were parked just beyond the RMPs could be seen examining the children. A tall, muscular man dressed casually in black pants and a short- sleeve shirt strode confidently toward the solo patrolman.

"What do we have here, Officer Brown?"

"One male, DOA found by three children; two boys and a girl; all siblings under the age of twelve, sir. They were playing hide-and-seek when they stumbled on it."

Standing a solid, heavily muscled six feet tall, Detective Mason Jones was an imposing figure–the kind of man who meant business. A seasoned detective, he routinely worked homicide cases.

Jaded by his experiences, he thought he'd seen it all. Nothing really ever surprised him anymore. This case was going to change all that. Right now, all he knew was that some children had chanced upon a DOA. He particularly didn't like it that young children found the body, but at the same time, all he really wanted to do was go home to his new wife and have a nice dinner. They'd argued over something stupid that morning and he knew he was wrong but his ego wouldn't let him admit it to her right then and there. Now, he was looking forward to not only making it up to her but making up with her as well.

Why is he taking so long to spit it out, the detective thought to himself.

Even though he had just arrived at the scene, he was already frustrated with not only the situation, but also the young officer. He just wanted to get home to his wife.

"Go on," he encouraged the patrolman as he stepped over the threshold and signaled him to follow.

"Yes, sir.

"Like I said before, the kids were playing hide-and-seek. Alex, age nine, wandered into a back room looking for a place to hide. According to his statement, he stepped behind the stove, and got a whiff of something that smelled bad. He said 'it got to him' but he thought it was just a dead rat and he wanted to see it. There were large pieces of discarded linoleum and broken bricks lying on the floor so he shifted the debris around and found the body."

Detective Jones raised an eyebrow. He knew there was a dead body in there somewhere but he couldn't see it from where he was.

The patrolman noted the look on Detective Jones' face.

"I think you'd better have a look yourself, sir."

"Alright, let's go do that then."

The patrolman and the detective walked together through what might have once been the entry foyer.

"You'd better take one of these, sir. The stench is pretty bad."

The young patrolman handed the detective a cigar.

Even after lighting the cigar to mask the odor, the detective still cringed. But that was nothing compared to what he saw. Movement in his peripheral vision seemed to slow to a crawl. He could hear the voices of all the technicians buzzing and movement blended together in a surreal moving mural.

He slowly approached the body for a closer look as he pulled on a pair of gloves.

The male victim was completely naked. He appeared to be about thirty years old, well built, tall and tanned. Though in an advanced state of decomposition because of the oppressive heat, the detective guessed the murder took place at least forty-eight hours prior to its discovery. He bent down to get a closer look and gently moved the victim's head to the side. There was bruising about the neck, forehead and forearms. The victim's knuckles were cut. His penis and scrotum appeared to have been either crudely sliced off or rodents had begun to chew at the bloody flesh. Blood had caked all around the area and on the upper thighs. It was hard to tell what had happened without a complete examination.

"Jesus! What kind of monster does this? I don't suppose we have identified the victim?" he asked the young patrolman.

"No, not yet, sir, but we did find an empty wallet."

"Ok. Maybe it was a robbery. Where are his clothes?"

"We didn't find any clothing, sir."

"The clothes may have had evidence on them. Could be why they were removed by the perp."

"That was my thinking, sir."

Jones rubbed his bald head. It was going to be a long night. It appeared that his make-up session with his wife would have to wait.

He nodded and turned to scan the crime scene once again. He watched the fingerprint specialists, crime scene unit experts, and medical technicians as they worked. It seemed he always did that while he pulled off his gloves. The ripping sound they made always impacted him and what he saw. It made grisly scenes like this one feel real to him. It was hard for him to believe otherwise; that something like this could happen to another human being.

He turned again toward the patrolman and said:

"Cover him up. I'm going to go see what I can get from the kids. If you need me, I will be home in about an hour. Call me there."

Frowning, the detective stepped out onto the street and walked over to where the ambulances were parked. He spent some time with each of the children separately. They all had different perspectives leading up to the discovery, but for each of those kids, the story ended the same way: dead body. Now, there was nothing more he could do but wait for the lab reports to come back. Letting out a deep sigh, the detective got in his car and headed home. He hoped he could still make it there before his wife went to bed.

In all his years of service to the NYPD, Detective Mason Jones had seen a lot of things but this, by far, was one of the most disturbing scenes he'd ever witnessed. He felt badly for those kids. This was the kind of thing bogeymen were made of. For that reason alone, he swore he would find out who did this no matter how long it took.

Chapter 23
Adina and The Foundation for Emerging New Life: 1990

"Are we all set for tonight's gala, Adina?"

"Pretty much. I'm just going to check on the menu at the restaurant and that'll be it. Is there anything you need me to do for you before I head out, Doctor?"

"Nope, I'm good. I'm very excited! This is going to be one for the records! I don't know how you managed to get all those donors to celebrate with us!"

Dr. Boulas was so proud of Adina. She had come to him a troubled teenager, but she worked hard, learned everything he taught her and transformed herself as the face of the Foundation. Recently named Director of Public Affairs for the Foundation, Adina's responsibilities included fundraising and marketing. She mastered these duties. She was even given a second office in a fancy building downtown where important meetings were held.

Tonight was the first Annual Independence Day Gala in support of the Foundation for Emerging New Life. Benefactors had quietly come forward in previous years with small donations in support of Dr. Boulas' work. But as the stigma of being afflicted with the AIDS virus lifted, more and more victims came forward and even more funds were needed in order to keep up with the growing epidemic.

Brainstorming with some of the doctor's hospital colleagues, Adina came up with the brilliant idea of a fundraiser and hoped to raise funds in excess of one million dollars. She commandeered their

Rolodexes and personally called notable citizens throughout New York City for commitments that they would attend. She knew some of the people she called merely agreed simply because she was incessant in calling and they just wanted her to stop. Some were impressed by her passion. Some were simply curious to see what this girl could pull off. And frankly, some of the ones she met with in person were mesmerized by her and couldn't find it within them to say no.

Dr. Boulas chuckled softly.

"What? What's so funny?" she asked her mentor with a smile.

"You're simply amazing, Adina! Now, run off and make sure to get some rest before the gala. It's going to be a long, busy night!"

Adina hugged her boss and friend tightly, giving him a kiss on the forehead.

Adina didn't like people in general but she had come to understand the doctor and felt that he deserved to be shown some sort of affection.

"I'll see you at the restaurant then!"

And off she went.

ॐ

Qi Restaurant
Times Square, New York City

In the heart of Times Square, the popular Qi Restaurant featuring Thai cuisine would be the perfect setting. The food was tasty and the service impeccable. The décor's central theme was white. The walls were matte where they weren't mirrored. The tables and bar were a high gloss and the barstools and chairs of clear Formica.

At the midpoint of the restaurant, a separate, large rectangular shaped seating area cut lengthwise through the restaurant. This arrangement elicited a sense of privacy to diners between glass-encased chandeliers. At the end of this long dining area, a large Buddha statue sat serenely, right hand up as if casting a blessing over all who drank and dined there.

Behind the statue, a silver beaded curtain hung between the main dining area, and a private room filled with plush burgundy couches were arranged to allow for intimate conversation. Signature clear Formica coffee tables were placed between the couches and additional ones were strategically located throughout the room. An abundance of tea lights flickered filling the room with a white aura. Just a whiff of sandalwood drifted through the room adding to its calm.

Adina absolutely loved this place.

She took a look around and was extremely pleased with herself, but she knew it could be even more perfect. She walked around the restaurant, her eagle eyes not missing a thing. She took notes down in her little pad. There wasn't a single corner in the whole restaurant she hadn't inspected.

Meticulously, she went over the minutest details for a long while. She took great care to speak with and thank every single person involved, starting with the chef and ending with the busboys she handpicked herself for this event. This was her hallmark; a strategy she perfected. She knew that in order to get things done the way she wanted, she had to show respect to each person involved, no matter where on the totem pole they sat, even though she felt nothing at all for these people.

Adina thought to herself: It never ceases to amaze me how elitist some potential benefactors could be. They fail to recognize one thing. When naked, we are all equal in status. But just for a little while if they ever find themselves naked in a room with me, I am the elitist. They all bow to me, not the other way around. As far as I'm concerned, that is when the party begins.

After meeting with the staff, Adina headed to the back office where the manager, Mr. Sansurin, was at his desk peering over ledgers.

"Hi, Mr. Sansurin!"

"Ms. Adina! How lovely to see you! Is everything to your liking?"

The restaurant manager's accent was thick and lispy. It took Adina a second to comprehend what he was saying.

"Yes, everything and everyone looks lovely! Perfection! Thank you for hosting our event. I am so grateful."

"Ms. Adina! You have been with us since the beginning; our greatest supporter! Our business has tripled since we opened and I believe it is all because of you!"

The proprietor was effusive in his praise of the woman he considered his good-luck charm.

"It's called *karma*," he emphasized. "Good fortune is like a pebble that ripples in a pond. I am happy to return the favor and I have faith in Buddha you will receive many blessings tonight. Your gala will be a huge success! Mark my words, sweet one."

"Thank you. I hope you're right." She gripped her clipboard to her chest.

Though she smiled at this humble man, her eyes betrayed the smile with their emptiness.

"I'll be going home to rest for a little bit, but if you need me for anything at all or if you or anyone in your staff have any questions, you know how to reach me."

"Ms. Adina, don't you worry about a thing! I will make sure you are not disturbed.

"Thank you. I will see you later."

"Yes, until then."

Adina left the office and headed to the restaurant's exit. As she stepped out on the street, she stopped for a moment and took a look around. The street was littered with tourists gaping at all the flickering lights.

Look at these fools, she thought to herself.

You can tell they've never been anywhere by the way they stop and stare.

She turned and walked to the train station and thought about what the restaurant proprietor had said about Karma and faith.

Faith. Karma. She didn't believe in any of that.

That's bullshit, she thought.

I've had to bust my ass to get where I am. There is no *faith* or *karma* in that. And, I'm going to fully enjoy whatever comes out of all that hard work; come what may.

∂∞⊱

Preceded by a loud crack of thunder, a bolt of lightning lit up the early evening sky sending shivers down Adina's spine. She straightened up nonetheless, put on a bright smile and shrugged off the unease that momentarily clung to her like a second skin. Benefactors of The Foundation for Emerging New Life began to stream through the front doors of Qi, each embracing her warmly as they did. A young man stood beside Adina holding a tray of cocktails meant to be the first of many to help release the purse strings.

"Welcome, Mr. and Mrs. Booth! Thank you for coming!"

"Why, don't you look lovely tonight, Mrs. Carver!"

"Jason Meade! How wonderful of you to join us!"

"Yes, Mrs. Luce! I'm very excited to host this event along with Dr. Boulas, who, by the way, is dying to speak with you!"

She made distinct eye contact with each entrant.

"What perfume are you wearing, Madam Ambassador? You smell divine!"

Adina played the role of the perfect hostess as her guests wandered in. She could care less for the women. All those compliments were for the benefit of the Foundation.

It's a win-win situation, she thought to herself.

Finally, the last of the guests had arrived and cocktail hour was in full swing. Adina turned to the waiter on her right.

Damn it! She had forgotten his name!

"I'm terribly sorry. Your name escapes me. Please remind me again."

"Chakrii. My name is Chakrii, and it's all right. It got crazy there for a moment."

"Chakrii, yes, that's right. I'm sorry."

She paused, her hand mid-gesture.

"Chakrii, please don't leave here before seeing me tonight. I want to express my regret in the proper manner. Now, can you please bring me a fresh flute of champagne? Those have been sitting on your tray for ages now. I'm going to go find Dr. Boulas."

"Yes, Ms. Adina, right away."

The hapless waiter walked away and Adina turned to scan the crowded restaurant. She felt beautiful and dangerous. Dressed in a floor length, red satin gown that hugged her curves, with an open U-drape that exposed her sinewy back, she commandeered every room. Her hair was swept up in a severe French twist with a few tendrils skimming her neck. She was iced with diamond studs in her ears, thin gold bracelets on both wrists, and gold, high-heel sandals.

Adina was very aware of the power she held over these very influential men and for that reason she was very calculating when choosing her outfit for this event.

Chapter 24
Adina: 1990–2000

The first-ever fundraising event for the Foundation for Emerging New Life at Qi Restaurant was a huge success, all thanks to Adina. The attendees were a very carefully targeted group of philanthropic types; Park and Madison Avenue residents–elitists. These were people willing to donate huge amounts of money to the Foundation in order to keep it running at its current location: none of them wanted to see AIDS-infected people in their own neighborhoods.

It was soon apparent that AIDS had no prejudice and because of that realization, it became high society's latest pet project. Now a national phenomenon, it was not just a problem for commoners to deal with. Actors, musicians, even politicians had to take notice because members of those circles were also being infected. Even hemophiliacs who received tainted blood in life-saving transfusions became ill and the stigma surrounding speculation about the disease began to die down as facts about the phenomenon emerged. Over the next ten years, events like this one became the norm and money was regularly poured into research.

This first event for the Foundation is where Adina lost her fundraising virginity. As a side benefit, over the ensuing years, she learned she could have her choice of playmates and in the process, raise a lot of money for Dr. Boulas. All she had to do was study the affluent, particularly the men. She had a knack for figuring out what their weaknesses were and effectively breached their vulnerabilities in order to achieve her goals.

People like these also frequently attended functions not unlike this one, making very generous donations to other charities and she needed them to make similar donations to her Foundation. She became involved in as many fundraising events as possible and learned as much as she could. It wasn't long before she became known as a star fundraiser.

While talking with a guest, Adina heard her name being called. She turned to watch a heavyset man with a full head of stringy dirty blonde hair amble toward her. She recognized him as the ambassador to the United Kingdom, Jason Meade.

Excusing herself from the woman she had been chatting with, Adina turned to face him.

"Hello again, Ms. Cruz. I didn't get a chance to tell you earlier, but I wanted you to know that this event is extraordinary. I'm very impressed by the turnout."

"Why, thank you, Ambassador. I will have to agree with you."

"May I also say you look ravishing? I wondered if you would save a slot for me on your dance card tonight."

About fifty, the ambassador was overweight and about five-foot-seven. The dawning of a potentially huge potbelly was showing behind his tuxedo jacket. His green eyes were small, beady and deep set. He had no facial hair and that was a good thing as his lips were almost invisible.

While waiting for a response from Adina, he lasciviously scanned her body as if she were a well-dressed bar code.

"Mr. Meade, of course I will. My card is pretty empty, as I've not had much of an opportunity to fill it. Come find me whenever you'd like. Now, will you excuse me? I must speak with Dr. Boulas."

"Of course."

Jason Meade took a step back and Adina smiled politely. She turned and headed in the direction where her boss was speaking with the CEO of a major cosmetics company. She knew the ambassador was watching her as she walked away, so she swung her hips with emphasis.

There! How do you like them apples? she thought.

☙❧

Later, as the end of the night drew near, Ambassador Meade approached Adina for his turn on the dance floor.

"May I have this dance?"

Adina laughed inwardly at the song that had just begun playing. Outwardly, she smiled at the Ambassador and in a show of acceptance, took his extended hand into hers.

'Thieves in the Temple,' huh? Title's appropriate, she grinned to herself.

"Certainly, Ambassador."

Taking advantage of the situation, Ambassador Meade made an elaborate show of bringing Adina into a tight embrace.

"I can't get over how stunning you look tonight, my dear."

His lust caught in his words.

"Thank you."

Adina rolled her eyes over his shoulder.

"Tell me something, Ms. Cruz, would you be interested in discussing the Foundation a little further after this event?"

"You want to have a discussion? What do you have in mind?"

"I want to become more involved in this cause. AIDS is a problem in my country as well and a topic of heated discussion. I have friends back home who would be interested in working with your Dr. Boulas as well as the Foundation. We think we can learn from what he's doing and duplicate a similar program across the pond."

"Well, that sounds exciting! Did you have anything specific you wanted to do? A fundraiser perhaps?"

The ambassador twirled Adina around the dance floor and she saw that the effort caused a thin line of perspiration to appear on his upper lip. He then pulled her so close that this smeared on her cheek.

She grimaced then turned it into a simper as they faced each other.

The ambassador continued talking. It was nearing the end of his dance.

"I will be in town for a few more days."

The music stopped, interrupting him. Gratefully, Adina pulled away and took a step back, but he held her hand in a sweaty vice. Beneath her polite smile, her mind was working.

You dirty sweat hog! I know what you have in mind. Just say the word. She churned the idea in her head.

"I'm staying at the Waldorf Towers. Why don't you meet with me there, say tomorrow? I can order an in-suite lunch and we can discuss the details then."

"Details?"

"I'm thinking a grant would do the trick; a very large grant for your Foundation. You see, I believe I have enough influence with a group of individuals. It would be easy to convince them to participate in creating one for the Foundation. I don't see how they could refuse. The good doctor could use this money to continue doing his work and reach many, many more people in need of his services if we're able to pull this off."

His eyes flashed at her.

"That is indeed very generous. I don't know what to say."

Ambassador Meade tilted his head, invaded her personal space and whispered.

"Say 'yes.'"

He bowed slightly and took Adina's hand, placing a light kiss on it leaving her feeling like a clammy mess.

"I'm leaving in three days. Think about it. If you think we can work together, give me a call at the hotel and we'll discuss the details."

"Very well then. I'll think about it."

"And when you're done thinking about it, you'll call me either way? I need to hear a decision from you."

"Yes, sir, I'll call you. Thank you for your generous offer."

Adina bowed her head slightly, took one step backward then turned around and walked away.

&⤳⤝

Two days later a limo collected Adina from her home. After a short drive, they pulled into the Waldorf=Astoria Hotel's carport. She waited in the back seat while the driver got out and walked around the rear passenger door to hold it open for her. He helped her out of the car then escorted her up to the ambassador's luxurious suite in the Waldorf Towers. When they reached their destination, the driver didn't even knock. He simply opened the door and led her inside where Ambassador Meade was ending a telephone conversation.

The driver asked her if there was anything she might need. She shook her head no so he bowed slightly and was gone in a moment.

This was Adina's first time in such opulent surroundings. She walked slowly around the perimeter of the room all the while gazing at the artwork, the chandeliers, the heavy drapes and the plush furniture. It was a lot to take in and she was very impressed.

Finally, the ambassador was done with his call.

"Hello! I am so happy you decided to meet with me!"

"Hello, Mr. Ambassador. Thank you for inviting me."

"Oh, please dispense with the formalities. I would like you to call me Jason."

"'Jason' it is then. Please call me Adina."

"Very well."

Jason smiled shyly.

Adina caught the change in his demeanor compared to how he behaved at the fundraiser.

He gathered himself before speaking again.

"Now that we've gotten that out of the way, can I offer you a glass of Chardonnay?"

"Yes, please. Thank you."

Jason acknowledged Adina's request with eyes downcast and a slight nod of the head. His heart skipped in a happy dance.

"Please take a seat. I'll bring it to you."

He waddled over to the wet bar where the wine had been chilling in a bucket and quickly poured two glasses. Done with his task, he handed her a chilled glass then took two steps toward a winged tip chair across from the identical one she sat in. A glass-topped table separated them. As he sank heavily into the chair, he accidentally passed a bit of gas.

Adina heard the sound and lowered her eyes. She fought hard not to react and took a sip of wine.

"Oh, this is delicious. Thank you."

After an awkward moment she spoke again.

"Ambassador, er, Jason, on behalf of Dr. Boulas as well as everyone at the Foundation, I'd like to thank you for this opportunity. Your idea of a grant is something we had been hoping for. We just never dreamed it would or could come from a group of individuals rather than an organization or a medical institution. We have submitted applications to all the major medical research facilities, but have yet to get a response."

"There is no need to thank me, Adina. Going through proper channels takes time. This particular grant would be created specifically for you, or rather, the Foundation.

"However, there is one small thing I would like to discuss with you."

Jason lips suddenly became dry. His tongue slid slowly along his lower lip to moisten it. He followed that with a nervous sigh.

"Oh? What would that be?"

Adina's mind went into overdrive. She could guess he was nervous, losing control.

Oh! This is going to be fun!

"Well, this is a bit embarrassing, but I must be honest."

He paused, looking towards the window.

"I've had nothing but thoughts of you since I first laid eyes on you at the fundraiser the other night. You are an exquisite woman."

Adina stared, emotionless.

He looked panicked, but continued.

"I've always wondered what it would be like to have a woman like you in my bed, and in control."

Adina fought back a smile. This is going to work out very well.

She set the glass of wine on the table between them and rose from her seat, feigning indignation. The action surprised the ambassador and his mouth dropped open.

"I'm sorry. I think I'd better go. Thank you for your offer. I am going to have to pass."

"Wait! Please! Please hear me out …"

"Ambassador, I believe what you are proposing is that I prostitute myself for the sake of the Foundation. You have misjudged me. This conversation is extremely inappropriate, and it is over."

Her eyes sought an exit.

"Please, Adina. Please let me finish."

He began to reach across for her, but stopped himself.

Now, she had him right where she wanted him. She knew all along it would turn out this way. She could tell by the way he fawned over her that he was malleable. She could potentially get whatever she wanted from him. All she had to do was manipulate the situation in her favor, and in the process, make him think he was getting what he wanted of his own free will. If she played her cards right, he would soon feel the need to make it up to her for the perceived insult.

"Very well then, go on."

Adina sat back down.

"I promise, you will not regret this.

"I live a solitary existence because of my work. I am constantly travelling around the world. I have no one to go home to, no one to talk to. I am very lonely.

"If you and I could come up with an arrangement, I promise you, you will not be sorry. I am deeply desirous of a companion I can be free with. I need someone who is not going to be afraid to make the hard decisions in the bedroom. I need to couple with someone who would be willing to explore the secrets of sexual abandon with me."

"Arrangement? What would such an arrangement entail?"

Her voice was tight.

"I make many decisions all day long, every day. Some of those decisions determine the outcome of life and death situations. At the end of the day, I am drained and I want to submit to someone. I don't want to have to make any decisions in the bedroom."

Adina could not believe her ears. This guy was a Submissive and he was looking for a Domme!

This greatly excited Adina. She had experimented with this lifestyle but found it difficult to meet people with the same interests. Most men she met in the life wanted to be Dominants and she refused to submit to anyone.

"Ambassador ..."

"Please—before I lose my nerve. There is something about you that makes me feel that you are the right person for me, for this situation. I see it in the aggression of your stride, the way you talk to people with certainty in your words; the way you command attention when entering a room."

He shifted a bit and his hands played together in his lap.

"I like that. It arouses me. Your tough reputation excites me to no end.

"If you agree, I will make a personal, initial donation of fifty-thousand dollars in the name of your Foundation. If after a few meetings you feel you can continue with me in this arrangement, I will double my donation and round up the first group of three other benefactors to make identical bedrock donations to the grant."

Intrigued, Adina responded.

"And if I refuse?"

"I would still spearhead the formation of the grant in the hopes that my actions would help convince you that I only want to serve you in any way that pleases you."

Adina nodded while the wheels in her head went spinning.

There! That's what I wanted to hear. He's admitting that he would allow me to do whatever I want to and with him. There is a God!

"This is all very compelling, Jason, but you are only making offers that benefit you and the Foundation. What benefit is there in this arrangement for me?"

Adina began to feel warm as she was now fully aroused: nipples hard, panties moist. She saw that there was great potential in this deal and squirmed in the chair where she sat. All she could do to be discreet at this point was cross her legs at her ankles.

"I'll give you anything you want. You just name it," Jason begged.

Adina lowered her head demurely for half a second. There was no outward sign that her heart beat in a staccato passage. When she looked up again, chin down, her persona had changed.

There was an edge to her look and a gleam in her eye. Her upper lip curled in a sneer.

Elegantly rising from her seat, her arms swinging to and fro slowly at her side, she moved toward and around him.

The ambassador followed her movements with an unblinking eye.

His armpits moistened.

His cock hardened.

The throbbing there caused him to lift himself closer to the edge of his seat. The excitement that rose within him as he watched her move was barely controllable. His stomach tightened and his breath caught in his throat.

Adina moved behind him and grabbed a handful of hair, pulling his head back forcefully. A gasp escaped from Jason's mouth and his eyes rolled back.

It was too much for him and he cried out with an orgasm.

She watched him for a moment.

"Fine. I accept your offer," began Adina.

Letting go of his hair, Adina ran a sole finger across the ambassador's cheek. He turned his head to kiss it. Adina let him then walked back to the chair she had been sitting in, making him linger in his juices.

"You definitely are in need of someone who can help you. However, before we go on, you must be made aware of my needs."

"Anything, I'll do anything. You just say the word," he panted.

"Very well."

"First, under the conditions that you have just outlined, this arrangement can only be for six months. At the end of six months, we will revisit the details.

"Second, you will provide me with a five-thousand-dollar a week stipend. I will spend that stipend however I see fit. Furthermore, I will provide you with a list of items that I will need in order to fulfill your desires and fantasies. *You* will purchase these items, no questions asked.

"And finally, meeting in hotels makes me feel cheap. I need you to rent an apartment for me in the city and you will rent it solely in my name.

"Agreed?"

"Yes. I told you. I'll do anything you want."

"Good. Now, stop squirming and go clean yourself up. I will remain standing here, waiting for you, my puppy, to show me where the bedroom is."

Nodding like a bobble head in the rear window of a car, Jason rose and went to the bathroom. He was in there just a short while and when he returned without pants on, he tried to take Adina's hand.

"Did I say you could touch me? From now on, you will call me Madam and you may not touch me unless I give you express permission. Understood?"

"Yes, Madam."

Jason almost drooled.

"Good boy. Now, take my hand and lead me to the bedroom. You need a good spanking; a taste of what's to come."

ॐॐ

Adina briskly washed her hands in the marble bathroom then dried them on the towel hanging on the warmer, appreciating its soft lushness. She caught a glimpse of herself in the mirror.

Ugh! I look a mess!

She reached over on her left and grabbed her pocketbook off the settee sitting against the wall then plopped it on the counter top. Chuckling softly to herself she reached in and pulled out her lipstick. She thought about the ambassador, his eagerness to please her and how she wouldn't let him touch her. She had to keep from breaking into a silly grin in order to apply a thin layer of lipstick. Once that was accomplished, she put it back in her pocketbook and ran her fingers through her hair, fluffing it out. One more, quick glance in the mirror and she turned to leave. Without a word to the ambassador who was still sprawled face down on the bed trying to catch his breath, she opened the door and stepped through it into the hallway.

The driver who had brought her there was standing just outside the door. He silently reached over to call the elevator for her. When it arrived she stepped in and simply stared out as the doors slowly slid closed. It wasn't until she was out on the street that she drew in a deep breath, and almost gagged on the smell of Mediterranean food being cooked by a nearby street vendor.

Casually, she walked over to the corner of Park Avenue, crossed and headed west toward Madison Avenue.

Time to go shopping ... Madam, she said to herself with a grin.

ॐॐ

Adina was in her glory. She loved the way having control over another human being made her feel. She spent many years with the ambassador and even played similarly with other men even though there may not have been any financial incentives. She simply enjoyed having her way with people, men especially, and particularly those who asked for it.

Jason was extremely useful to her. He provided her with any and every little thing her heart desired. During those first six months, she continued living at home with her parents for several reasons.

She wanted to put away a healthy nest egg and she wanted to see how much she could get from the ambassador before fully committing to this situation with him.

But there was nothing to worry about. Jason kept his word and she kept hers. As promised, he made his first donation to the foundation and then helped Adina set up several additional fundraising events so as not to raise suspicion regarding the sudden influx of money; and the money did indeed flow regularly. Dr. Boulas could not be happier.

"What a stroke of luck to find such a benefactor in Ambassador Meade, don't you think, Adina? If I didn't know any better, I would say you charmed the pants off of him! You've made such wonderful connections!"

Adina's eyes shot up at the doctor, but she remained silent.

"Did you know you were so gifted in marketing and fundraising?"

Then she relaxed and chuckled.

"No, I don't think it's a gift. All I had to do was wiggle my hot, brown Puerto Rican butt a little and flutter my eyelashes at these guys. They always go weak in the knees when I do that."

Adina enjoyed the shocked look on the doctor's face, so she continued teasing him.

"They all think they're so powerful until they encounter an exotic beauty like me!"

Though seemingly speaking in jest, Adina was actually dead serious. She knew half these men fantasized about being with a "hot Latina" but would never allow themselves to be seen in public with one or even admit they had such fantasies. So, she played into their fantasy, but it would cost them and she let them know up front that it would.

Still slightly shocked, Dr. Boulas chuckled nervously at Adina's comments. He should've known better than to be surprised by what comes out of her mouth.

"You are something else, Adina. Why don't you take off early today? It's Friday and it is beautiful out. You should spend the day outside."

There was no way they could spend the day together after an exchange like that.

"I can't. I still have so much to do!"

But Dr. Boulas persisted.

"It'll keep. Go on now, I insist. I'll see you on Monday."

"All right, then. Thank you.

"Have a nice weekend!"

"You as well, Adina. Go on now! Go!"

A smiling Adina left the office.

Out on the street, she stopped to dig out her pager. She sent a page to the ambassador, who happened to be in town. She used her code letting him know she was on her way home and he should meet her there in an hour. Within minutes, he replied with his code for yes.

☙❧

The doorman held the door open for Adina as she approached the front entrance to her building.

"Good afternoon, Ms. Cruz! You're home early! It's nice to see you."

"Good afternoon, Billy."

"There's a flower delivery for you in the package room."

"Oh, really? How nice. Please have them brought to my apartment as soon as possible."

"Sure thing! Bye now! Enjoy the rest of your day."

"Thank you, Billy, you as well."

Adina's two-bedroom, well-appointed apartment was on the eighteenth floor of one of several luxury high-rise buildings overlooking the East River. She loved her apartment, her refuge. It was comfortable, quiet and nobody bothered her because everybody was too busy with his or her own lives to notice her.

When she told Jason this was the apartment she wanted, he didn't think it was opulent enough but she insisted and, as was his pattern, he gave in to her.

She poured herself a glass of white wine and kicked off her shoes a few minutes after walking in. Soon a maintenance man was ringing the doorbell; he was there to deliver the flowers that Jason had sent her. She didn't even have to look at the card. She knew they were from him because he sent her flowers regularly. It was one of her requirements.

She placed the vase on the large glass table by the window and went for a quick shower. A short time later, she stepped out of the shower stall wrapped in an oversized towel and went into the spare bedroom. The walk-in closet in this room was big enough to hold an art deco vanity where she kept her make-up. It sat near the far wall glittering with multi-colored diamonds created by the bright make up lights she had installed above the mirror.

Along the walls of the interior of the closet there were various storage areas. On one wall there was a section where rods were installed to hang exotic lingerie. Opposite that section there were shelves where she kept shoes of all types. Between the two walls, drawers were installed where she kept other accessories used in sex play.

The king sized, four poster bed was between two picture windows. The bed sat so high, she needed a small step stool to get on it. The bedspread was custom red sateen. Pink thousand-thread-count Egyptian cotton sheets lay underneath it. Against the headboard was an assortment of plush pillows and above the headboard hung a portrait of her naked self. It was artfully and tastefully done.

She thought about Jason as she got ready. She had no real feelings toward him. He was just a convenient vehicle she was using to arrive at her success.

❧❧

"Jason, sit up and look at me."

The man's body was sore but he was satiated and sexually drained. Still naked and lying face up on the floor; his flaccid penis lay limp against his thigh.

He wasn't allowed to cuddle with her on the bed after sex play, but he hoped to one day be invited to do so by Madam. Obviously, today was not the day.

He sat up and raised his eyes to her while he remained silent and waited to hear her command.

"Did you enjoy our session today?"

"Yes, Madam."

"Is your butt sore?"

"Yes, Madam, but I like it like that."

"Good. What about your balls? Do they hurt?"

"Yes, Madam."

Jason dared not look away.

"Good. The pain will serve as a reminder that you belong to me–the one you will serve until you are no longer needed or wanted. Now, get cleaned up and get out of here. I need to rest."

"Yes, Madam."

He paused and drew in a breath.

"May I speak please, Madam?"

"You just did."

Jason blinked furiously. If she saw him cry, she would be displeased.

"Oh, for chrissakes! What is it?"

"I have to leave for Europe in two days. I just wanted you to know that."

"Fine. Now go on, you can rise now and get out of here."

He scrambled to his feet and grabbed his clothes not daring to ask when he would see her again, but wondering nonetheless. Once in the bathroom he bathed quickly. When he was done, he left without saying anything to Adina because that was the way she wanted it.

❧◈

This is the lifestyle that Adina indulged in. Over the next ten years, she continued to play the role of Jason's "Madam" but as she became more and more comfortable in the game, she acquired additional short-term subs, some of them people that she met through joint fundraising activities with Jason and his consortium of benefactors. Some she picked up at bars that catered to the lifestyle. She spoke openly about her subs to Jason. She never lied. She enjoyed that it bothered him that he wasn't enough for her. But he truly believed that if that was what made her happy, then he would live with it. He was just happy to have her in his life.

By 1999, Adina had become very successful as Director of Marketing and Fundraising for the original group of benefactors and now her schedule was teeming with office meetings of all kinds. Many similarly organized groups attempted to duplicate Jason's genius business plan but they all inevitably and regularly failed within a short period of time. There was one thing in the business plan that no one knew about and that was the relationship she had with Jason who remained loyal to her and happy to do her bidding. His sexual tastes notwithstanding, he was a powerhouse in this field and undoubtedly the driving force behind their success.

One night, after closing on a particularly difficult deal they'd worked on late into the evening, the group decided to go out to dinner and celebrate together. Damien Childs, a member of the consortium as well as her ad hoc sub, suggested a restaurant in Riverdale. He raved about the food. It was rare for Adina to socialize with them and it was even more of a rarity for her to be out in public with Jason. But she was confident that he knew the rules and would know how to behave.

She wasn't at all concerned about Damien.

When it was time to leave the office, they split up in two and drove to the Bronx in separate cars.

The name of the restaurant they were going to was "Rhys' Pieces."

Chapter 25
Adina Falls in Love with Riverdale: 2000

On the drive up to Riverdale from her Harlem office, Adina was silent. Michael, the most obnoxious of the group, wondered aloud why she was so pensive. She told them she was tired and would probably feel better once she had eaten. She added she needed to have a glass of wine to help her relax and get her blood flowing again.

She returned to gazing out the car window as she rode along morosely with her colleagues. Soon, they were pulling into the parking lot of the restaurant and walking together toward the door. Adina took in her surroundings. She noticed how green this part of the Bronx was and inhaled the October air, deeply appreciating the freedom she felt at that moment.

An upper middle class neighborhood, Riverdale is located in the northern-most, west-end section of the Bronx. Teeming with residential homes and small businesses, it is visibly cleaner than most neighborhoods south and east of the area and sported manicured lawns in front of scattered private homes. All of the buildings in the area were well maintained. Some high-rise buildings contained professional offices and some even housed gyms. She could tell there was a nice mix of residents: professionals like the ones she was having dinner with, young families, the elderly and the retired. Everyone she saw walking the streets seemed comfortable in the area. She did not sense any threat or danger. The neighborhood felt safe.

All she observed caused her to fall in love with the neighborhood and she made a mental note to look into it a little deeper; maybe even explore the possibility of living there.

Adina's stomach grumbled as they reached the entrance. She couldn't wait to get something to eat and hoped she wouldn't be disappointed after all the raving about the food back at the office.

Located just off the highway in a cul de sac trimmed with flowering bushes and strings of white twinkling lights hanging from them, Rhys' Pieces was very nicely decorated. Dark mahogany booths lined two walls and a matching bar with a ceiling to countertop mirror lined the far wall. Behind the bar was the kitchen and to the left of the entrance was the coat check.

The restaurant was still crowded even at nine o'clock at night. She looked around and spotted a few families with children that were a little bit older but not yet teenagers.

The group chose a large booth opposite the bar and settled in. A short while later, a young man came over to take their drink order.

"Welcome to Rhys' Pieces. I'm Rhys, and I'll be taking care of you tonight."

Michael was the first to speak.

"Nice to meet you, Rhys. Are you the 'Rhys' in Rhys' Pieces?" He sneered.

"Yes, sir, I am."

Michael looked at Rhys as though he had two heads.

What's wrong with this asshole? I need to calm down. It's best to ignore him, Rhys thought.

Standing a little straighter and centering himself, he spoke again.

"Sometimes I like to wait tables in order to get feedback from our patrons."

Rhys handed each of them a menu as he spoke.

"May I take your drink orders now?"

He went around the table and efficiently took everyone's order. When it was Adina's turn, his heart quickened. It wasn't just that she was a captivating woman but the sudden feeling of kinship he felt with her gave him pause. He felt as though he had known her his whole life, but he couldn't place her. He kept a poker face.

"And you, young lady, what is your pleasure?"

He asked the question and it seemed to him as though it was an eternity before she responded. Their eyes had locked and so it seemed, her ability to speak as well.

Finally, she did and it was the sweetest sound he had ever heard.

"Chardonnay. May I have a glass of Chardonnay please?"

"Of course you may! Coming right up!"

Rhys hesitated half a second before turning on his heel and walking away. This woman mesmerized him.

Adina hardly noticed him except for the fact that he seemed to hesitate a bit when he looked at her, as though he wanted to say something.

Hmm. Another one bites the dust. Let's see what his story is.

☙❧

Adina thoroughly enjoyed her dinner. The raving earlier about the food was not exaggerated. She ordered Italian–"The Godfather Special"–one of three cuisines offered. Of the others, the orders were split between "Native Fare" and "Variedades" on the menu. She could have either of those anytime, but she had a weakness for Italian food, so she had to have it. When dinner was over, she convinced her colleagues to leave without her. She didn't say so to them, but she had become curious about Rhys and wanted to stick around and talk with him; see what he was about.

"I'll be fine. I'm just going to have one more drink at the bar before I go home. I'll be just fine. I'm sure Mr. Rhys can call me a cab when I'm ready to go."

"Are you sure, Adina?" Jason asked, concern written all over his round face, showing his thoughts: We're in the Bronx for chrissakes! I don't know what I would do if something happened to her.

Correctly reading Jason's expression, Adina faced her colleagues and looked each one in the eye while reassuring them. She lingered just a second longer on Jason's face and he appeared to relax.

"You guys should go. Let's plan on a short conference call first thing in the morning to make sure we're all set to begin this next phase."

Everyone agreed on a time and with a round of "good nights," the men left. Adina sauntered over to the bar and slid onto a stool.

"Hello, again," said Rhys in greeting.

"Hello, Rhys. I thought I might have a nightcap."

"Well, that's great! What's your poison?"

He grinned and leaned on the bar while waiting for her order.

"Nothing heavy. How about you make me a white wine spritzer?"

Adina was back on her medication; she shouldn't be drinking. She promised herself she wouldn't go overboard since she'd already had wine with dinner.

"White wine spritzer–coming right up!"

While preparing Adina's drink, Rhys looked at her reflection in the mirror of the back bar. It was nearing eleven o'clock and the restaurant had quieted down. He scanned the bar and there were only a few people scattered around it. All the tables were empty. Then after stealing another peek at her, he set her drink before her.

Why does she feel so familiar to me?

"Here you go. It's on the house."

"Thank you very much. Do you have time for a chat? I hate to drink alone," Adina said with a flirty smile.

She couldn't help herself.

"Sure. What's on your mind?"

"Tell me about this neighborhood. I've never been up here and it seems so quaint."

"Quaint? I wouldn't call it 'quaint'."

Confused, Adina tilted her head questioningly.

"I mean, this *is* the Bronx, you know. But, the neighborhood does have a rich history. There are beautiful parks lining the Hudson River. Some of the mansions further north have been named historical landmarks and the neighborhood continues to grow. As a matter of fact, there is a new housing complex going up not too far from here."

"Is that right? Do you know what type of housing? I mean is it public housing? Government?"

"Well, I heard rumors they were condominiums and that the exclusive realtor is actually taking offers from potential buyers, sight unseen. They can't actually show the units because most are still being constructed. They are using basic floor plans in the hopes that people will purchase the unit, then finish it themselves."

"If all that is true–you did say you heard a rumor–if what you are saying is true, the idea of making these units attractive to potential buyers by way of a floor plan template is exceptionally ambitious and potentially disastrous."

Rhys shrugged as he chuckled.

"I guess. Do you know much about realty?"

"Not much, but I know about marketing and selling a product."

Rhys nodded.

How do I know this woman, he wondered.

Adina spoke again.

"Do you know who the realtor is? I'm intrigued."

"As a matter of fact, I do. Hold on a sec. I think I have her card sitting on the register."

Rhys walked away from Adina. She looked down at her drink. She hadn't touched it–that was a good thing. It was getting late and she was beginning to feel tired again.

"Here you go," he said as he handed her the card.

"Thanks. I should get going. Can you call me a cab?"

"Sure. There's a service around the corner. They can be here within a few minutes."

"Great, thank you. And thanks for the chat. I'll just wait outside; I need some fresh air."

"Thank you for coming by. I'll go call your cab."

"By the way, name's Adina. I like it here and I'll be back soon."

"Nice to meet you, Adina."

"Good night, Rhys, and thank you once again."

"Good night, Adina."

Adina. Wow! What a beautiful name. A beautiful name for a beautiful lady.

Adina hopped off her seat and headed toward the door. She had waited less than a minute before her cab pulled up and she jumped in.

"Good evening," the driver greeted.

"Good evening. 57 Sutton Place, please," she directed the driver and settled in to the back seat.

ॐॐ

Early the next morning, Adina rose and went to the gym. When she returned, she called her colleagues as promised the previous evening to discuss final details of the latest deal. It was a short call and ended within twenty minutes.

"Enjoy the rest of the weekend everyone," Adina said in closing and disconnected the call before anyone could respond. She wanted to make one more call.

ॐॐ

"Good morning, Riverdale Real Estate. How may I help you?"

"Good morning. May I speak with Ms. Kalani?"

"One moment please."

The line went silent and within a few moments the realtor was on the line.

"Sharon Kalani. How may I assist you?"

"Good morning, Ms. Kalani. My name is Adina Cruz. I understand you handle real estate for the Riverdale Circle Condominiums?"

"Yes, ma'am. Are you interested in purchasing a unit?"

"Actually, I was hoping to get an appointment to meet with you before making that decision. When are you available to see me?"

"I'm available all day today. Is three o'clock good for you?"

"Yes. That's perfect. I'll see you at three p.m. Thank you."

ॐॐ

The meeting with Ms. Kalani lasted over two hours. According to the realtor, the six- building complex consisted of two garden apartments, two bi-level townhouses and two towers each twenty floors high. The project would be finished in three months' time. Currently, it was only forty percent sold but there was an anticipated ninety-five percent occupancy rate within a year. Adina listened intently and thought the rate of occupancy was ambitious given the current climate within the real estate market, but she didn't care. She was really taken by the neighborhood.

Ms. Kalani went over the amenities with Adina: concierge service; laundry and dry cleaning services on the premises; a package room; an on-property gym; a parking garage that can also accommodate guests; and a full service beauty salon. Each building had its own maintenance worker as well as a superintendent who was on call twenty-four hours a day. Finally, there were two ATM machines on the premises. She would never have to leave the complex if she didn't want to except for groceries and they could be delivered.

After discussing the services offered by the complex's management firm, Ms. Kalani showed Adina a mock-up of what the property would look like once it was completed. They reviewed floor plans and afterward Adina was offered a tour. She accepted the invitation and placed the proffered construction helmet gingerly on her head then followed the agent out the door.

She was so impressed that by the end of that meeting, she had written a check for thirty percent of the purchase price as a down payment. Once all the paperwork and background investigation was complete, she would be the proud owner of 1212 Delafield Avenue, one of the newly built garden apartments, in the Riverdale Circle Condominium complex. She decided she would not do any additional construction, and if all went well, she could legally move in the first day of the new millennium.

She was fine with that date because she was ready to begin a new phase in her life and the almost three-month window would give her ample time to make some changes.

"Thank you for meeting with me, Ms. Kalani. I look forward to the New Year. This is a great way to end the decade!"

❧❦

It had been ten glorious years since Adina's first fundraiser on behalf of The Foundation for Emerging New Life, and her life as a Domme began. It was when she discovered a whole new side of who she was. She learned that she enjoyed having control over others and was happiest when others catered to her every whim. When they didn't comply with her wishes as she commanded, she discovered that she enjoyed inflicting punishment–preferably punishment that included some kind of pain. She got off on the suffering of others at all levels in the bedroom, and Jason Meade was especially eager to teach her the intricacies and the rewards that came with that kind of sexual tension.

But now it was time to end it with Jason. He was much too old for her. He had served his purpose.

It was right after the Christmas holiday and before the New Year when she broke the news to him.

"Come sit on the bed with me, Jason. I want to talk with you."

Jason could not believe his ears. This is what he most wanted from his Domme. He wanted her to hold him; cradle him against her breast.

"Yes, Madam."

Jason sat gingerly on the edge of the bed. He had to wait for her to invite him to come closer.

But the invitation never came. Adina's lips were moving, words were coming out of her mouth, but they were not the words he wanted to hear. His face went slack and his mouth was agape.

"Jason? Did you hear what I just said?"

Jason could not believe his ears. He had followed all the rules. His heart broke into a million little pieces. His lips quivered. It was all he could do to keep from breaking down.

Merry fucking Christmas!

"Madam. May I ask a question?"

"What is it?"

"Madam, did I offend you in some way? Please. I beg of you. If I did, just tell me what I can do to make it up to you. Please, Madam."

A tear escaped from his eye. He brushed it away quickly. He knew she saw it.

Jeez! I hoped it wouldn't turn into waterworks. What a pussy!

"Jason, you did nothing wrong. People change. Their needs change. I've changed and I've tired of this situation. It's time to move on. Do you understand?"

"Madam, are you sure there isn't anything I can do to keep from losing you?"

"Are you questioning my desire? This is my wish. You will find someone else. I'm sure of it.

"Now, put on your big boy pants and leave."

He watched her in horror.

"Now."

"Yes, Madam. One more thing."

"What?"

Adina was abrupt.

"Though you have broken my heart, my wish for you is that you find whatever you are looking for. My wish is that you never have to experience the pain you have just inflicted on me. Yes, I enjoy pain, physical pain. This emotional pain is far too much for me to bear."

Adina nodded slightly.

"You have had your say. Thank you for all you have been to me. Now, please leave."

Jason did not respond. With a trembling hand, he reached down to where his clothing lay in a heap, grabbed them and left the room to dress. When he was done, he silently left Adina's apartment.

Later that evening, Adina turned on her television set. A popular movie about the hunt for a serial killer was on. She put the remote control down and settled into her couch to watch. A few minutes later, the screen switched to a news reporter standing in front of the United Nations.

The reporter began speaking.

"We interrupt the regularly scheduled program to bring you this breaking news. Ambassador to the United Kingdom, Jason Meade, was found dead today in his hotel room at the Waldorf Towers. His chauffeur and valet, Mr. Byron Palmer, found his body in his suite. There was no suicide note.

"Mr. Palmer stated that when he last saw the ambassador he was in good spirits. He added that he knew of no reason why the ambassador would take his own life. He had no further comments.

"We will continue to monitor this situation and bring you the latest as it develops. We return now to your regularly scheduled program."

Adina sucked her teeth and turned off the television set.

That's the way to handle a break-up, Jason. Way to go!

Six weeks later, Adina moved into her garden apartment at 1212 Delafield Avenue in Riverdale, The Bronx.

Chapter 26
Tomas "Tommy" Ortiz

Tomas Ortiz, or Tommy as he liked to be called, is the newest resident in one of two Towers at the Riverdale Circle Condominiums. A commanding presence, he was always conscious of his height. Even while in primary school he was the tallest in his class. He always stood proud and radiated a high level of self-esteem rarely seen in someone with his background.

Now in his early forties, Tommy was not overly muscular but he stayed in shape with regular visits to the gym and weekly basketball games with his best friend, Mason Jones. His velvety dark skin and deep set dark brown eyes fringed with long curly lashes and sharp facial features were the envy of men and women alike. He resembled a young Denzel Washington with a Hispanic flair and was often confused for being black. Well groomed, he kept his now graying-at-the-temples curly hair and manicured goatee closely cropped.

He rarely dated and his last relationship ended over five years prior. As a lover, he was generous, kind and understanding. But he was also an emotionally intense lover. He didn't handle break ups well, often becoming desperately despondent due to his separation anxiety issues.

On the other hand, when he was in a good place emotionally, he didn't take himself too seriously. He was a lot of fun and most women clamored for his attention; that is, the ones who weren't astute enough to take notice of his emotional issues.

A graduate of New York City's John Jay College with a Bachelor of Science degree in Computer Information Systems in Criminal Justice and Public Administration, he was what some would call a nerd. He read any and everything he could get his hands on, particularly computer related material. This quirky nerdiness was a plus for him and helped with his work at the police department where he was employed as an information systems designer. He definitely knew his way around a computer.

At college, he took courses in gender studies for extra credit in an effort to understand his own psychology. This field intrigued him because it helped him understand how gender and sexuality influence human identity both historically and culturally, ultimately shaping a person's human development and behavior.

Tommy did not have gender identity issues, but he had often wondered if he would have handled the trauma he suffered as a young boy the same way if he were a girl.

All was not rosy for Tommy while he was growing up an only child in Spanish Harlem. His was a troubled childhood. His father was a teacher who drank; a strict disciplinarian. His mother, a homemaker, was a passive parent. Theirs was a shotgun wedding after his mother became pregnant as a teenager, so there really was no love there.

When Tommy was nine years old, he lost both parents in a car accident caused by his drunken father who lost control of his car. His best friend's family took him in and raised him as a son.

Though it took a while for Tommy to adjust, his years with the Joneses were as happy as they could be considering the circumstances. Mason was an only child and he and Tommy were best friends since first grade. He was ecstatic to now always have his best buddy around to play with. They shared everything. However, he was slight as a young boy and withdrawn, frequently the target of bullying by the neighborhood punks.

When Tommy was sixteen, he used a broken beer bottle during a fight to cut the face of a gang member in Mason's defense. The gangster was badly injured. The police became involved and after meeting with a judge, Tommy was sent to juvenile hall for two years. He finished his primary education there and it was at "juvie" that Tommy got his first taste of computer technology.

His love affair with computers began.

During what was considered his senior year in high school, the police department implemented a cadet program as a way to interest new recruits. The program's biggest incentive: a number of college credits for any future college student with an interest in law enforcement. In exchange, the student had to agree to work for the police department for a period of two years.

Because it had always been Mason's dream to be a police detective, he took advantage of the program. Upon graduation, he joined the police academy and graduated with high scores as a rookie cop. He absolutely loved police work. As boys, he and Tommy took turns playing cops and robbers. They constantly talked about what it might be like to fight crime.

Tommy never forgot those conversations and they inspired him to choose a career in police work. But he didn't want to work as a uniformed policeman, as he knew something of the ugliness you can encounter on the streets of New York City as a cop. He felt strongly that he could be a much better asset behind the scenes in their growing technical department.

A job as a technician with the police department was not part of the cadet program, but Tommy joined the program anyway. Upon graduation, he approached the program director and inquired about working behind the scenes at his local precinct. At that point, their technical department was very small. However, recognizing the explosion of the technical and computer industries, they agreed to give him an entry-level job during his years at John Jay College. They also gave him a small scholarship on the condition that he would work at the station for five years to help build the department. He agreed and continued working part time with the technicians already employed by the precinct and learned everything he could while he completed his studies.

Upon graduation, he was given additional responsibilities and steadily rose up the ranks, finally supervising five people at a precinct in Riverdale two years later, and that was the position he was in when he met his angel, Adina.

❧

The year was 2000. Mason was recently transferred from his home precinct in Manhattan to the 54th Precinct in Riverdale. He requested the change so he could be closer to his best friend who was a supervisory technician there.

Claudia, Mason's wife of ten years, spent a full, busy day making phone calls and planning a surprise birthday celebration for her husband. She had just one more phone call to make and she saved it for last because aside from her husband, the person she was about to call was her favorite person in the world.

Tommy knew how to celebrate, plus he was family. Having him there meant a good time was guaranteed.

"Hello, handsome. How are you doing?"

"Claudia, you need to stop calling me handsome. Your ugly husband is going to be mad. He's probably got the phone tapped and will be here shortly to kick my ass! You're putting my life in jeopardy."

Claudia giggled.

"Aw, come on, Tommy! If you'd get a girlfriend, I wouldn't have to make these calls in order to stroke your ego!"

"Now, you see? Was that nice? What do you want?"

"You know I love you, Tommy. We both do."

"I know. I was just kidding. But, seriously, what do you want? I got work to do, woman!"

"Damn! You don't have to be rude!"

They both laughed heartily for a long time. This is what happened whenever the two of them got together–sparks of happiness burst all around them.

"What!? Speak woman!"

"All right, all right! I wanted to let you know that I'm throwing Mason a surprise birthday dinner tomorrow night and your presence is required. No excuses, do you hear me?"

"Girl, you know I wouldn't miss it for the world. Where is this shindig?"

"I found a really nice restaurant right near your precinct. It's called Rhys' Pieces. Do you know it?"

"I've heard good things about it."

"That's right! You're an adult now–a property owner! Woo! Hoo!"

"Well, it was time for me to grow up, ok? Now what do you know about this place?"

"I heard nice things about it too, especially about the food, and you know I like to eat! I'm so happy I was able to rent it out for the evening."

"Whoa! You got it like that? Jeez! You must be in lurve!"

"Would you stop it? You know I'd do anything for Mason."

"I know. It's a beautiful thing."

"Yeah," said Claudia dreamily.

"Anyhow, I spoke with Mr. Rhys himself. He gave me a discounted price for the rental because it was for a policeman. Apparently, he's got great admiration for the NYPD."

"Wow! He does?"

"Yep."

"No, he doesn't. I think he's some kind of serial killer who's trying to stay close so that he doesn't get caught!"

"Damn, Tommy! You have some imagination! You could confirm that yourself once you finish moving in to your new condo. Then you can spend all your free time looking for evidence of your theory. You might even get some press if you're right.

"And, if you look good on camera, you might even get a girlfriend!"

"There you go again with the girlfriend shit. I just haven't found the right one, ok? Besides, God only made one of you."

"Aw! Ok, you got me. I'll stop teasing you."

"So, can I count on you to detain Mason—and I used the term loosely—until I give you the call that everyone is there? Obviously, it's a surprise. It would be nice if you could kind of steer him there for, say, an after-work drink?"

"Of course! Anything for you my princess! It's a date. See you tomorrow."

"Thanks, Tommy. Love you!"

"Love you back!"

Tommy hung up the phone with a big ole cheesy grin on his face. Claudia and Mason were the only family he had.

∂∞∕

"Yes, Mrs. Jones. I am very pleased we are able to accommodate you. I will be here to oversee the event and make sure that everything goes as you wish. Thank you again for thinking of us. I look forward to meeting you tomorrow.

"Good-bye."

Rhys hung up the phone. He did something he had never done before. He didn't usually close Rhys' Pieces for private parties, but this was an exception.

Lately, he had been having trouble tamping down his desires. He needed to find a release soon. He was doing so well! It was because of that woman who had been at the restaurant a few weeks earlier.

Adina. He couldn't get her out of his head.

Rhys ran his hands through his hair.

What is it about that woman? It's not like I want to have sex with her. It's frustrating to constantly be thinking of her and not know why! She's driving me crazy!

ॐ∽

Mason hung up the phone.

Where the hell is she?

Claudia hadn't answered. It was their date night and his birthday but they hadn't yet confirmed their plans. He left her a message asking her to call him back then he logged off his computer.

He thought maybe Tommy was still around and could go for a quick drink.

ॐ∽

It had been a long day for Tommy and he was tired. He almost regretted agreeing to stall Mason. He yawned as he tidied up his desk.

His phone buzzed.

"Hey, Tommy! What are you still doing here?"

"Hey, buddy! Yeah, it is kinda late, but it's all right. I was going to swing by your office. Wanna go for a quick drink?"

"I was about to ask you the same thing. I just left Claudia a message to call me back. I would love a cold one. Where do you want to go?"

"Have you been to that Rhys' Pieces yet?"

"No, I haven't. Do they have a bar?"

"Let's go see. I should really check it out since I'll probably be a regular if the food's good."

"Sounds good to me. I'll swing by and pick you up."

As soon as he hung up with Mason, Tommy sent a text message to Claudia letting her know that they were heading there. She responded almost immediately saying she and the guests were all set and ready for their arrival.

❧❧

"Does it look like it's closed to you? It looks dark inside."

"No, can't be closed," replied Tommy to his friend as he pulled open the door.

"See? It's not closed. After you, sir."

Tommy bowed elaborately and signaled Mason to enter first.

"SURPRISE!!" came the loud greeting as he crossed the threshold.

He was taken completely off guard when his wife rushed him to give him a warm hug and kiss.

"Happy birthday, baby!"

"So this is why you didn't answer your phone! Was this all your doing?"

"Yes, indeed, and you deserve it!"

Claudia pulled her husband along to the center of the restaurant where all his friends from the precinct were gathered with raised champagne glasses. Somebody handed him a glass, which he raised as well.

"Wow! This is amazing! Thank you all for your good wishes. A special thank you to my lovely wife for putting together such a shindig."

Mason turned to face his friend.

"And to Tommy. Man! You are good, my brother! You did not let on at all!

"Let's all eat, drink and be merry!"

❧❧

RJ busied himself at the bar; wiping down imaginary spills. He eyed the participants of the party but paid special attention to the celebrated detective.

He put down the rag and waited for an opportunity to introduce himself to the man of the hour.

"Excuse me, Mrs. Jones?"

"Yes, Mr. Preston."

"Please call me Rhys."

Claudia nodded with a smile on her face.

"Is everything to your liking?"

"Yes! Everything is perfect, Rhys. The food is delicious! Thank you so much!"

"It was my pleasure to accommodate you."

Rhys was shaking Claudia's hand when Mason came up behind her and kissed her on the back of her neck as he pulled her into a bear hug.

"Ooh!" squealed Claudia happily.

"Honey, this is Rhys Preston, proprietor of this fine establishment. Rhys, this is my husband, the esteemed Detective Sergeant Mason Jones."

Detective Sergeant? Nice, Rhys thought.

"So nice to meet you, sir. Should I call you Detective or Sergeant?"

"Nice to meet you as well, Rhys. You can just call me Mason. Thank you for helping the missus put this together. It must have been short notice. That's the way she operates."

Mason kissed his wife on top of her head.

Rhys smiled for his audience.

"As I told your lovely wife, it was my pleasure. Please feel free to come back whenever you like. I assure you every visit will be perfection!"

"Well, that's nice to know. I may just do that. Thanks, again.

"If you'll excuse me, I'd better go mingle."

"I'll see you later to settle up any additional expenses," Claudia said as she and Mason walked hand-in-hand toward the crowd.

Rhys was left standing there. He ran his hand through his hair and turned toward the coat check to see if the attendant wanted something to eat or drink.

That's when he saw her. She was peering in through the front door, accompanied by a young man. He didn't look familiar, or rather, he didn't look like any of the men that were in the group she was with on the night he met her. His heart pounded as he strode confidently to the entrance of the restaurant.

Be cool.

"I'm sorry. We're closed tonight; private party."

"Rhys? Hi, Rhys. Don't you recognize me? It's Adina. I was here the other night, remember?"

"Oh. Adina! Hi! I'm sorry–the lighting; I didn't recognize you."

"Hi. Are you closed? I was telling my friend Wade here about your restaurant and figured rather than talking about it, I'd bring him so he could see for himself what I was crowing about."

Rhys nodded at Adina's friend.

A friend? People call their boyfriends "friend." Is this her boyfriend? He wondered.

Adina looked at Rhys, she wondered why he blocked their way in. She knew he would step aside any moment now because no one ever denied her anything. When Rhys didn't step aside, she pouted her lips slightly and batted her eyelashes.

"That's really sweet of you to speak so well of my restaurant, but I couldn't possibly let you in today. There's a private party going on. I do hope you come back soon."

"I'm dismayed, but I understand. I'll come back another time."

"Have a good evening."

"Good night, Adina. Thank you for understanding."

Rhys closed the door and watched as Adina and her friend walked away. He was disappointed he wouldn't have the pleasure of being around her that night.

Chapter 27
Adina and Wade Sturgis

"That was disappointing. Do you have any ideas?" Adina asked Wade.

"Well, we're in luck! There's a piano bar at The Vue Hotel in the city. The pianist featured tonight is very popular. If we go now, it's still early enough that we can get a cozy table in the back."

"Sounds good to me. Let's get a cab."

"Great!"

Wade Sturgis, an investment banker, was handsome, young, virile and sexually open to experimentation. He is average in height and well dressed. He wore a small gold hoop in his ear and a devil's patch Adina found titillating. He had an old world charm about him that sort of reminded her of her father. They met while she stood in line at the local bookstore one afternoon not too long before that night. She really wasn't much of a reader, but she wanted to purchase a selection of books to decorate her new apartment.

A short time later, their cab pulled up in front of The Vue Hotel, but just before getting out, Adina turned to her companion.

"You up for a game?"

"Anything for you, my princess."

The term of endearment caused her heart to skip a beat. Her father used to call her that and at that moment she missed him terribly.

"What do you have in mind?" Wade continued, bringing her back to reality.

"How about I go in first, find that table in the back you talked about and when I'm comfortable, I want you to approach me as though we've never met. We could play "pick up."

"Ooh, you bad, bad girl. This sounds exciting. Yes! Let's play!"

Adina smiled. She reached across to caress Wade's face then elegantly exited the cab. She straightened her skirt and strutted into the hotel lobby. Upon entering, she looked around and was impressed with the décor. The music was soothing and she followed its sound to the Piano Bar. Once at the bar, she immediately noticed it. Just as Wade said, there was an empty booth in a dark corner. She made a beeline for it.

A few minutes later, Adina looked up to see Wade standing before her.

"Excuse me. May I join you?"

"Of course."

"Are you here alone tonight?"

"Not any more."

Wade chuckled and held out his hand.

"My name is Wade. Yours?"

"Adina."

Adina let him take her hand in his and watched as he kissed it.

"Adina. A beautiful name for a beautiful lady."

"Thank you."

A waiter came over and took their drink order. She ordered a dirty martini; Wade, a scotch on the rocks. The palpable buzz of muted conversation in the room all around them made the fantasy all the more exciting for her. The pianist played softly in the background as Adina eyed Wade.

Let the games begin! She thought.

"So, Wade, what brings you here tonight?"

"Well, I was feeling a bit lonesome and wandered in here to find you, my angel."

"Is that right?"

"Yes. It is."

The waiter returned with their drinks. They clinked glasses.

"To adventures," toasted Adina.

"To adventures," countered Wade.

They each took a sip, eyes locked.

"Tell me, Adina, when you ventured out of your home into the cold, cruel world tonight, what did you expect to find? Is there any chance you thought you would find a playmate?"

"Well, I had hoped so, but I wasn't holding my breath. If you're insinuating you might be that playmate, then you are a pleasant surprise."

"I'm full of surprises, Ms. Adina."

"Oh? I'll tell you what. I'm going to go to the little girls' room and when I return, I'd like you to show me what you've got in your little bag of tricks. How's that sound?"

"Sounds good to me. But let me assure you, there is nothing little about either my bag or my tricks."

Wade winked. He hardened just thinking about the things he would do with her and his heart pounded in his chest. His tongue slid like a snake along his lower lip. Then, he bit it–hard, sexily. Adina watched the spot where his teeth left their mark go from white to pink again.

She inhaled deeply and squirmed. Her heart beat a fast and hard tempo in her chest. She cleared her throat to finally speak in a whisper.

"I'll be right back."

Wade nodded. It was just enough time for Adina to gather herself.

"I'd like to drink champagne when I return, please."

"Yes, ma'am. Whatever you want."

Like mercury, she slid out of her seat and seductively walked to the ladies room, knowing full well that he would be watching.

When she returned the lounge was a bit darker.

Wade spotted her walking toward their table so he rose and helped her back into her seat. Once he was sure she was comfortable, he slid closer to her and put his right arm around her shoulder and his left hand on her lap under the table, covered by the heavy white cloth. Not getting any resistance from her, he caressed her thigh over her dress. She moved his hand underneath her hem.

A smile crept across Wade's face but Adina didn't see it. She was pointedly avoiding any opportunity to glance his way. Her eyes were on the pianist. This presented a challenge for Wade.

He touched her chin with two fingers and she allowed him to turn her to face to him. But when he tried to kiss her, she stopped him.

"This is the last time tonight I will lay eyes on you. You can play with me until either I tell you to stop, or I stop you myself. After that, I will do as I please with or without you, and you will comply with my wishes. Understood?"

Wade was taken aback.

"I love a challenge," he said and kissed the tip of her nose.

Adina turned her attention back to the pianist.

Wade's hand was now riding up Adina's naked thigh so slowly gooseflesh rose on her arms and her nipples hardened. She inhaled deeply. It had been so long since she had felt anything like this that she thought she might lose her own challenge.

When he reached her apex, she spread her legs slightly and licked her lips. Encouraged, Wade used his fingertips to circle her naked diamond. When he tried to draw back the curtains that led to the treasured wet cave, she snapped her legs together tightly.

"You broke my hand," he said jokingly.

Adina held on to her poker face and stared straight ahead.

"My turn. Relax."

When she was done playing with Wade, Adina discreetly reached across the table for the cloth napkin and wiped her hand clean. Out of the corner of her eye, she noticed he was leaning back in his chair, his lips parted. She rolled her eyes, grabbed her pocketbook and without looking at Wade or saying a word to him, she left the table and headed to the ladies room.

Wade watched her go, anticipating a triumphant return.

He thought: Shit! That was amazing. I can't wait to get her home tonight.

But Adina didn't return to the table that night and she never saw Wade again.

That was just the way she rolled.

Chapter 28
Adina Settles in Riverdale:
2000

Now settled in her new apartment, Adina enjoyed herself as she acclimated to her new environment. She started each day at the on-property gym always arriving just after sunrise. The gym was a huge selling point for the real estate company. Featuring ultra-modern equipment, the Riverdale Circle Condominiums was only the second complex in the Bronx to offer such an amenity; a coup for sales. At that time, it was rare to see, even in Manhattan, such an offer made to its residents.

This particular Sunday morning, Adina slept in. It was nearly ten o'clock when she awoke and prepared for her daily ritual. Soon she was out the door, earphones in her ears and cassette player at the ready. She liked to listen to '80s disco music while she exercised. It inspired her to work harder to keep her youthful figure, and it remained so even though she was in her late thirties. Thanks to her dark complexion, sometimes she was carded at bars and restaurants when she ordered alcohol. This annoyed more than flattered her.

When she arrived at the gym, it was crowded. The only place she could go for a workout was at a treadmill near the free weights. She took a deep breath and walked toward it, intent on placing her cassette player in the holder to keep from having someone come along and jump on it before she could wipe it down.

"I'll keep an eye on it for you."

The rich, baritone voice startled her and she turned around.

"Excuse me?"

"I said I'll hold it for you so no one takes it right out from under you," the man said.

"Thank you," Adina responded and started to turn away.

"On the other hand ..."

She turned back. Impatient. Curious.

"I could just let someone jump on it and we could chat while you wait."

This time he smiled. She was dazzled by his brightness.

Who is this guy? she wondered.

Undeterred, he put down the weights he was working with and stood on the treadmill.

"Go on now. I won't let anyone on here."

This time he winked.

She smiled shyly. She would have melted if she didn't have to move.

What the hell is wrong with me? I'm acting like a schoolgirl!

She returned to the treadmill, antiseptic spray and a wad of paper towels in hand but the handsome stranger did not move.

She kept bouncing back and forth between being awed by him and being nasty to him.

What's wrong with me? she thought.

"Sir, would you please remove your body from my treadmill?"

Taken aback, the handsome stranger threw his head back and laughed heartily. Adina joined him in cautious laughter. Eventually, they both stopped laughing and the man stepped off the machine.

"Tomas, the name's Tomas Ortiz, but everybody calls me Tommy."

"Adina, Adina Cruz. It's nice to meet you, Tommy."

Adina smiled and swayed slightly on the balls of her feet.

Hmmm. A charmer. This could be interesting.

"So, Tommy. Now that the introductions have been made, can you get off my machine?"

Adina curled her full lips and waited for him to make way.

"Yes, ma'am! Whatever you say, ma'am!"

Tommy jokingly gave Adina an exaggerated salute and stepped off the machine, but remained standing in front of her. She hadn't yet told him to get lost.

"I've noticed you before. I see you bust your ass in here. I also noticed something else too, you know."

Tommy grinned.

"Oh? And what might that be?"

"Two things: One, you're intense. You get lost in whatever you're listening to on your cassette player. It's obvious you're very focused on your workout. It's a beautiful thing to watch."

"Yes, now you said there were two things you noticed. What else?"

"I also noticed that you're not wearing a ring."

Adina blushed.

"So ..." Tommy began to speak again.

He had to. The moment he mentioned the ring, he felt awkward.

"... how about we acknowledge one another from now on? We could be gym buddies. I've just moved in and I don't know the neighborhood or anyone in it. I think it would be nice to have a gym friend."

Adina didn't respond and Tommy wanted to find a hole to crawl into. He was that pimply, pre-pubescent boy with the crush on the prettiest girl in school everyone reads about. He would kick himself if it would make him feel better.

"Sure, Tommy. Let's be gym buddies," Adina replied sarcastically.

"Are you teasing me?"

"Yes. I am."

Tommy frowned playfully, but he felt a bit dejected.

"Now, if you don't mind, I'd like to start my workout. You can go back to your weights now.

"Thank you for holding down the treadmill for me. I'll look over at you every once in a while and wave hello. How's that?"

"Oh, you got jokes! Ok. I deserved that. Nice to meet you, Adina. Have a nice workout."

Tommy wasn't sure if she was serious. If she was flirting, she sure had a strange way of doing so.

He stepped aside to let her on the machine, and walked back toward the free weights never taking his eyes off her. She didn't seem to notice.

⤜⋘

Adina wiped down the handles and the screen on the treadmill monitor, turned on her cassette player and started her workout. Soon she was running in tune with the music that played in her ear like a soundtrack to the movie of their encounter. It played over and over in her head. She dragged her eyes over the length of Tommy's body while he bench pressed in time with his heavy breathing.

She thought to herself: Who am I kidding? He is handsome. I'll make it up to him. Who knows, he may be just what I need.

Twice during her workout, Adina waved hello at Tommy, then ignored him. The rest of the time she kept thinking that she would approach him afterward.

I wonder if he would still be interested in me looking a mess.

But, she didn't figure on him not being there when she was done. Oh well, next time.

⤜⋘

Adina Cruz Rosario rocked Tommy's world and turned him into that panting schoolboy with a crush and a hard-on. The instant he saw her he knew he had to have her no matter what. She had been on his mind since the first time he laid eyes on her. And on that day, when he least expected it, there she was. His be all; end all, his *beshert*.

Yeah, his beshert. Though not Jewish, that was the only way he could describe what she was to him–his soul mate. The one person he was meant to be with and no matter what happened, they would work it out together.

He knew he screwed up. Badly. He couldn't figure out how or where he went wrong, but he knew he had to fix it.

Tommy sighed as he put his key in the door. He was sweaty and desperately needing a shower. On top of that, he was hungry. Though it was Sunday, he wanted to stop by his office to check on a project then afterward, maybe swing by Rhys' Pieces for a late lunch.

⤜⋘

Adina finished her workout and walked through the complex back to her garden apartment. She showered and went through a pile of mail that had been growing at her desk all week. Famished when she was done, she decided to head over to Rhys' Pieces to grab a bite to eat. She hadn't been there since the night with Wade when it was closed for a private party. She really wanted lasagna that night, but she couldn't get in. Needing no further inspiration beyond that memory, she dressed and headed out.

Standing at the entrance, Adina's eyes scanned the restaurant. It was pretty empty, but she opted to sit at the bar to eat.

"Well, hello, Adina. How have you been?"

Rhys was jovial in his greeting.

"Hello, Rhys. I'm well, how about yourself?"

"Better now that you are here. What can I get you?"

"I'll have the Godfather Special and a Coke, please."

"Coming right up. Coke's on the house; you can have unlimited refills.

"Pick a table, I'll bring it right over."

"Can I have it at the bar?"

"Sure, you can! I'll be right back."

"Thank you."

Sighing, Adina reached into her pocketbook. She had a new-fangled gadget pager thingy that allowed her to receive emails and organize her calendar electronically on it. She spent the time waiting on her food doing just that.

"Here you are, pretty lady."

So engrossed was she with this new technology, Rhys startled her when he spoke.

"I'm sorry."

"Oh, it's all right. I was wrapped up in this thing."

Adina waved the gadget dismissively.

"What is that?"

"It's called an Owl. It's supposed to help organize my life."

"Oh?"

"Yes, it allows me to receive alphanumeric pages. I can also organize my calendar as well as send and receive email."

"Really? Wow, isn't modern technology something, huh?"

"It sure is. It's amazing."

"I can't imagine why someone would want to have one of those things unless they're a doctor or a lawyer. You don't look like a lawyer to me; you look too honest. I'm going to guess you're a doctor. Am I correct?"

Adina chuckled at his comment about looking honest.

"No, I'm neither. I organize fundraising events for an AIDS foundation in the city. It's not really a nine-to-five job. One of my foundation's benefactors is an executive with the company that created this thing. Though it's not yet available for the masses, he gave me one since my schedule is so busy. I guess he did it out of the kindness of his heart."

She held it up to demonstrate. "You are correct in assuming that doctors and lawyers might use one of these things. They were the first group of people to test the prototype."

"I'm impressed."

Adina smiled at Rhys and reached for her appetizer.

"Enjoy your salad. I'm going to go check on your lasagna."

"Thank you."

Rhys headed back toward the kitchen just as Tommy walked into the restaurant.

৵৽

Holy shit! Today is my lucky day!

Tommy nearly yelped at the sight.

He had only just seen her at the gym, but as fate would have it, there at the bar was Adina eating a salad. He stood frozen in place for half a second then gathered up the courage to approach her.

"Excuse me, Ma'am? Is this seat taken?"

Adina froze; her hand stopped half way between her plate and her mouth. She put the fork down and turned to her left. Her heart skipped a beat.

"You again."

Tommy smirked.

"No, it's not taken."

"May I join you?"

"Suit yourself."

Tommy slid into the stool beside her. He contemplated moving in closer to her but decided against it.

He pondered while watching her: I'm not going to let her make me feel bad. That wall did not go up by itself. It's just a protective barricade. I know it's really not who she is.

Within himself, Tommy rationalized Adina's behavior toward him but he stayed put except to turn slightly toward her. Determined, he was the first to speak.

"Adina, maybe we got off on the wrong foot earlier today. Have I done or said something to offend you? What did I do to make you act this way toward me?"

"Well, let's see. How about stalking me?"

"C'mon! That's pretty dramatic."

"Well, you've admitted that you had watched me work out, and that you enjoyed doing that."

"Seeing you at a gym on a property where we both live–and I know you live at the Riverdale Circle Condominiums because only residents can use it–does not constitute stalking!"

"What? Are you a lawyer?"

"No, I'm not a lawyer."

Tommy was becoming extremely frustrated, but he was damned if he was giving up.

"Look, I didn't stalk you."

He waited for some sort of reaction from Adina. None came, so he continued.

"Can we just start over?" He shifted uncomfortably.

"And how do you propose we do that?"

Without responding, Tommy rose from his stool and walked away from Adina toward the exit door. He stepped through it, took a few steps out front and came back into the restaurant. When he re-entered, he walked confidently toward Adina who sat watching him, stunned.

A smile slowly cracked her icy glare while Tommy approached.

"Hello, pretty lady. Is this seat taken?"

Out of nowhere Rhys appeared at the bar with Adina's lasagna.

She's sitting with someone. Who is this guy? The last time she was here she was with some other guy. She's always with some guy.

His brow furrowed.

"Here you are. Can I get you anything else?"

"No, thank you. This looks great!"

"Well, enjoy."

Rhys turned to address Tommy.

"And what can I get you, sir?"

"I'll have what she's having, thank you."

"Sure thing. Anything to drink?"

"Just a Coke, thank you."

"Good. I'll be right back."

Rhys turned to go back into the kitchen. He could hear Adina and her friend laughing.

Hmm. They're amused. Isn't that nice. What's so fucking funny?

Rhys could feel his temperature rising. He was getting upset and fought to stay in control. He remembered the man sitting with Adina at the bar. He recalled that he was there the other night for that cop's party. He wondered if she knew him, and what he was doing with her.

Rhys wanted to talk with her and now he couldn't because this idiot guy was there. He became restless for this guy to hurry up with his meal and leave. He hoped maybe Adina would stick around and talk with him for a while like she did the first time she was there.

A few minutes after taking Tommy's order, he returned with his lasagna and placed it in front of him. Tommy declined anything else, so Rhys turned and disappeared again into the kitchen.

えぐ

"Hmm. This looks delicious!"

"It is," responded Adina.

"But not as delicious as you, I'm sure."

Adina smirked, then smiled.

"So, Tommy, what do you do for a living?"

"I work at the 54ᵗʰ Precinct."

"You're a cop?"

"No. I'm a civilian employee. I oversee their technical department. I write code and do research."

"Interesting. Technology is a booming industry now. But it must be pretty boring being cooped up in an office all day long with just computers for companionship."

"Actually, it's not. It really is quite interesting and there are other people who work with me. What about you? What do you do?"

"I work for an AIDS foundation in the city. I'm a fundraiser for AIDS research."

"Now *that's* interesting. AIDS is a monster. I've lost friends to the disease. You're doing a good thing. I'm impressed, but that shouldn't surprise you."

Adina smiled. This guy's not so bad.

They continued chatting, laughing and eating their meal together, and when they were done, they sat at the bar for hours and talked some more while they drank wine.

Rhys was beyond frustrated. It was obvious he would not have an opportunity to spend any time with her.

Finally, Tommy got up the nerve to ask her out.

"So, Adina, can I ask you a question?"

"What's that?"

"Would you have dinner with me sometime? I'd like to get to know you."

Without hesitation Adina responded, "Sure. That would be nice."

Adina reached down for her pocketbook, pulled out a business card and a pen. On the back of the card, she wrote her home number and handed it to him.

"I've got to get going, but here's my card. My home number is on the back. Call me."

"Great. Thanks! I will."

"Good. I'd better go. Did you see which way Rhys went?"

"He's in the back somewhere. But don't worry about it. I'm going to have another drink. I'll take care of your bill."

"Really? Why would you do such a thing?"

"Because I like you and I enjoyed my time with you. I'm happy we got a chance to chat. Don't worry; ain't no thing."

Tommy smiled his megawatt smile again.

"Ok. I accept. Thank you. But now, I really have to go. Talk with you soon!"

"Yes! Absolutely."

Tommy rose to give Adina a chaste kiss on the cheek. She returned it, smiled and left. He was surprised she let him kiss her. He was ecstatic but he knew he would have to take it slow with this one—she was a keeper.

☙❧

Two days later Tommy called Adina and asked her out to dinner. She didn't need much encouragement and agreed. He discovered over time that they couldn't have been more different. Through sheer determination, mostly on his part, they managed to make it work for a few months. Ups and downs? Like most couples, there were many. Eventually the downs became a bigger part of their relationship.

Adina was extremely controlling and seemed confused about what being in a relationship entailed. She often found herself battling with Tommy regarding not only her social life but her sexual life as well, and this affected him. It wasn't long before the bomb exploded.

"I don't understand why you would want to do this. Why aren't you happy just being with me? Why do you want to go out with other men?"

"Tommy, I am not wearing a ring."

"Is that what you want?" Tommy interrupted.

When Adina didn't respond, he continued.

"A ring? Do you want to get married? Let's get married then!"

"No! I don't want to get married! I especially don't want to marry you if you feel pressured to do so. You just don't understand!"

"You're right! I don't understand. Why don't you explain it to me?"

"Tommy. Look, there are things I like to do. I have a need to be in control in the bedroom. You haven't been exactly amenable when

- 234 -

I try to introduce something new! Sex with you isn't as satisfying to me as it is with someone who is more like me; someone who is more open-minded than you are."

The words came at him like a slap in the face. But he managed to maintain eye contact with her. He didn't blink once while she continued.

"Look, I enjoy your company, I do. I have fun when I'm with you. I laugh when we're together and I feel comfortable around you–as long as we aren't having sex."

"So, you think I'm not good in the sack? I don't satisfy you? Tell me what you need! Tell me what you want me to do!"

Frustrated, Adina paced the room.

Back and forth, back and forth. They had been together close to a year at this point and he even had a key to her apartment, where they were at the moment having this discussion.

Adina bit her lower lip. She needed to think.

He was attentive to her in the bedroom and sometimes she didn't mind the vanilla sex, but more often than not she was left wanting more. She wasn't good as a submissive, even in vanilla sex. Why couldn't he understand what she was saying?

"Tommy, I need you to be more open-minded. Let's try amping it up a little bit."

"What? You want to tie me up? Blindfold me?"

"Yes. That and more."

"More? More!?" Tommy was now yelling.

Adina was now really confused.

Yes, she liked to be the one in control.

Yes, she liked to inflict pain.

No, she didn't like to cuddle afterward.

But at the same time, Tommy made her feel things. He made her feel wanted, even loved and she couldn't handle it. He made her feel the way Benny did so many years ago and he ended up disappearing from her life. Benny's imprisonment all those years ago arrested her soul. She couldn't let that happen again. If she let herself submit to Tommy emotionally, and he ended up leaving her, she knew she would slip into that darkness she had fallen into when she was seventeen. She would probably end up in an institution again. She couldn't let that happen. She had to protect herself.

"Adina, my heart is invested in you. I love you. Always have. I have loved you since the day I first laid eyes on you.

"I don't want to sound like a heartsick puppy, but the truth of the matter is, there isn't anything I wouldn't do for you. I just can't be the person you want me to be. It doesn't feel right in my soul to do those things. Please try to understand that."

Adina's heart broke into a million pieces just to hear Tommy pour his heart out to her like that. He was Benny all over again. She couldn't deny that she had fallen in love again for the first time since forever. She had no choice but to come clean.

She fought the tears welling up in her eyes. She knew she would lose him as soon as she told him what was in her heart.

"Tommy, please. Let's just sit down and be calm. I want to try and make you understand. After I tell you my story, if you want to leave forever, then that is your choice. I won't stop you."

"Adina, you're scaring me. What are you about to tell me?"

"Please, Tommy. Just sit down. Please?"

Adina sat crossed legged on the floor in front of Tommy. He sat on the couch. She took his hands in hers. His face was pale. Eyes? Red and watery.

She sat this way for two hours while she told him the whole ugly story: how she met Benny, the life lessons he taught her, his arrest, her miscarriage, and her stay at the mental institution. Then, too: her suicidal tendencies, how she has to be on medication for the rest of her life, and finally how alone she felt in the world after her parents followed each other in death even though she was estranged from them.

She didn't omit a thing.

She explained how inflicting pain onto others was her way of protecting herself; how this was the only way she felt she could remain sane. She told him that the same way he felt about submitting himself to her in the way that she wanted didn't feel right to him, being without it didn't feel right to her.

When it was all said and done, she collapsed into a ball and sobbed. Tommy sat next to her on the floor, put his arms around her and cried with her. He didn't let her go.

"Oh, baby. I'm sorry; so, so sorry.

"Let's try something. If you agree to what I'm about to propose, and if it doesn't kill me, we can get past this."

Adina looked up at Tommy, confused. She was sure that once she told him about her past he would be out the door. But he was not only still there; he was talking about working things out.

"What? Don't you want to leave while you have a chance? I just gave you an out!"

"Leave? Where am I going to go? I told you. I love you. We can work through this."

He searched for the right words.

"Listen, it sounds to me as though you just need some time to figure out what works best for you. I'm willing to give you a year to do that. Do whatever you need to do to come to a place where you can decide how you want to live your life. I would love to be a part of it, sweetheart, but if you choose not to have me in your life, then I will accept your decision. No questions asked.

"Get it out of your system. We'll talk about it again in a year and decide at that point what we're going to do.

"Deal?"

They were quiet for a long time.

"What? Are you telling me that you're all right with me dating other men? Doing what I've been doing?"

"No. I'm not saying that. What I am saying is that you need to decide what you want without me sweating you. I am willing to take a step back for one year and let you do you. At the end of that time, as I said, we'll decide together what to do next.

"As hard as this is going to be, as much as this arrangement will hurt me, I love you enough to let you go and have you figure it out on your own."

Adina found herself standing on a precipice. She was scared out of her mind. If she continued on with her lifestyle as she had been, then she risked losing him. How many people ever get a second chance at love? Not many. She knew that. But, unlike the other men in her life, she didn't want to hurt him. She would gain nothing from that. If she allowed herself to fall into the abyss again, she might as well commit suicide. There would be no coming back and life was not worth living without him.

"What about you, Tommy? Can I still see you or will you go away?"

"You hold the cards, Adina. Whatever you want."

"I don't want you to go, but I don't want to hurt you either."

"Don't worry about me. It's like I told you: you do you. I'll still be here. We'll still see each other, do things together. We live in the same complex. It just won't be the way it's been.

"You just have to do one thing for me."

"What?" Her brown eyes spilled over.

"Don't give me any details. I don't want to know. I don't think I could bear it."

Adina crawled into Tommy's lap. She held his face in her hands and looked into his eyes searching for some hint he wasn't serious but could find none. She began to cry again and he kissed her hard, passionately.

She pushed him down onto the ground and made love to him—vanilla love. When she reached her climax, she convulsed long and hard; shaking like a leaf with his every caress, then finally collapsed on top of him.

She realized that the only other person who could make her come like that was Benny, and she sighed.

That was her last thought before she drifted off to sleep.

❧❦

Tommy lay awake under her an hour later, still and wide-awake. Tears streamed down his face.

What have I done?

❧❦

"Tommy has a girlfriend!"

"You're kidding! How come you know this and I don't? And, hello to you, too!"

Mason hadn't even gotten completely in through the door when his wife assaulted him. He hadn't seen her so excited in ages.

"I'm sorry, honey. I'm just so damned excited!

"Come. Let me tell you all about it."

Claudia took a hold of Mason's hand and led him into the living room.

"So, I called Tommy today just to see how he was doing. I was concerned about him, you know? It's been months since I'd spoken with him."

"Honey, he's just been busy at work. I see him working late nights at the office all the time."

"That may be so, but I called him anyway."

"What did he say?"

"He said he met a woman a while ago."

"Really? Where?"

"At the gym in the complex where he lives. He also said that they'd been spending time together–getting to know one another."

"Mm-hm ..."

"I don't know, but this one seems promising. Didn't he tell you about her?"

"He did say he met someone. They've had a few meals together, but I didn't get the impression that it was anything serious. Your imagination is in overdrive, sweetie."

"It's not my imagination. There's something going on with him. Call it woman's intuition. You know I'm never wrong!"

She clapped her hands together once and pronounced, "I'm going to invite them over for dinner."

"Whoa! You wait a minute. Don't you think that would send the wrong message?"

"Wrong message? It's just dinner. What's wrong with that?"

"I know you, Claudia. Don't you go getting any ideas, woman!"

"I just want to see him happy, that's all, like us! C'mon, baby!"

"How do you know he's not happy?"

"I didn't say he was unhappy, now did I? I just said I wanted to see him happy like us. You know, in a solid relationship."

Mason was powerless when his wife put her mind to something. He had no out.

"Ok. How could I refuse?"

Claudia clapped like a little girl.

"How's Friday night look to you?"

"Do I have a choice?"

"Nope!"

Mason nodded in defeat.

"Good! I'm going to go call him right now."

Claudia got up on her tippy toes, kissed her husband happily and skipped away.

Mason sighed, shook his head and smiled. Fucking woman. You gotta love her.

ᕲᕤ

"Hey, handsome! Whatcha doin'?"

"Working hard, Claudia. What's up?

"How's your lady friend? What's her name again?"

"Adina. She's fine."

"I bet she is."

Claudia giggled but Tommy didn't respond.

I don't know how long I can keep up this charade, he thought.

"Tommy, Mason and I were wondering what you guys were up to this Friday night. I think it would be nice to get to know Adina seeing as you and her are spending so much time together."

"What? You want to interrogate her? See if she's up to snuff? What are you up to, Claudia?"

"Nothing!" responded Claudia indignantly.

"I just want to be friends with her."

"Yeah, right!"

"Tommy listen, if she makes you happy, then we're happy. You're family. *We're* a family: you, Mason and me. You're my brother-in-law. You're right. I do want to make sure she's good enough for you.

"So, I'm making dinner for you guys on Friday night and I won't take 'no' for an answer."

"Claudia ..."

"Nope. I'll see you guys on Friday, say around eight o'clock?"

"Do I have a choice?"

"Funny, Mason asked me the same question when I approached him with this. You should know better than to ask. Neither one of you ever have a choice when I ask for something. You got that?"

Of course Claudia was kidding and Tommy chuckled. He loved her like a sister.

"Fine. You win. I'll see you Friday night."

"Bring wine ... red!"

"It better be a steak dinner!"

"You bring the wine, I do the cooking. Don't worry about it."

She clucked at him.

"Love you!"

"Love you back."

❧

Adina applied a thin layer of lipstick to her full lips. She fussed with her hair as she took another look in the mirror. She was all set to leave when the phone rang.

"Hello?"

"Hi, Adina. It's Tommy."

"Tommy! Hi! How are you?"

Adina felt her stomach tighten. Two somersaults later she was cognitive again. She loved the sound of his voice and always had a physical reaction to it.

"I'm well. How are you?"

"I'm ok."

"Just ok?"

The words caught in Adina's throat. How could she respond to that without giving away how confused she felt?

"Um, I was just heading out the door."

"Oh. I'm sorry. I was calling to ask you if you wanted to join me for dinner at Mason's Friday night. Claudia's cooking. She's a great cook."

Tommy kicked himself. He sounded like he was trying to convince her to join him before she even said no.

"Mason? Your cop friend?"

"He's more like my brother; and his wife. I told you about them, remember?"

"Yes, I remember, but considering our situation, do you think that's wise? I don't think we should be sending out the wrong message."

"Adina, there are no messages to be sent. I'm asking you out to dinner as a friend. We're just friends having dinner. How about it?"

Tommy waited for a response. He was rubbing his forehead so hard he was getting a headache.

Adina contemplated the invitation. She would love to see him. It's been months since they'd spent any real time together. And, she had to admit to herself that she was miserable sharing only a polite, passing hello at the gym and just wasting time with those guys who let her humiliate and boss them around.

The realization that she missed him sent her into a tailspin.

"I would love to have dinner with you Friday night," she spoke softly into the phone.

Tommy heavily released a sigh of relief.

"Great! I'll pick you up at seven-thirty. Is that good for you?"

"Perfect."

"Good."

Tommy hesitated.

"Adina?"

"Yes?"

"I miss you. I hope you're taking care of yourself."

Adina put her hand to her throat.

"I miss you, too, Tommy. I'll see you Friday."

"Ok. Good night."

"Good night, Tommy."

She couldn't stop saying his name.

Chapter 29
Adina and Rhys

She's back again; and with yet another guy. Boy, she dates a lot of men.

Rhys continued wiping down the glassware while periodically glancing over at Adina's booth.

"Jimmy, I'll take care of booth three," he yelled at the waiter on duty.

"Are you sure?"

"Yeah, why don't you go home?"

"Really?"

"It's not too busy. I can handle it. You'll still get paid for your shift. Don't worry. Go on now, have a good night."

"Ok. Thanks, boss. I'll see you tomorrow."

Rhys waved off his waiter and proceeded to make two dry martinis for booth three.

"Welcome back. Here you are."

He maintained eye contact with Adina.

"Thank you, Rhys. How are you?"

"I'm well, Adina. Nice to see you again."

"I love this place."

"That's good to know. I'll be back shortly to take your order."

When Rhys returned, both Adina and her companion placed their orders from the Italian menu. He ended up talking the whole time they were there and Adina daydreamed about Tommy. She didn't hear a word he said. It was extremely difficult for her to stay focused on the chatter.

Finally, when dinner was over, they stood in the parking lot talking; or rather, her date was trying to convince her to go back with him to his place.

"I promise you won't regret it. I want to please you. Whatever your wish is my command. You could do with me as you please if you'd just join me at my place, " he whispered in her ear.

"I'm sorry, I don't think so."

"What? What do you mean?"

Her date was shocked.

"Just that: I don't think so. That is my wish."

"Are you sure?"

"Are you doubting my desire? You go on. I'll call you."

Adina now regretted even coming out with him. When she first met him, she thought he would be interesting but he didn't evoke in her the desire to want to spend time with him or to control him. She now saw him as a puny man who was constantly whining and moaning about nothing. She wondered if she just didn't have it in her any more.

There had been a few more men like this guy over the past year, but none captured her like Tommy did. She could physically be in attendance with any other man, but her mind was always elsewhere; her mind was always on Tommy just as it was that night.

I'm going to see him on Friday, she thought. Then to herself, a whisper: "I can't wait."

A rent-a-car pulled into the parking lot and let out a woman with red hair, bright red smeared lipstick and a clingy cocktail dress. They watched her teeter on her high heels—so drunk she was barely on her feet.

Adina turned to her date. "You should go. Get the attention of that driver and let him take you home."

"Well, what about you?"

"I'll be fine. You go on. I will be in touch."

Skeptical, he waited. Then relented.

"Fine. Good night, Adina."

"Good night. Thank you for dinner."

Her companion got into the cab and she watched it pull out of the parking lot. When it was out of sight, she turned and walked back into the restaurant. The woman who had been dropped off earlier was making a ruckus at the bar. Adina took a seat as far away as she could get.

She half-smiled. Let the side show begin.

Rhys spotted her immediately and walked the length of the bar to where she sat. Adina spoke first.

"Didn't know you offered live entertainment."

"I don't."

"What's going on?"

"She's upset because I won't sell her a drink. Instead, I offered her coffee on the house to sober her up. She's not having it."

Adina threw back her head and began to laugh.

The drunken blonde hollered over, "Gray! Is I'm fa-fuc-kucking funny ta you, ah, lady?"

Adina's raised eyebrows, tilted head and smirk let the woman know, in no uncertain terms that she was not to be messed with.

"Excuse me?"

Sensing a fight, Rhys quickly stepped over to the woman.

"Look, if you're not going to drink the coffee I've offered you, you cannot stay here and insult my patrons. I'm going to have to ask you to leave."

The woman tried to sit up but swayed in her seat. She licked her lips and again tried to remain upright and speak. She sat a little straighter but she couldn't do both and slurred her words, her body sinking and her head bobbing with each one.

"I'rll talk it block! Tank jewel."

Rhys poured a cup of black coffee and set it in front of her.

Rhys shook his head and returned to Adina.

"Do you get that a lot?"

"Not really. I've never seen her here before. I hope she sobers up soon.

"What can I get you?"

"A glass of Chardonnay, please."

"Sure. Coming up."

Rhys was surprised to see Adina return, but he was not displeased.

Maybe we'll have a chance to chat if this woman doesn't screw things up for me.

"Here you go.

"What happened to your friend?"

"Oh, I sent him home. Didn't feel much like company tonight."

Rhys nodded.

"I understand. You're becoming quite the regular here."

"Yes, I like it here. It's comfortable."

"That's nice to hear."

He paused, and leaned down in front of her.

"If I may be so bold, may I ask you a question?"

"Sure. What's on your mind?"

"Well, I think you're a very nice lady. Very attractive, and no, I'm not trying to make a pass at you."

Adina looked at him skeptically.

"But, please forgive me; I'm concerned about you."

"Oh? How so?"

"It's the gentleman you were here with tonight. He's been here before and he's got a reputation for being quite the ladies' man. He is not a very nice man either. A few nights ago, he was here with another woman. They had a disagreement and I had to interfere. He was manhandling her. She ended up leaving in tears.

"I didn't want to say anything while he was here, but I kept an eye on him, you know, making sure he didn't try the same thing with you."

"I appreciate your concern and if you had approached me on a bad night, I might have told you to mind your business ..."

Rhys lowered his eyes; Adina continued talking.

"... But the truth of the matter is that I don't know why I even accepted his invitation tonight. I don't really know him well at all. He's a business associate.

"I don't know why I'm even saying this, but my boyfriend and I are going through a rough patch right now. He knows I date. We don't have any secrets.

"I don't know why I do the things I do; why I am the way I am."

This last statement caught Rhys' attention.

He thought to himself: What does she mean? Is she like me?

"I'm sorry, Adina. Do you want to talk about it?"

When Adina didn't answer, Rhys kept trying to convince her to stay. He thought they had something in common no one else did. Maybe they could help each other.

"The restaurant is empty except for our friend over there. I can encourage her to leave and we can talk if you'd like. I'm a good listener and I promise, I won't judge."

"That's very kind of you. Thank you. I don't have many friends."

A sudden movement caught Adina's eye. The drunken woman had slipped soundlessly out of her stool and onto the floor.

"Oops! You'd better go see if she's ok."

"Be right back."

Adina didn't wait around. She was upset with herself having divulged so much to the owner. She left a ten-dollar bill on the bar and slipped out.

☙❧

"Are you all right?"

"I meant to do that," the drunken woman spat. "I wanna sleep ..."

Rhys picked the woman up and put her in a booth.

"Well, you can't sleep here. Let me get you some water."

Rhys rose from his crouched position and when he headed back behind the bar for a wet towel and a glass of ice water, he noticed that Adina had left. Twice in one night she slipped out before he could notice and it was the second time he had missed the chance to talk to her. This infuriated him.

"Here you go."

He gave the woman the water and when she drank it all, he placed the cold, wet rag on her forehead. She protested violently.

"Ma'am, you need to stop fighting me. You have to sober up and leave. The restaurant is closed now."

Defeated, the woman nodded.

"You just sit here for a few minutes. I'll be back."

Rhys took one last disgusted look at this mess of a woman. She was the reason why he wasn't getting to know Adina better. His anger rose like a hot flame straight up through his core. He ran his hand through his hair in frustration, sighed deeply and headed toward the cash register.

She should be the one to disappear, not Adina. She had better be ready to leave by the time I'm done with this; otherwise I'm not sure I can control myself. That fucking bitch!

૏❦

After he closed out the cash machine, Rhys stepped out around the back to bring out the garbage. The next day was garbage day and he wanted to make sure to put it out before closing up for the night. She was out there, the lush who had slipped out of her stool earlier. The reason Adina had left.

She called out to him.

"What are you doing here?" he asked.

"I wanted to thank you for helping me," she said slowly, trying not to slur her words.

"You can thank me by going home and sleeping it off."

She stumbled over to him, draping her body against his and rubbing her face along the length of his neck. She ran her hands along his chest, finding his nipples through his sweater and squeezed, hard.

He tried to fight his feelings, but his body betrayed him.

Grabbing her hands, he shook her free.

"Stop it! Get your hands off of me!"

She persisted; wrenching herself free from his grip and just as quickly wrapped her hands around his neck and forcefully kissed him.

Like a movie, he saw flashes of memory before his eyes. He was back at that park again the same as he was with Brenda so many years ago. She had done the same thing, but she did something else too. Brenda had gotten him all worked up and when it was time to finish the act, she couldn't. Instead she laughed. This woman even looked a little like her ... or did she look like her because of the way she behaved?

"Take me home with you," she whispered. "Let me show you how much I appreciate you caring for me."

Rhys couldn't believe his ears. It was Brenda all over again. The familiar ache, the throbbing, was back. He was quickly losing control. He had been so good.

Without thinking, he said aloud, "Why is this happening now?"

"What's wrong? Don't you want to feel good? I can make you feel good," she slurred.

Blinded by the desire to take this woman by the throat and squeeze, Rhys grabbed a hold of her hand and dragged her back to his place above the restaurant. All he could think of was feeling life ebb from her as he squeezed. He was sixteen again and he was in that park with Brenda.

He said calmly, "I guess drowning wasn't enough for you. I'm going to get it right this time."

She didn't even hear the threat.

Rhys hadn't been with a woman since the day he killed her, only men. But now she was back as this whore pushing herself on him.

When they entered his apartment, God came running, tail wagging. Rhys only stopped long enough to pat him on the head and rub his stomach.

"What a fucking ugly dog!"

"Fuck you, bitch!"

Rhys backhanded her across the face, his knuckles cutting her cheek, a thin line of blood slicing it. She wiped the blood away, and licked it. She had a weird look in her eye that infuriated him.

Bitch ain't scared.

He grabbed a hold of her hair and dragged her into the living room where he threw her on to his couch. The woman violently bounced up and down, which caused her to bite her lip. It was now bleeding as well. She sucked on it.

"Oh! So you like it rough, huh?" she asked with a glint in her eye. "Go for it then!"

"Bitch! Take off your clothes."

The woman stood and seductively removed her dress, slowly sitting back down, legs spread. She put one hand on her crotch, running her middle finger around her opening, the other hand twisted a nipple as she held Rhys' gaze.

Rhys stood before her, his mind racing, his stump throbbing. Looking down at this supine, vulnerable being, he put his hand on his waistband and undid his zipper.

He pulled his pants down together with his underwear in one fell swoop. This act seemed to suddenly sober her up and she focused on his knob, which was directly in her line of vision. Like a child, she pointed at him, confused, wondering what the fuck—

At that moment, Rhys saw nothing but red. This woman *was* Brenda and the rage of that day came rushing back at him.

He pounced on her, grabbing her by the neck. She clawed at his hands in a futile attempt to save her own life but the more she scratched and scrambled, the tighter he squeezed; and the tighter he squeezed, the more excited he became. He felt life ebb from her, just like he wanted it to. When she went limp, he climbed on top of her, humping until his thigh muscles cramped and then slipped to the floor. With no relief in sight, pained and curled on the floor at the foot of the couch he rubbed and pulled and tugged to no avail.

Finally irate and exhausted, he scampered to his feet, standing over her, breathing heavily. It had happened again, rather, it *didn't* happen again.

Rhys paced, wearing a path on the carpet. He had a conversation with her in his head:

Where did you come from? I don't even know your name!

You laughed and that's why you're in the predicament you're in. I should never have brought you here.

I'll tell you what the problem is. You're not good enough for me. You recoiled as if I were some sort of disgusting animal. I'm not an animal! You recoil from snakes, other animals not human beings! I am a human being! I have skin, not scales! What's so disgusting about me?

You're the one with the problem! You couldn't do what was necessary to make me cum! Is it because you aren't able to?

Well, here's news for you: You're nothing but a drunken whore!

Seeing the agitated state his master was in, God paced circles around him, panting, waiting for some sign he needed assistance, but none came. Rhys just continued pacing back and forth, back and forth running his hand through his hair.

He looked over at the woman who lay dead on his couch. Her blank eyes stared back at him and he had to turn away. He couldn't bring himself to look at her.

She lay on his couch naked, eyes open and mouth agape. He couldn't bring himself to touch her, close her eyes. He didn't want to dress her, but he had to. When he reached for her dress, he saw how torn up his hands were and he thought of Adina.

I can't let her see me like this.

He had to force himself to go near her and then he thought about what to do with the body. It had been years since he lost control like that.

Blood was caked on the woman's lips and God was now sniffing around the body. He too began to show signs of agitation, but he periodically lapped at the blood until it was wiped clean.

"Hungry, boy?"

God wagged his tail in affirmation.

"You haven't had a treat in a long while, huh?

"Don't worry. You've been a very good boy and Daddy's going to show you how much he appreciates it."

With that, Rhys gathered up his knives, a roll of duct tape and a new bundle of plastic wrap he used in the restaurant for fresh meat. He went downstairs, started up the RV then came back upstairs. He dressed the woman then pulled her upright. He put an arm over his shoulder, grabbed her shoes and pocketbook then half-carried her downstairs and into the RV.

RJ drove east to the Bronx/Lower Westchester border ending up on a dark desolate shoulder on the interstate. He cut the lights and went to the rear of the RV. The woman's dress had fallen slightly in front and a full breast popped out in all its morbid glory. He unfurled his knife holster and pulled out the sharpest butcher knife he had. He quickly sliced the breast clean off her chest, blood running free on to the plastic.

No silicone. Good. This is for God.

He wrapped the breast in brown paper then in plastic and put it in a cooler. Next, he grabbed his knapsack and got out of the RV with an empty container he sometimes used to fill with gasoline.

In case someone sees me, it will look like I ran out of gas and walked to a station, he thought.

He was in a loading zone where butchers and fishermen sold their wares. Scanning the area, he searched for heavy objects like bricks or something he could use to weigh down the body, when he spotted a construction site a few yards away.

There was a pile of concrete chunks and stone in a dark corner. He gathered up as many as he could carry in his bag and walked away. A few minutes later he was back in the RV and wrapping the woman and concrete stone neatly and securely.

He drove to the next shoulder overlooking the Bronx River and parked. He waited a bit to determine the traffic pattern. When he decided there was no danger of being caught, he jumped out and quickly tossed her over the railing.

He waited a moment but then realized that if her body didn't sink there was nothing he could do about it. He put the RV in gear and drove off.

☙❧

Rhys whistled with relief as he walked through the door. He picked up God's bowl and filled it half way with dry dog food then he unwrapped his latest victim's breast and put it on a cutting board. After slicing it in half, he grabbed a curved salad chopper and began to rhythmically chop up half into small pieces, put them in God's bowl, mixed it well with his dry food and put it down for him. When he was done, he wrapped up the other half–first in wax paper, then plastic wrap–and put it all in the freezer.

God looked up at his master gratefully and licked his mouth then proceeded to eat his meal in less than five gulps.

Chapter 30
Adina and Tommy

She had been daydreaming at her desk when the ringing phone jangled her nerves.

"Good afternoon. This is Adina Cruz."

She'd dropped "Rosario" from her name long ago because it was unusual to be a Latina of power in the business world, let alone one with two ethnic last names. People got confused and they flip-flopped it. It made things simpler to use just one name.

"Adina? Hi. It's Tommy. How are you?" He switched ears and gripped the handset.

"Oh, Tommy! Hi! I'm sorry I was distracted."

"You sound it. So, how are you?" he repeated.

"I'm fine, how are you?"

"I'm excited about seeing you on Friday. That's why I'm calling—to make sure we're still on. We are, aren't we?"

"I still don't think it's a good idea, but if you're amped about it, then I'll be there."

"Well, I am amped and I don't think you have anything to worry about."

"If you say so. Can you remind me of their address again? I don't know if I have it. I have a general idea, but ..."

Tommy interrupted her.

"Why? Don't you want to ride with me over there? I mean, we live in the same complex; we're going to the same place ...

"Do you have something to do afterward? Somewhere to go?"

Adina remained silent.

"I'm sorry. I shouldn't have asked you that. Do you have a pen and paper handy?"

Adina felt like shit. She didn't usually worry about other peoples' feelings, but Tommy was different. He reminded her so much of Benny that she naturally succumbed to whatever he wanted.

She reconsidered.

"You know what? You're right. Why don't you pick me up at seven thirty?"

"That sounds great! I'll see you then."

"Great. I have to go now."

"All right. Bye then."

"Bye. Oh, and Tommy?"

"Yeah?"

"I'm looking forward to seeing you."

"Me too."

Adina smiled and said good-bye then hung up the phone. She tried to get back to work but it was useless–she couldn't concentrate on the budget she was working on. She rose from her seat, poured herself a glass of water and walked over to the window. Her mind drifted to the last time she and Tommy made love. He was so tender, so loving and took care to make it last. It was as if he was making love to a virgin. For the first time in a very long time, she felt loved, cared for and protected. At that moment, she was a real woman; not the semblance of one who cared for no one but herself.

She was a mess emotionally that night having just poured her heart out to him. They each had explosive orgasms and afterward he cried too. She knew that because she felt his chest move with the ragged breathing as she lay on his chest, but she never mentioned it. The memory caused her to hug herself. The dam broke and she dropped to the floor in a heap and cried for a long time. Unmoored thoughts played on a loop in her head: I don't know what to do! I don't know how to be without inflicting pain on people. I don't want to hurt him, but I can't stop doing what I do because it makes me feel alive.

She knew her feelings were schizophrenic. She felt disjointed as though there were two of her battling each other for control.

She had stopped her medication just after that night with Tommy and she was becoming more and more despondent.

She rose from the floor, took a deep breath and straightened up. She stepped into her private powder room and splashed cold water on her face, re-applied her lipstick and got back to work.

✧✧

Tommy hung up the phone with a huge grin on his face. He was still smiling when Mason walked into his office.

"Hey, Tommy! What's the cheesy grin for? Adina?"

"Yeah. I just confirmed our date on Friday."

"Look at you! You're in lurve! Ha! Ha!

"I'm happy for you, my brother. Claudia's looking forward to meeting her and quite frankly, I am too."

"I'm a bit nervous about this."

"Why?"

"Mason, I'm going to tell you something, but please–don't judge."

"You know me; no judgments here. What's up?"

"Adina and I are kind of on a break, so ..."

Mason interrupted.

"On a break? What's that about?"

"I love her ... but ..."

"What? What is it?"

"Adina has had some issues in her past that affect her behavior in a relationship. She's confused about some things."

"What do you mean 'issues'? Is she confused about being with men or women? If it's women, then that might turn out to be a good thing for you." Mason waggled his eyebrows.

"No! Mason!"

"Then what? Spit it out, man!"

"She has certain sexual tastes I'm not into."

Mason raised an eyebrow.

"Ok ..."

"She's been experimenting with some mild BDSM."

"I still don't see anything wrong with that. You know, I've got an extra pair of handcuffs. You can have them."

"Jeez! Why did I even say anything?"

"Ok. I see this is an issue for you. Talk to me."

"I gave her a year to figure it out. I don't see her as often as I'd like and it drives me crazy when I'm not with her because I don't know what she's doing or who she's doing it with."

"Whoa! Whoa! 'Who she's doing it with'? Are you saying that she's seeing other people?"

"Mason, she likes to dominate, to inflict pain and she's got 'friends' who like to be dominated. She sometimes sees them."

Tommy hung his head.

"I was stupid to let her do this. I'm going to lose her."

"Tommy, listen to me. Don't you think it is better that you know early on what she's like? If she comes back to you and you decide to get back together, then it will all be worth it. If she doesn't, then it wasn't meant to be. Lots of people go on breaks in relationships. Don't sweat it."

"You're right. I've got to get back to work. Talk later?"

"Sure. My day's over anyway. I did forty-eight hours straight. I'll see you tomorrow night."

"Get some rest."

❧◆❧

The doorbell rang. Adina looked at her watch. 7:25 p.m. It could only be Tommy.

Always on time.

She took one last look in the full-length mirror. She wore a simple black sheath with a sheer straight neckline in the front and cutout "V" in the back. A small, heart-shaped pink diamond dangled brightly from a thin white-gold chain. She centered it right above her full breasts. Her hair, in a loose bun atop her head, exposed the matching earrings that twinkled in her ears. Her feet were adorned with simple black pumps.

She shuffle-ran to the door and opened it.

"Hi, Tommy. Come in. Why didn't you use your key?"

Tommy greeted her with a kiss on the cheek and a warm hug. He ignored her question, instead commenting on her scent.

"Mmm! You smell wonderful! Is that new perfume?"

"No. It's Opium, my favorite. My dad gave me a bottle when I was sixteen and I've worn it ever since for special occasions."

Tommy was happy to hear this.

"So, this is a special occasion, huh?"

"Any time I'm with you is special. Ready to go?"

Tommy's heart lit up but, again, he remained silent about her comment.

"Sure. Let's go."

Adina grabbed her bag and a fur-trimmed shawl instead of a coat for the unusually warm January evening. They would only be outdoors briefly–from the car to the Joneses and back. Taking it from her, Tommy draped it over her shoulders then held the door open for her. In the car, they listened to oldies music and had lighthearted conversation about the singers. They arrived at Mason and Claudia's brownstone in Harlem right on time.

❧

The buzzing at the door alerted the Joneses that their guests had arrived.

"Promise me you won't say anything, Claudia. I mean it. It is none of our business what they do. Do you hear me?"

"All right! I hear you! Jeez."

"Good. Now smile."

She practiced an outrageous and cheesy grin on her husband before reaching the door and he rolled his eyes.

❧

"Welcome! Come in!"

Tommy and Mason shook hands and Claudia stepped around them to greet Adina.

"And you must be Adina! It is so good to meet you! I'm Claudia."

"It's nice to meet you as well, Claudia. You have a lovely home. Thank you for having us over."

"Why, thank you. And having you guys over, well, we should do this more often!

"Mason, did you say hello to Adina?"

"I'm about to!

"Adina baby! Come here and give a real man a hug!"

Adina smiled and embraced Mason as Claudia hugged Tommy.

Adina simpered and churned a bit internally: Oh my gosh! What have I gotten myself into? These people are so normal!

"So, Tommy, where's the wine I asked you to bring?" Claudia asked.

"Right here, Momma Bear. I brought two bottles of chilled Chardonnay and a bottle of Merlot because I just know you made steak, right?"

Claudia rolled her eyes.

"Yes, I made steak. Let's break open one of these bottles of Chardonnay until we're ready to eat."

They all went inside and it was light banter and getting-to-know-you conversation. After a while, Claudia asked Adina to help her in the kitchen with the salad.

"Adina, do you mind chopping the vegetables over there?"

"No, not at all."

Adina reached for the carrots, rinsed them out over the sink and patted them dry. She took a potato peeler to task but after about thirty seconds she could feel Claudia eyeballing her. Claudia would not be a good poker player.

"Is there something wrong?" Adina asked her.

"Well, there is something I want to say to you. You can tell me to mind my business, and I won't be upset, but I've got to get this off my chest."

All sorts of alarms went off in Adina's head. She switched to a knife and began slicing green peppers.

"What's on your mind, Claudia?"

"It's Tommy."

"What about him?"

"He's in love with you, Adina."

"I love him, too."

"Then why the break?"

"That's none of your business."

"Ok, I'm sorry. But know this. Tommy and Mason are tighter than brothers. That makes him my family. He's a good guy and I don't want to see him hurt. You feel me?"

"I feel you. Is that all?"

Adina was unperturbed.

"I just wanted you to know how it is."

"You did indeed."

"Is this enough salad?" Adina asked, dismissing her.

☙❧

"Thank you for having us over. Dinner was delicious."

Adina was entirely annoyed with Claudia, but she was cool throughout.

Initially, she was angry with Tommy, but she couldn't see it in his personality to be the type to go blabbing about their relationship problems, even with people he was close to.

She took a long, hard look at Claudia and how she carried herself. The dinner conversation faded into the distance and she busied herself with appearing interested as her mind fidgeted:

Hmmm, I wonder if she's using the cuffs on him? The way she struts about is annoying. She's nothing to worry about. I can handle her.

Tommy's stretching and the winding down of voices brought her to. Then parting words, hugs and the typical see-you-out-see-you-soon pleasantries.

Finally, they were out the door, getting into the car and driving off. A relief.

☙❧

Mason banged into the kitchen. "I noticed the chill in the air. Did you say something to Adina?"

Claudia scrubbed violently at invisible dirt.

"What! I just wanted her to know not to mess with his feelings. What's wrong with that?"

"I told you not to say anything! Why can't you ever keep your mouth shut!?"

"Whoa. You know how Tommy is. He gets so wrapped up in the women he's with. She needed to know that he had family that loved and supported him. She needed to know that she had people, namely me, to answer to if she fucked up. What's wrong with that?"

"You acted ghetto, Claudia. He's a grown-ass man! Mind your business! I want you to call her, in the morning–first thing–and then I want you to apologize. Got it?"

"I got it, I got it."

"I'm sleeping on the couch. I'm so pissed off at you right now. You always do things your way without a fucking care how your words and actions affect other people."

Claudia was stunned. She couldn't understand why he was so upset. She was just trying to protect Tommy.

᠄᠄᠄

"Adina, I'm so sorry about Claudia's behavior tonight. I don't know what got into her."

"It's all right. She loves you, Tommy, and she doesn't want to see you hurt. No one is ever going to be good enough for you as far as she's concerned. Besides, I'm not worried about it."

Tommy nodded and reached over to squeeze her hand.

"Can I ask you something?"

"Sure."

"There are two months left on our agreement. I admit, I've been going crazy wondering what you've been up to, and if you've been ... you know. I want you to know that when we do get together like this, it is only about your company. I'm not looking or hoping for anything more; though, if anything did happen, I would be over the moon."

"I made an agreement with you and I always keep my word."

"And I appreciate that, Tommy. You have no idea how much I do."

Tommy drew his lips into a tight line.

"Adina, I was wondering: are you happy? I mean, the lifestyle, the domination thing. Is that something that you want for the long term?"

"Tommy ... " She looked up at the ceiling.

"Ok. Ok. I won't push it. It's just that we're getting close to the end of our agreement, and I just wondered where I stood–where *we* stood–and if we have a chance, that's all."

"Tommy, I have mixed feelings about it. And I miss you too. There has to be a happy medium."

"Well, you just showed me that you've been thinking about it. I'm good with that."

It was time to change the subject.

"Do you want to go somewhere for a nightcap? I really don't want this night to end with this conversation."

"That's a good idea. Let's go someplace close to home?"

"That sounds good."

"Music?"

Adina nodded. She didn't want to talk any more. She needed to think.

Tommy reached down and turned on the radio then focused on the road. His mind was racing as well.

ℜ℞

"Hello, Adina, Mr. Ortiz."

"Please, call me Tommy."

"'Tommy' it is then. What can I get you?"

Adina turned to Tommy.

"Let's live! How about Cognac?"

"Cognac? Why don't you order?"

Adina turned to Rhys.

"Can we have two 'Between the Sheets'?"

Tommy was thrown.

Between the Sheets? What the fuck was that? Was that a message?

"Don't think I've ever made that drink. What's in it?"

"It's Cognac–Remy Martin please, white rum, Cointreau, and lemon juice. Shake three ounces of each over crushed ice. That should be enough for two. Garnish with a slice of lemon and voila!"

"Got it. Be right back."

Tommy watched Adina, doe-eyed.

"Wow! That's exotic. Go to many fancy functions, do you?"

They both laughed out loud.

"It's strong, but I'll think you'll like it."

That night, Adina went home with Tommy.

⚶

Two months would pass after Adina went home that night with Tommy. A night 'between the sheets' indeed.

⚶

Friday afternoon, finally!

Adina sat restlessly in the conference room. It was Adina's and Tommy's anniversary and the night that their agreement came to an end. She'd promised him earlier that she would be home, where he was preparing their dinner, at a decent time. She couldn't wait to see his face when she told him that she was giving up the life and committed to working toward a more stable relationship with him.

She decided then she can give up any hope of being a Domme in the bedroom with him, but she still thought she could slowly introduce him to other things that weren't so aggressive. There were feathers, food, handcuffs, a playful slap on the ass ... plenty of ways that she could still do some of the things she enjoyed doing. She was sure he would be open to some of those less-than-vanilla activities.

The meeting ended and after polite farewells she was finally in the cab heading home. She was happy and she realized she hadn't been this happy since Benny.

Little did she know that would be her last day on Earth.

⚶

Tommy let himself into Adina's apartment. He had two arms full of groceries, flowers and wine for their anniversary dinner.

She's going to be here in an hour. Everything has to be perfect, he thought. He whistled and nearly beamed with anticipation.

And it was. Adina arrived right on time. She seemed happy. There was brightness in her eyes, a glow in her face. She looked angelic through Tommy's lovesick eyes.

Dinner was perfect: grilled steak, garlic mashed potatoes, buttered string beans with roasted almonds, a rich port and an unexpected proposal of marriage after Adina gave Tommy the news that she was committed to a stable, normal relationship. They made love under the moonlight and then Adina asked him to stay the night for the first time.

Tommy left her bed only to go home and get a change of clothes for work the next day. He was only gone twenty minutes at most and left his apartment still feeling the voltage from their frenzied lovemaking. He was lost in thought about engagement rings, weddings and honeymoons as he walked back to her place, when suddenly he remembered that he hadn't locked her door behind him. He hoped she had. A little bit concerned, he rushed to return to his fiancée.

When he reached her door, he found that it was still unlocked and chastised himself for being so careless. He felt something at his feet but dismissed it. He turned on the foyer light and caught sight of his beloved Adina lying in a pool of blood on the beautiful parquet floor. The scarlet blood horribly contrasted against its pale blonde color.

Tommy dropped to his knees beside his beloved and let out a sound that would send chills down the spine of a stone statue.

In agony, he reached for his cellphone and called his best friend. "Mason will know what to do," he cried.

But Mason could do nothing for either of them. Tommy was the main suspect and was shortly arrested for the murder of Adina Cruz Rosario.

Chapter 31
Tommy's Devastation

Weeks passed before Tommy was cleared of Adina's murder. A thorough investigation showed that although his fingerprints were everywhere, and his semen was found within her, there was also evidence pointing to another person being in the apartment.

The stickiness Tommy felt on the light switch when he turned it on upon his return to Adina's place was pre-ejaculation fluid. Its DNA did not match his. Though DNA from skin cells scraped from under Adina's nails belonged to both Tommy and the unknown person, there was also DNA from the blood of the other person. Additionally, she did not have tears in her genitalia indicating forced sex.

Three types of hair were found in the bedroom: Adina's and Tommy's were positively identified. The third hair type potentially belonged to the perpetrator's. That same hair type was found on Adina's forehead and in the foyer.

The battered condition in which her body was found did not jibe with what Tommy told the police about their evening together. To lend credence to his assertions, he had no marks on him. There was no evidence of a fight on his own body.

At this time, there was no way of knowing exactly whose DNA it was but it was discovered that it matched DNA found at the scene of two other murders. One was a male whose genitals had been cut off. His rotting body was found in an abandoned building in Brooklyn. He had skin under his nails.

The second was a woman found floating in the Bronx River a year prior. Her body was not in an advanced state of decomposition due to the plastic wrapping she was in, so the crudely sliced breast was obvious. She too had skin under her nails.

In addition, dog hair was also found on her face near a cut that looked like it had been wiped clean. The DNA in each of these cases matched the DNA collected at Adina's crime scene.

Now there was evidence of a string of murders linked to the unknown suspect, who by virtue of the sheer number of murders–Adina's making it three–was now deemed a serial killer.

The one thing that they found intriguing was the fact that there had been a body part cut away in all the cases except for Adina. The detectives deduced that the reason for this was either lack of time or the killer knew her. Adding credibility to this theory was that Adina's hair had been positioned to cover up a bruise on her forehead, a seemingly caring gesture.

The water that had overflowed in the tub could explain the reason she was found naked. She was apparently getting ready for a bath when she was attacked.

In the other case, the woman was dressed.

But these were details that were kept confidential.

Everyone involved in this investigation was frustrated. None of the evidence they had was identifiable so they had to let Tommy go.

Mason was in the courtroom when Tommy was released. He let out a whoop so loud he was reprimanded. Embarrassed, he stepped out of the courtroom and waited for Tommy to complete the process of his release. Afterward, Mason put his arm around Tommy's shoulder and they walked out of the courthouse together. Luckily, there was no press standing on the steps and a short while later, they were driving uptown toward Claudia and Mason's home in Harlem.

"We'll get the son of a bitch who did this, Tommy. I promise you. You just hang tight. We. Will. Get. Him."

Each word of Mason's promise was punctuated with a fist to the steering wheel.

"I give you my word."

"I can't believe she's gone, Mason. We were going to get married."

Tommy dropped his head into his hands and sobbed like a little boy. Mason reached out to squeeze his best friend's–his brother's–shoulder. His heart ached for him.

Seeing his friend in this condition, Mason decided to drive around for a bit. He thought that if Tommy declined to stay with him and Claudia, he wasn't going to just drop him off at home to wallow in his pain. He himself had no appetite but thought maybe Tommy was hungry. Whatever he was fed in jail couldn't have been nourishing. He stole a glance at his childhood "bestie" who was staring out the window, silent and morose. After a while, Tommy realized they were nowhere near his home. He had assumed Mason would take him home.

"Mason, where are we going?"

"I just thought we'd ride around a bit, you know, give you a chance to breathe after spending time inside." He paused and looked over at him.

"Is there somewhere you'd like to go?"

"Yeah. Home. My home."

"Tommy, why don't you stay with us for a little while? I don't think it's a good idea for you to be alone. We would love to have you, and Claudia's already set up the spare bedroom for you. You know how she is. What do you say?"

"I appreciate the offer, but I disagree. I should go back to the apartment and get started on settling Adina's affairs." He made an unconscious shift toward the door.

"Tommy, I know you were close, but maybe you could wait a few days before doing that, huh?" Mason begged.

"No. I think I need to do this as soon as possible.

"You know, I've been thinking. I haven't really done anything with my apartment because of work, but Adina has done a beautiful job with hers. I've decided to sell my apartment and move into hers."

"Tommy, are you sure? I mean, why?"

"Why not, Mason? Her apartment is smaller, cheaper than mine, and that's where we were the happiest.

"I don't want to talk about it anymore," Tommy said, his voice cracking.

"Ok. Ok. I understand. How about we compromise? Stay with us a few days, just until I can get the foyer cleaned up, please? The chalk outline is still there and the ..."

"... the blood," Tommy finished.

"Yeah. The blood. Tommy, I can get a cleanup crew in there within forty-eight hours. You can move in afterward, ok?"

Tommy began crying again.

"Ok. But please Mason, don't try and change my mind."

"You got it."

Please, God, change his mind, he prayed.

Relieved for the moment, Mason queried:

"Hungry?"

"Not really, but I could use a drink."

"All right, then. A beer might open up your appetite. There's an Irish Pub just a few blocks from here. They make the best, crispiest fish and chips in town. It's the middle of the afternoon. It shouldn't be too crowded right now. How about it?"

"No. Let's go to Rhys' Pieces."

"Why there?"

"Adina loved it there. I want to be where her spirit is."

"All right."

Tommy sighed deeply.

Mason reached over and put his hand on his friend's chest, over his heart.

"For the record, buddy, Adina's spirit is right here. Don't you ever forget that, you feel me?"

"I feel you."

Tommy's response wasn't just colloquial. The promised protection that came with that love made him cry again. Mason patted Tommy's chest then put his hand back on the steering wheel.

⤞⤝

When they arrived at the restaurant, it was fairly busy. It was early evening Friday. There were a few people sitting at the bar and scattered booths had families in them eating early dinners. They chose a table near the back. Though people in the neighborhood knew about the Riverdale Circle Condominium murder, no one recognized him as having been the accused. Tommy was grateful for that.

It felt like they were sitting a long time before anyone came by to wait on them even though Rhys noticed their arrival. He thought to himself: What are they doing here? And why isn't he in jail?

Rhys breezed by their table with a tray of food and stopped only long enough to tell them that he would be right back.

"I wonder why that guy is always the one to tend to our table," Tommy said.

"What do you mean?"

"I mean, look at the way he's always doing something. He's always either tending bar or taking care of one table or another. He always took our order whenever Adina and I came here. Why haven't we ever been taken care of by a waiter? It was always him."

Mason turned and watched Rhys hustle about then turned back to Tommy.

"You don't like him, do you?"

"I have no opinion of him. Adina seemed to like him and he was always attentive to her; always respectful. I don't know. There's something weird about him. He was just too nice to her."

"Tommy? What are you saying?"

"I'm not saying anything, just that he was too freaking nice to her." He lowered his voice to a whisper. "I'm going to ask him about that first chance I get."

"Whoa, listen. You're angry. I don't know what I would do if I were in your shoes. I understand that you need someone to blame. You want justice. But this guy, Rhys? He's just a restaurant owner who took a shine to Adina. You can't be mad at him. She was a beautiful, beautiful woman. She was a human testament of your good taste. Don't go starting something you'll regret." He stared down at his menu. "I don't like him. There's something strange about him and I'm going to find out what it is."

The next thing Tommy knew, Rhys was standing before him. He looked up and saw his mouth moving but the words that came out of the hole in his face were garbled.

"Excuse me?"

Mason tensed.

"I was just saying how sorry I am for your loss. Adina was a beautiful person and I hope they find the killer.

"If there is anything I can do, please do not hesitate to ask."

Tommy stared at Rhys in deadly silence.

Why does he keep running his hand through his hair?

"Why do you keep doing that?"

"What?"

"Run your hands through your hair?"

"I ... I ..."

Mason interrupted the potential inquisition. "Can we have two Coronas with lime please?"

Tommy looked at his hands crossed on the table, then up at Rhys, thinking: You're hiding something and I'm going to find out what it is.

Rhys looked relieved not to have to answer Tommy's question.

"Yes, two Coronas. I'll be back shortly."

Rhys was a nervous wreck.

৯৯৯

A week after Tommy's release, he held a funeral and memorial service in Adina's honor. He was amazed at the people who went to pay their respects. Well known politicians, entertainers, prominent doctors, medical researchers, and even patients at the Foundation who were well enough to travel showed up. He was very touched. At one point, Dr. Boulas pulled Tommy aside to talk with him.

He was very old now and seemed much feebler with the emotion of Adina's passing.

"She will be missed. She was feisty but she was good at her job. I grew to love her as if she were my own daughter. If there is anything you need, anything at all, young man, you be sure to come to me. I will do everything in my power to help you."

"Thank you, Dr. Boulas. She spoke kindly of you and enjoyed the work that she did for you and the Foundation. She once told me that you saved her life by hiring her as your intern when she was in high school. She was very grateful."

"She had no idea, did she?"

"What do you mean?"

"Poor child saved my life as well. She was so eager to learn she inspired me to continue with this work and she made us what we are today. I had no idea we would end up as big as we are."

Tommy nodded. It was nice to see that other people loved his Adina and saw her inner beauty just as he did.

"Oh! Before I forget, here is the key to her office. Feel free to go anytime you like to collect her things."

"Thank you, Doctor. I will make it there on Saturday morning, if that's all right with you."

"Of course, whenever it is convenient. I assure you, no one will bother you."

"I must leave now, before it gets too late."

"She loved you very much, Tommy. Hold on to that love. She is in your heart and therefore with you all the time. Don't you ever forget that, young man."

Tears welled up in Tommy's eyes. She had spoken to the doctor about him. It was obvious. He shook the doctor's hand and watched him get into his limo then roll away.

Chapter 32
Tommy Makes a Discovery

The following Saturday, having had no sleep, Tommy arrived early at Adina's office to collect her personal belongings. It was eight in the morning when he flicked on the light and swept his eyes around the room. There had been a thunderstorm the night before, and the sun was just starting to peek through the clouds. The shadows in the room played with his imagination.

Tommy slowly walked the perimeter of the room, closely examining photos, certificates and awards hanging on the walls as he did so. He ran his fingertips along the edge of Adina's desk and then walked around it to sit in her chair that faced the window and slowly lowered himself into it. He shifted his weigh, closed his eyes and took a deep breath. He could smell her perfume in the room. He lovingly caressed the armrests in an attempt to soak her up.

The rays of sunlight blinded him for half a second and he squinted. He rose and lowered the blinds just enough so that he could sit at Adina's desk comfortably but not plunge the room back into darkness. Now back in Adina's chair, he pushed himself away from her desk, stretched out his feet in front of him and laid his head against the leather headrest. His sorrow flowed from his eyes before he could bring his hands to his face.

I don't know if I could do this today. How am I supposed to go on living without her?

Even though the sun was now shining brightly, he had slipped into an abyss so dark that pulling himself out of it would be difficult. A soft knock on the door temporarily brought him back home.

"Good morning, Tommy."

"Good morning, Dr. Boulas. I didn't mean to disturb you."

"Not to worry. I was looking out for you. Come have a cup of coffee with me."

Tommy almost declined but then realized that Dr. Boulas loved her as well.

"That would be nice, Doctor. Of course."

Together they walked over to the pantry in silence. The doctor poured himself a cup and told Tommy to help himself. That was the only exchange between them until they sat at a table near a window.

"Tommy, you don't have to do this today."

"I do, Doctor. I want to settle Adina's affairs as soon as possible so I could try to put my life back together."

"Are you going keep your residence? It might be a good idea to consider selling. It will be hard to live there after what's happened, don't you think?"

"I have put my apartment up for sale."

"Good. What do you plan to do about Adina's apartment?"

"I'm keeping it. I didn't know that Adina named me sole benefactor in her will, so I have a right to do with it as I please. It pleases me to keep it. Most of my personal belongings have been moved there already, but I haven't completely moved in, nor have I slept there yet."

"Tommy, is that a good idea? Keeping it?"

"I want to be where she was last happy."

"I doubt her last moments were happy."

Tommy shifted and tensed up. "She was happy with me before she was killed. That is what I choose to remember."

"I loved her too, Tommy, you know that. She was like a daughter to me. My heart broke when I heard what had happened. My first thought was that I was no longer going to start my day with some witty comment from her.

"She was a pistol, you know! Everyone here loved and respected her. Whatever happened that night, whatever condition she was in when you found her—I don't want to know the details—just know that she will be a huge loss to us all.

"I can see how devastating this has been for you and I want to support you. Please know that I am here for you. Whatever you need, no matter what it is, no matter what time of day, please, please ... "

The doctor's words hung in the air. His voice cracked and he couldn't go on. Tommy sat there silently, his hand over the doctor's. Finally, when he found his voice again, Dr. Boulas spoke.

"You are my only connection to her. If you feel like talking, venting, screaming, crying–whatever you need, I want you to come to me. Deal?"

There was a twinkle in the doctor's teary eyes.

Tommy had a frog in his throat and his chin fell to his chest. His body shook as he sobbed uncontrollably. Dr. Boulas rubbed his back and let him release his pain all over his shirt. They stayed like that for a long time.

Eventually, they finished their coffee; each lost in their own thoughts and memories of a woman both loved but each had a different view of. Afterward, Tommy returned to her office to pack her things.

ॐॐ

Tommy wiped his brow, put his hands on his hips and looked around. The walls in Adina's office were now bare. The bookshelves only contained Foundation-related documents. All that was left to do was to clear out her desk. It would take several trips to his car to load it up.

He put an empty box atop Adina's desk and sat down. He began by emptying out the lower drawers and tossing personal contents into the box. Makeup, aspirin, an extra pair of panty hose, a pair of flats, a mirror, a hair brush, hair accessories, lotions ... all the things women can't do without.

He mentally talked himself through the process: I should maybe toss this stuff. It's not like she's going to need this ... No. I will keep it all so that I can keep her memory alive. One more drawer and I'll be done.

Tommy pulled open the middle desk drawer. There he found a ruler, batteries, a few loose rubber bands, and a novelty USB drive with her initials glued on with tiny crystals.

Hmmm. I wonder if this contains Foundation business, he wondered.

Tommy fired up Adina's computer. After a few seconds, the log-in window appeared demanding a password. He tried her birthday and each of her parents' birthdays but none of those dates worked. He thumbed the drive and put it in his pocket.

I really don't think a bejeweled thumb drive is going to contain Foundation documents. I'll check it out at home. I'll return it if it does.

࿊

When he arrived home from collecting Adina's belongings, he organized what he would keep, what he would donate and what would go into storage. He was getting ready for his evening shower when the flash drive fell out of his pocket as he undressed. After placing it on the desk next to his computer, he showered. When he was done, he poured himself a drink and sat down at his computer.

The flash drive wasn't protected. There were two items on it. One was a calendar showing activities spanning the last year, and the other was a spreadsheet. The spreadsheet was four columns wide; the first column bore four names. The second, third and fourth columns had personal data corresponding to each name, including height/weight and contact information; a place alongside it with what appeared to be a date next to it and the last column listed what he could only imagine were sexual preferences for each of the names.

One name, Jason Meade, had a star next to it along with the number one and a range of numbers: 1990–1999. Tommy assumed this was the length of time she spent with this person.

Tommy stopped scanning the screen to jog his memory.

Wait a minute! Isn't Jason Meade that ambassador that committed suicide ten years ago? Was she the reason?

Tommy stared at the computer screen in the study of his apartment. He reached for the scotch on the rocks he had been drinking and took a gulp. He looked at the screen again, stunned by what he saw.

Elbows on his desk, he rubbed his temples with his fingers then rose.

What if one of these guys knows who might have done this? What if one of these guys killed Adina?

Right then and there Tommy decided he would contact these men and see what he could glean from them. He wouldn't tell a soul until he had some concrete information.

Chapter 33
The "Investigation"

"Yes, Mr. Sturgis?"

"This is he."

"Yes, my name is Tomas Ortiz. I'm calling from the 54th Precinct in Riverdale."

"The police?"

"What can I do for you officer?"

Tommy never said he was a police officer but did not correct the man.

"As part of the investigation into the murder of Adina Cruz, we are interviewing all her friends and colleagues."

"I don't know how helpful I can be. I really didn't know her that well."

"We will decide that, sir. Sometimes the smallest detail can be helpful."

"Well, if you think I can help, I'll do what I can."

"Good. It's almost lunchtime. Why don't you meet me at 1259 Riverdale Avenue here in Riverdale, say one o'clock?"

"That works for me."

"I'll see you then. Oh, by the way? I won't be in uniform. I'll be the one at the small table in the back with the blue striped shirt.

"I look forward to meeting you, Mr. Sturgis. Thank you."

Tommy didn't wait for a response and hung up.

He had spent the day contacting these men and was able to set up meetings with them all except for Jason Meade. Tommy was right. He was the ambassador who had committed suicide and judging by the dates next to his name and the date he killed himself, it was safe to assume he was despondent over Adina. But ... he would never know for sure now. So many unanswered questions.

He looked at his watch. He had over an hour before he had to be at the restaurant to meet Wade Sturgis. He went to Adina's spreadsheet and dialed the next number on the list.

Mr. Childs? Damien Childs?"

"Yes?"

"Good afternoon. My name is Tomas Ortiz. I'm calling from the 54th Precinct in Riverdale ..."

And so it went. Tommy was able to set up meetings with all three men remaining on Adina's spreadsheet. He was hoping to gather enough information that would allow him to find her killer. What he found interesting was that all three men assumed he was a policeman, and he did nothing to dissuade them.

∾∾

Tommy entered Rhys' Pieces and took a seat at the lone table in the back.

"Nice to see you, Tommy. What can I get for you?"

Tommy did not like Rhys at all. There was something about him that he didn't trust. He decided to interview the men on Adina's spreadsheet at Rhys' Pieces partly because it was Adina's favorite restaurant. He thought that if he brought these men there, he might be able to discern something from their body language. Plus, he wanted to keep an eye on Rhys. He was determined to find out what it was about him that raised his hackles.

"Just coffee, please. And, Rhys, I'm going to have a couple of meetings here. I'll be monopolizing this table this afternoon."

Rhys became nervous and wondered why Tommy would have his meetings at the restaurant. Why not his own office? But he did not let on.

"Of course. Stay as long as you like. I'll be right back with your coffee."

"Thank you."

Tommy had just finished his second cup of coffee when his first appointment, Wade Sturgis, showed. That conversation went quickly and about an hour later Damien Childs appeared. Tommy's conversations with both these men were painful. They each spoke about how good Adina was at fundraising, how respected she was in the AIDS community and how creative she was with her fundraising ideas. Neither one of them gave any indication that their relationship with Adina was anything other than professional, but he knew better.

☙❧

All the while, Rhys kept an eye on Tommy. He found it strange that he would be meeting with men who Adina had previously brought to the restaurant. Then he saw Benjamin Bradford walk in. That was the guy he tried to warn her about.

He shot a glance over his shoulder with narrowed eyes. What the hell was going on?

☙❧

"Mr. Bradford, how well did you know Adina?"

"Oh, I knew her very well."

This guy was definitely not like the two Tommy had just interviewed. He certainly was not someone she knew from work.

"Did you meet her through work?"

"No."

"Well, how well did you know her?"

"I knew her in the biblical sense."

He smirked and tapped at the table with his fingertips.

Tommy fought with every fiber in his being not to punch this motherfucker's lights out. This was one vain son of a bitch.

"Why don't you take me back to the beginning? Where, exactly did you meet Ms. Cruz?"

"I met her in The Village, The Garage. She was some freak! She liked to control; inflict pain. She was known in BDSM circles as a tough Domme."

Tommy's nostrils flared.

"I'm not ashamed to admit I'm in the life," he continued.

"I wanted her to hurt me, but for some reason, she didn't care too much for me. We had one interlude and that's it. She was gone in the wind."

Tommy's lips went into a tight line.

"Did you know her like that? Are you one of her subs?" Benjamin asked Tommy.

Tommy inhaled deeply but remained silent.

Benjamin continued the taunt.

"No answer. Well, you must know then that she was good as a Domme. A right bitch. Thinking about her is making me hard right now. When she got down to it, there was no one better than her."

Tommy jumped up and hauled off with a right hook to the guy. Stunned but shaking it off, he lunged across the table at Tommy. Tommy dodged then knocked the table aside so he could get full contact. Head down, he rammed like a linebacker on training day. Benjamin took hold of Tommy but Rhys and another waiter broke up the fight before too much damage was done.

"You!"

Rhys pointed at Benjamin who was hunched over trying to catch his breath.

"I want you out of here and I never want to see you here again!"

Rubbing his jaw, Benjamin stared Tommy down and walked out without a word.

When he was gone, Rhys turned to Tommy who was shaking the pain out of his hand. He banged it up pretty bad but it landed–well worth the discomfort.

"Let me take a look at that."

Tommy's hand was swollen and red.

"I'll get you some ice. Have a seat at the bar."

Tommy obeyed. When Rhys came back with the ice, he also gave Tommy a highball of scotch on the rocks. Tommy nodded his thanks and gulped it down. Rhys waited to see if he wanted to talk, but Tommy remained silent. Rhys finally spoke.

"Tommy, listen. Why don't you let the police handle the investigation?"

He paused. His eyes went unfocused, remembering.

"I know it must have been terribly hard on you to find her lying naked in the foyer the way you did."

Tommy's attention spiked. But he remained stoic.

His heart skipped in his chest and he felt the back of his neck prickle with alarm.

Tommy tensed but didn't look up.

This Rhys guy knows something. I have to find out what it is.

∽∽

Rhys remained outwardly calm. The words came out of his mouth too fast to stop them. He slipped.

Shit! I fucked up! I fucked up! His mind clamored.

I don't think he noticed. He's too upset. He couldn't have noticed my slip, Rhys thought. He needed to know what Tommy knew.

He put his hand on Tommy's shoulder.

"I'll tell you what, Tommy. Why don't you come hang out at my place tonight? This whole ordeal must be stressful for you. You need to take some time to relax. We could catch a game on the television or throw back a few beers, maybe talk? You have to get your mind off things for a bit."

He had to find out what Tommy knew. He had to find out if he was a suspect.

Tommy had to think quickly. He had to talk with Mason. Rhys knew something, he was sure of it now. Nobody knew the condition Adina's body was in. How could he have known she was naked? How could he have known she was found in the foyer? Either Rhys did it or knew who did, so he agreed.

∽∽

"You did what? Tommy, have you lost your mind?"

"I had to do something, Mason!

"I got into a fight with some jackoff at the bar. He gave me some ice for my hand and a drink. Then he said something about the murder scene that nobody knew. He knew how her body was found and said something about how hard it must've been for me to find her that way. How would he know the condition she was in unless he was there or knows the person who was?"

"Ok. You have a point. But Tommy, did you know that you can be arrested for impersonating a police officer?"

"I didn't say I was a police officer. I said I was with the Precinct. These men assumed I was a cop. I didn't correct them, that's all."

Mason shook his head in disbelief. But there was no time for reprimands. He had to follow through on what Tommy was telling him.

"Let me assemble my team. Don't you go over there until I tell you I'm ready, do you understand?"

"Mason, we have to do this today. I told him I'd see him after closing."

"Shit! Wait for my call, do you hear me?"

Mason grabbed Tommy by the shoulders and shook him like a rag doll.

"Wait for my call!"

Tommy shook Mason off.

"I'll wait for your call."

లిలిఈ

Tommy sat on Rhys' sofa while he went into the kitchen to get a couple of beers. His ugly ass dog sat right in front of him, staring and panting. Rhys said his name was God and that he was his trusted companion. What kind of shit was that? Was he fucking having sex with it?

Rhys walked in.

"Go to your room, God," he commanded.

And the dog trotted off after one parting glance over its shoulder.

Rhys handed a bottle of beer to Tommy and sat on the other side of the room from him.

"You know, Tommy, if there's anything you want to talk about, I'll listen."

"There's really nothing I want to talk about. My mind is always on Adina and I think after a while people are going to get tired of me talking about it."

"I won't. You can talk to me."

Tommy just looked at him. The tape that was holding the wire against his chest was beginning to itch. He moved forward to sit on the sofa's edge. That's when he noticed it. Rhys was wearing an ankle holster but he couldn't tell what kind of gun was in it.

Rhys spoke again.

"You know, I felt a special connection with Adina as well. It's the strangest thing. You know how sometimes you meet someone and you feel like you've known them your whole life? That's the way it was for us. We were starting to get close.

"She was a beautiful soul, but of course, you know that."

Rhys seemed to go into a daze. By now, his eyes were closed. Tommy let him continue.

"I didn't like one bit all the men she kept company with. I mean, she only brought four–not including you–to the restaurant but I'm sure there were others."

Rhys began to get agitated. His eyes flashed.

"Those fucking idiots didn't love her the way that …"

Rhys stopped mid-sentence, realizing that he was with Tommy.

Tommy finished his sentence. "They didn't love her the way you did."

Rhys closed his eyes again.

"The way I do."

Tommy could not sit there any longer and listen to this man. He rose from where he was sitting, startling Rhys. He walked toward the window and pulled the shade back. He saw the unmarked car parked out front. He stole a peek down toward the parking lot and saw two plainclothesmen standing together. Down the street, he saw a radio car.

He turned to Rhys whose eyes were still closed.

"Rhys?"

Rhys turned and looked at him.

"It's obvious you cared a lot about Adina. But, I have a question for you."

"What's that?"

"Do you have any idea as to who might have done this to her?"

"There is no possible way I could know that, Tommy. Why do you ask?"

"Did you have anything to do with it?"

"Tommy, that's absurd."

"Then how did you know what condition her body was in when I found her?"

"I read it in the papers."

"No. You didn't read it in the papers, Rhys. That information was withheld from the public. How did you know?"

"I told you, I ..."

Rhys doubled over to his ankle holster, pulled out the gun and flashed it at Tommy.

Fuck.

A crash at the door.

A flash of light and Tommy torpedoed to the ground.

A cacophony of noise: screaming and fireworks.

Then, loud humming layered with screaming and the persistent ringing. Another burst of white fire.

Growling!

The evil iridescent eyes spider-veined red.

Fangs snapping.

More ra-tat-tat in quick succession.

A yelp, a thump.

Then.

Nothing.

Nothing but blood and movement all around him.

Suddenly he was on his feet, dazed. The walls became a slow-motion carousel as he turned to view the carnage.

"For mortal men there is but one hell, and that is the folly and wickedness and spite of his fellows; but once his life is over, there's an end to it: his annihilation is final and entire, of him nothing survives."

Marquis de Sade (1740-1814), L'Histoire de Juliette, ou les Prospérités du Vice, pt. 2 (1797)

Chapter 34
The Notebook

The Briarcliff Home for Long Term Care
Westchester County, New York

Roger slowly rocked back and forth in his rocking chair. He sat so stiffly it appeared as though he were engrossed with the heavy snow as it fell softly to the ground. But, that wasn't the case at all. Fragmented thoughts continually floated around in his head and lit a light in his brain.

Isn't today December 12th? Whose birthday is it?

The old man struggled to remember whose birthday it was.

Ah! Roger! No ... that's me.

Where's Alegria?

When he was younger and had all his mental faculties, all loved Roger, known as a caring doctor. He brought such joy to so many people. He once tried to count how many families he'd helped, but there were so many, he had to keep a written record in a little black book. It was the only way he was able to keep track of them all. This is where he kept all their names, birthdates and where their new homes were located. This was the little black book he nicknamed *Alegria,* which was Spanish for "happiness."

It's been a while since he'd last seen it.

Barbara must surely know where it is, he thought.

He decided he would ask her about it next time she came around to visit.

The sound of wheels desperately needing to be oiled caused him to blink and turn. There was that dreadful woman dressed in white with the funny hat again. She pushed the noisy cart toward him.

"It's time for lunch, Dr. Cohen."

"Is it lunchtime already? Where's my wife? You know I don't like to eat alone."

He squinted at the woman before asking, "Why do you insist on calling me 'Dr. Cohen'?"

The nurse bent down at eye level.

"Your wife is gone, Doctor. We both know that, don't we? And the reason why I keep calling you Dr. Cohen is because you are a doctor; a very well known and respected doctor. Don't you remember?"

"I was? Well, if you say so. Where has Barbara gone?"

The nurse sighed, rose and gently rubbed her patient's shoulder reassuringly. Today was a bad day.

"Would you like me to sit and have lunch with you today? I'm famished and it would make me happy," the nurse offered.

"That would be nice. Thank you. Please sit."

Now in his eighties, Dr. Cohen has been living at the Briarcliff Home for Long Term Care for five years.

Barbara was diagnosed with pancreatic cancer a year before he arrived. It was during that time, she saw early signs of dementia. She settled their affairs and prepared. Arrangements were made for him at Briarcliff. Barbara admitted herself when she could no longer take care of them both.

All of their assets were placed in a trust fund solely for the purpose of paying for their care, including the survivor of the two for the rest of either's life. Whatever was left after they both passed away was to be donated to the facility with the intention of helping patients who were less able to pay.

ɤɥ

While Roger Cohen enjoyed lunch with his nurse, three teams of six laborers were assigned the task of tearing out departments at the old Metro Region Hospital building. It had to be cleared: medical equipment, files, furniture, and bookcases. Whatever was recyclable, they recycled.

One team was assigned the administration and maintenance departments; another team was assigned the emergency and surgery departments; and the third was assigned pediatrics; geriatrics and ob/gyn. They had to be out of there within a week.

Late on the last day of the project, the only area left to clear out was the ob/gyn department. There was just one office left to gut. Three of the laborers volunteered to stay and finish the job.

Dr. Cohen's old office was located in this area. He was well known for his inability to throw anything away. A hoarder of the worst kind, his office was the hardest to tear apart. He had four huge bookcases nailed right to the wall that needed to be torn off. Some of the bookcases had drawers and storage space with solid oak doors. It was heavy work.

They disassembled drawers and shelves. Doors were taken off hinges before the back pane could be removed. The back pieces were secured to the wall with metal anchors. After a while, one wall was cleared and they took a dinner break.

Jack picked up a slab of wood to place in a pile when he saw something taped to the underside of a shelf. He ran his fingers along a small, neatly taped black spiral-bound notebook. Carefully peeling the tape off, he pulled the notebook away and fanned the yellowed pages as he skimmed the handwritten notes.

"Hey, guys! Look at this!" he called to his buddies.

The one named Samson stopped what he was doing.

"What's that?"

"A notebook. They probably forgot it was here.

"Yo, check this out. There's a list of names and dates and maybe money amounts for something."

"Let me see."

Jack handed him the notebook. Samson opened to a random page and started to read aloud:

"Otherwise healthy herm... herma–fro-something child; Hispanic, dark caramel complexion; fraternal twin of healthy baby girl. Surname Rosario born December 12, 1962; Metro Region Hospital; New York yeah, yeah ... P-A."

He paused as his eyebrows knit together.

"Ten thousand dollars? Can this be for real?"

"Oh, shit! What is this? Looks like someone sold a freaking baby!" The other chimed in.

He quickly read some more of the entries in the next few pages. They all contained descriptions of babies: their birthdates, names given at birth by their parents, place of birth and then another location followed by a dollar amount. It looked like most of the children were born at Metro Region Hospital. Some merely had the word "home" written next to their date of birth.

"What do you mean *a* baby? Dude, it looks like somebody sold *lots* of babies!" responded Jack.

"Shit! I wonder whose notebook this is?"

"We're in a doctor's office. Must belong to some doctor."

"Yeah. Do you think this is real? Think we should call the cops?"

"I don't know," Samson said.

Samson didn't really want to get involved. He just wanted to get the job done, go home and have a few beers while watching a movie on his brand new big screen television set. He wiped his forehead with the back of a gloved hand.

They decided to call the police.

ॐॐ

"Hi, honey. Are you done getting all pretty for me?" Mason cooed into the phone.

"Yes, baby, I am. Are you sure this is a good idea?" Claudia asked.

"Well, it would be worse to not acknowledge the date and leave him alone in his misery. The way Adina died is horrible but at least he knows who did it."

"She wasted her life, Mason. She threw it away and she hurt Tommy in the process," Claudia responded to her husband.

"Honey, look; I know you weren't crazy about her, but they were going to get married."

"I know. I guess you're right. Have you spoken with him today?"

"I spoke with him briefly this morning. He tried to beg off, but I wouldn't hear of it. I'm on my way out. I'll swing by and pick him up first and bring him with me to pick you up."

"Ok. I'll be ready to go when you guys arrive. Ring me when you're close and I'll meet you outside. This way he won't have a chance to hesitate."

"Ok. I love you, babe."

"Love you, too. Bye-bye."

Mason hung up the phone. He inhaled sharply and looked at his watch. He toyed with the idea of calling Tommy first but decided against it. Better to just show up at his place.

He rose, grabbed his coat and started for the door when the Captain stopped him. He had an envelope in his hand.

No. No. Please. Don't give me something to do, he silently begged.

"Captain? You look pissed."

"Detective, I just got this. It's a notebook with handwritten notes some construction workers came across at the old Metro Region Hospital. Check it out, would you?"

"Sure. What kind of notes?"

Mason turned the envelope over in his hands.

"Names, places, dollar amounts and dates going back almost fifty years. I don't know what it all means and I want you to look into it."

"Is there any urgency to this?"

Mason tried to keep his tone casual.

"Though I don't think you have to do anything with it tonight, you should get started on it as soon as possible."

"Well, I was just on my way out to dinner with Tommy and the wife."

"Tommy? How's he doing?"

"As well as can be expected, sir."

Mason tried to trim the conversation so he wouldn't be late.

"Would it be ok if I looked into this first thing in the morning?"

"That's fine."

"Is there anything else, sir?"

"No. That will be all. Enjoy dinner and give Claudia my love, and best wishes to Tommy."

"Thank you, sir. Will do."

Mason tucked the envelope into the inside pocket of his coat without looking at it and headed toward the elevator.

∽∾

Tommy paced back and forth in the living room of Adina's apartment. His life had been hell since her death. He was broken and he knew he couldn't continue living this way. His precious Adina would have been forty years old today. They might even have been married right now if it wasn't for that animal, that deranged monster.

He walked over to the couch, sat and slowly scanned the room. He saw Adina everywhere he looked. The whole apartment was exactly as it was that night.

Everyone thought he had to be crazy to keep Adina's apartment, but it didn't seem crazy to him at all. This was important for him. He wanted the freedom to look at her shoe collection and remember how childishly happy she was whenever she bought a new pair. There must've been at least forty pairs in the closet she had designated just for footwear and accessories.

Adina's smiling face floated before him, bringing a smile to his, then tears. That happened a lot.

When his cellphone began to buzz, he didn't answer. He couldn't.

Rising from the couch, he headed into Adina's bedroom. The first thing he saw was the naked bed and recalled the last time it had been used. It was the last time he made love to her. Memories of what they did, what they talked about–his arms ached to hold her.

He recalled her passion that night. For the first time, she asked him to stay the night. He lay in the bed and imagined her beside him.

He rarely slept a full night in it. He couldn't.

He sat in the dark thinking about her, recalling happy times.

He would often pull out old photos and re-live those moments.

So there he stood in the room where his life had completely unraveled.

Traces of the black dust left behind by the fingerprint and crime scene experts could still be seen on some surfaces like the dresser, the walls and windowsill. The items from atop the dresser that crashed to the floor during her struggle with Rhys were now in storage with some of her other possessions.

He turned to the mirrored closet doors and opened them; his reflection warped. Inside were her suits, dresses and other outfits all hung neatly. He touched some of the pieces lightly, brought other pieces to his nose and inhaled deeply. He could still pick up the scent of her perfume.

He went back out to the foyer where she died and sat down right on the spot where he found her body. He lovingly touched the surrounding area where her brains had spilled out and then he lay face up. He tried to mimic the position she was in. He couldn't explain, even to himself, why he did that. A single tear slid down his right cheek then rolled down into his ear. Brushing it away, he rose and walked to a small table by the window. He pulled open the drawer, reached in and removed a Glock.

He walked back over to the spot in the foyer and lay down again.

I'm coming, sweetheart. Happy birthday, baby.

He held the gun to his temple and pulled the trigger.

Epilogue

Mason arrived at his office bright and early. After Tommy's funeral he took some time off to go through his things and put the apartment on the market. This was the hardest thing he'd ever had to do, save his parents' funeral, but he was now ready to throw himself into his work.

He pulled out his middle desk drawer and reached in for the little black notebook his Captain had given him a week earlier and flipped through the pages. One entry got his attention.

Eyebrows knitted together, he reached for the telephone and dialed his home number.

"Hey."

"Hi, babe. How's it going? Are you ok?" Claudia asked; concern in her voice.

"I'm fine. Can you I ask you to do something for me?"

"Sure. What do you need?"

"Could you go through Adina's things and see if you can find her birth certificate? I'll need you to read it to me when you do. I'll wait for your call back."

"Honey, what's going on? Adina's been gone almost two years. Her case was closed, wasn't it?"

"Please, Claudia. Not now. I'll explain later. I've got a hunch."

"Ok. I'll call you back, but it may be a while."

"No problem, but please look as soon as you can, ok?"

"Ok."

"Thank you."

Mason dialed another number.

"Yes. This is Detective Sergeant Mason Jones, Homicide. I'm calling about a murder case. Vic was Adina Cruz Rosario. Yes, the home invasion. Could you please pull up everything you've got and send them to my attention as soon as possible?

"Yes, it's urgent. Yes ... Thank you."

He pressed another button.

"Good afternoon, this is Detective Sergeant Jones, NYPD, Homicide Division at the 54th Precinct. A necropsy was performed on a dog that was shot and killed in a shootout."

"Name?"

"Preston, Rhys John Preston aka RJ Preston."

"I have the file, sir."

"Good. Check to confirm that human remains were found in the digestive tract of the dog."

"Yes, sir. There's a notation referencing 'undigested human remains in the contents of the stomach'."

"Good. I need you to send me that file as soon as possible."

"Yes, sir."

"Thank you very much."

Mason grabbed his coat and left the station house. He was going to see this doctor at The Briarcliff Home for Elder Care.

When Mason arrived at the home, he was advised that Dr. Cohen had passed away in his sleep just that morning. Disappointed, he headed back to the precinct. He hoped that the records he requested had arrived. He was back at square one.

When he arrived at his desk, the items he'd requested were waiting for him.

Every detail of Adina's murder is here, he thought. A person's life and death concentrated down to a box.

He went straight for her DNA report.

Then he pulled the DNA report on Rhys' DNA; then, he pulled Tommy's.

Hmm, interesting, he thought. Let me see something.

He pulled the necropsy report. There had been undigested human flesh in the dog's stomach. DNA testing was done and it was determined not to be a match for Adina.

Good.

He knew that would be the case, but he wanted to double check, in case there was something he missed.

His phone rang.

"Claudia? Did you find Adina's birth certificate?"

"Yes. I have it in front of me. What do you need to know?"

"What hospital was she born in?"

"Metro Region."

"That's what I thought. I'll call you back."

"Mason ..."

Mason didn't hear his wife call his name. He had already hung up.

He shuffled papers around on his desk. Finally he zeroed in on the file he was looking for–Rhys' tax forms.

Date of birth: December 12, 1962–the same date as Adina.

He picked up the doctor's notebook and re-read the entry that caused him to pull all those documents from the files in the first place.

Otherwise healthy hermaphrodite child; Hispanic, dark caramel complexion; fraternal twin of healthy baby girl. (Surname Rosario); born Dec 12, 1962; Metro Region Hosp.; New York, NY/Lebanon, PA; $10,000.

Mason sat back in his seat, incredulous.

He ticked away the signs he missed as he flashed back to his surprise birthday party at Rhys' Pieces.

Rhys told him and Claudia that originally he was from Lebanon, Pennsylvania. He said he started working at the restaurant when he first arrived here ten years earlier.

The old man he worked for sold him the restaurant.

Around this time, Mason had been called to a crime scene in his old precinct in Brooklyn where a group of children playing 'hide 'n' seek' encountered a naked vic whose penis had been cut off.

It was horrific and he hadn't made the connection earlier.

Same M.O.

Mason called the file room and asked for that file as well. He feared it would confirm his suspicions.

And there was one other discovery.

Soon after his birthday party, a woman with a missing breast was found floating in the Bronx River. She was examined. Hair and skin was found under her nails. In addition, canine hair was found in hers.

Mason's thoughts turned to the shootout.

The coroner discovered Rhys was a hermaphrodite. He had both female and male genitalia and neither was functional because his organs never reached maturity.

Rhys was the serial killer living among them.

Rhys was also Adina's twin brother. He was the child sold at birth to that family in Pennsylvania.

Both were now dead, one at the hand of the other, never knowing they were blood.

Mason put all the files together again. He had to file a report.

Tommy was his friend, his brother. He deserved to be honored. He deserved to be remembered for the person he was, not part of some misunderstood natural ... unnatural? he wondered ... circumstance.

In his report, his recommendation to the matter did not warrant further investigation. Everyone involved was dead.